He had no doubt that this woman might rip his life, and his heart, apart if he let her.

And still...he wanted her. He wanted her to be *his*.

A furrow appeared between her brows.

"Shane..." His name was a whisper on her lips.

"Say that again."

Melanie's eyes darkened, and the furrow faded as a smile teased her lips. Her voice was stronger this time.

"Shane. What are we doing?"

"Damned if I know, but I'm not stopping unless you tell me to."

He waited, and she didn't say a word. His head dropped until his lips touched hers. He waited again, until she tipped her head up to meet his. Her lips parted for him with a sigh, and still he hesitated. Was he afraid for her? Or for himself? This moment...this moment felt big. She murmured his name against his lips, her arms wrapping around his neck. And he was a goner.

Dear Reader,

This book is the third and final book in my The Lowery Women series. This book is also one of the last four Superromances to ever be released from Harlequin. There have been so many terrific Superromances through the years, written by wonderful authors (my "Super Sisters") and edited by some of the best in the business. My emotions are all over the place between pride and sorrow to be in this final group of Supers.

I owe a tremendous debt of gratitude to my two Superromance editors. Victoria Curran is the person who said "yes!" to my debut novel, *She's Far From Hollywood*. I will never forget her enthusiasm and wise advice. And speaking of wise advice, my current editor, Karen Reid, got me through books two and three with wonderful guidance and vision.

As they say, when one door closes, another opens. If you enjoy the small-town setting of Gallant Lake, New York (the setting for this book as well as *Nora's Guy Next Door*), I'm happy to say I'll be writing more Gallant Lake stories for Harlequin Special Edition.

So...this is truly bittersweet. I'm thrilled to be part of Special Edition going forward, and very sad to be saying goodbye to Superromance. I hope you enjoy this story, and that you'll want to read more about the people of Gallant Lake.

Wishing you forever love,

Jo McNally

JO McNALLY

—

The Life She Wants

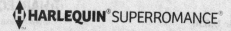

HARLEQUIN® SUPERROMANCE®

Recycling programs
for this product may
not exist in your area.

ISBN-13: 978-1-335-44928-3

The Life She Wants

Copyright © 2018 by Jo McNally

Printed in U.S.A.

Jo McNally lives in coastal North Carolina with one hundred pounds of dog and two hundred pounds of husband—her slice of the bed is very small. When she's not writing or reading romance novels (or clinging to the edge of the bed), she can often be found on the back porch sipping wine with friends while listening to great music. If the weather is absolutely perfect, Jo might join her husband on the golf course, where she tends to feel far more competitive than her actual skill level would suggest.

She likes writing stories about strong women and the men who love them. She's a true believer that love can conquer all if given just half a chance.

You can follow Jo pretty much anywhere on social media (and she'd love it if you did!), but you can start at her website, jomcnallyromance.com.

Books by Jo McNally

HARLEQUIN SUPERROMANCE

Nora's Guy Next Door
She's Far From Hollywood

Visit the Author Profile page at
Harlequin.com for more titles.

Writing doesn't happen in a vacuum. It takes a team, and I've had the best possible team for The Lowery Women series.

To Victoria and Karen with gratitude.

CHAPTER ONE

"MELANIE, CAN I skip this necklace? It seems like overkill to me."

"Mel, you don't really expect me to wear these shoes, do you?"

"Melanie, this dress is way too short for a grandmother."

"Mel…"

Melanie Lowery closed her eyes and took a long, slow breath.

If this was Paris or New York City, this type of fashion-model rebellion would never be tolerated. But Mel wasn't in Paris. And while technically in New York state, she was nowhere near the fashion district. The three women in front of her were not professional models. They were her cousins, and they had volunteered to help her market this collection.

They were doing her a *favor*.

She could *not* scream at them.

One more deep breath.

"Amanda," she said—as calmly as possible— to the petite blonde in the blue sheath, "it's not a necklace, it's an extension of the dress that happens to fasten around your neck. That jeweled bib is what makes the dress special. So please. Just. Put. It. On."

The tall redhead standing by the door wore a flowing floral gown. Bright orange stilettos dangled from her fingers. Bree's face said it all, but Mel stopped the inevitable flow of opinions before it began.

"Bree, I picked those shoes specifically for that dress. They match the clutch you'll be carrying. It's *almost* like I planned it that way." She tried to keep the sarcastic edge from her voice, but failed.

"Pull in your claws, Mel. It's not the color I'm worried about, it's the crazy heels. I can't walk in these things."

"Seriously? I've seen you walk Hollywood red carpets in higher."

"That was a lifetime ago. There's not much call for stilettos on the farm." Bree patted her protruding belly. "And don't forget my passengers. Twins, babe. *Twins.* They're wreaking havoc with my balance, not to mention my ankles."

"Okay, Bree, I get it. Twins."

Her business partner and best friend, Luis Alvarado, was already digging through a tangled pile of accessories in the corner of the room. These were his dresses her cousins were wearing to the charity gala tonight. Well, his with a little influence from her. Actually… Bree's dress was nearly *all* Melanie. It had been her idea to go old-school with a beribboned empire waist and the flowing organza to accommodate Bree's pregnant figure. With her dark red hair falling free and her sun-kissed skin draped in the colorful poppy print on ivory, Bree looked like an exotic goddess.

"Here we go!" Luis stood triumphantly. "Wear these nude flats, honey. Just watch the length of the dress. I don't want you to trip over it." Mel bit back a smile when Luis held out the delicate shoes in his meaty hand. His muscular build made him look more like a linebacker than a fashion designer. Of course, with his long, dark hair and that milk chocolate skin, he could also be the cover model on some romance novel. But the man was a genius with fabric. He was already respected in smaller circles, and soon the entire fashion world would know his name.

"Nora." Mel turned to face her eldest cousin, who was frowning at herself in the mirror while tugging at the hem of the dark red cocktail dress. "You may be a grandmother, but you're *forty*, not eighty. That length makes your legs go on forever, so *please* stop yanking it out of shape!"

Amanda slipped her arm around Melanie's waist. "Mel, you're not even dressed yet, and dinner is in half an hour. We may not be models like you, but we'll be fine. Go get your dress on, and we'll all meet outside the ballroom in thirty, okay?" Amanda turned serious, giving her a quick squeeze. Mel knew what was coming next. "Are you okay?"

"I'm fine. There's adrenaline happening, but it's good adrenaline so far. No temptations. A two at most." Amanda nodded at the use of their code. "Two" meant Mel was completely under control. No one was more concerned about her ability to cope with a pseudo fashion show than she was. This might be a charity event with loved ones by her side, but it was still bringing her perilously close to a world that nearly destroyed her the first time around. Tonight was a test, and everyone in this room knew that. Luis came up behind her.

"You may be at level two, but you're putting me at DEFCON *twelve* in that outfit. Go change! *Dios mio*, my reputation will be ruined if you wear that getup tonight." He nodded at her black leggings and bright green Gallant Lake T-shirt. Her damp hair was covered with a white towel. Maybe Luis had a point—she was cutting it pretty close.

She patted the hand he'd rested on her shoulder. "My makeup is done. All I have to do is put my hair up, shimmy into that magical dress you designed and I'll be good to go."

Luis nodded toward the door. "Go get yourself

magical in a hurry, girl, and I'll go check on the *real* models."

Tonight was an unconventional fashion show, happening concurrently with the awards gala that capped off four days of golf and other events at the Gallant Lake Resort. Everything benefited the Travis Foundation for Veterans, founded by Mel's cousin Bree a year ago. Since many of the attendees were well-heeled socialites and celebrities, Bree had asked Melanie to come up with a unique fashion event that would make the women happy while not boring their husbands. She and Luis had hired ten models to stroll silently around the tables tonight wearing fashions from their new collection. Her cousins, who were all on the foundation's board of directors, would also be wearing Alvarado designs.

"Earth to Mel? Stop daydreaming and get dressed." Luis gave her a friendly smack on the behind. He was the only man on this planet who could get away with touching her like that.

"Okay, okay!" She reached out to straighten Bree's hair on her way by, and got a scathing look in return that froze her hand in midair. Those pregnancy hormones were making Bree downright scary. "Right. See you all downstairs."

The suite she was using as a dressing room tonight was at the other end of the hall. She'd had too many years of changing her clothes while people watched to *ever* do it again, even with family. Mel was just swiping the room key when she heard low voices coming from around the corner, where the larger suites were located. The female voice sounded young. It also sounded tense, which was what caught Mel's attention.

"I don't *want* to go to this dinner, Gary. I don't feel like parading around in front of a bunch of old people again. *Please?*"

The answering voice was smooth, but with an undercurrent of anger that set off all kinds of alarms for Mel.

"Shane says you're going, so you're going, cupcake. If you behave yourself, maybe we'll start practice a little late tomorrow. And I'll take you to breakfast, okay, Tori?"

Mel's entire body went still, including her lungs and her heart. The words were innocent enough, but the tone was off. And it was much too familiar.

Mellie, baby, why don't you stop by my place before the photo shoot, and we'll work on some of your poses, okay?

She swallowed hard. This wasn't about her. It was about Tori. A girl she didn't know, hadn't even seen yet. She moved closer to the corner, trying to decide what to do.

"Umm…sure, Gary. But I still don't want to… What are you doing? Let go…"

Oh, *hell* no. Mel quickly stepped around the corner and took in the scene. Tori was fifteen or so, with a tall, athletic build and thick blond hair pulled back into a ponytail. She was wearing a Hello Kitty T-shirt that was two sizes too small, as if she didn't know she'd grown breasts, and skintight running shorts. Her arms were folded across her stomach.

Gary was probably in his fifties, with graying hair and a slim build, barely as tall as Tori. He stepped away from her the minute he saw Mel, his facial expression morphing from anger to a smarmy smile. Unfortunately for him, Mel had a PhD in smarmy men. Especially smarmy men who took advantage of teenage girls. Blood was pounding in her ears, and sweat tickled her scalp.

You need to loosen up a little or these photos won't work. Come over here and let me give you a little back rub, kiddo. And help yourself to the champagne. No one's watching...

She'd spent years with men like Gary, with no one watching out for her. She'd be damned if she'd let another girl be put at risk behind closed doors or hidden around corners where no one was watching.

"What the *hell* do you think you're doing?"

Gary raised his hands in innocence. "Everything's fine here, miss. You know how kids are. I'm just trying to get her to dinner on time."

Was this just a family squabble? If so, was it any of Mel's business if the guy was being gruff? Did all families fight like this? She really had no idea. She just knew Tori was being pushed to do something she didn't want to do, and Melanie couldn't ignore that.

"Are you her father?"

"No." Tori answered quickly and quietly, moving closer to Mel, her eyes focused tightly on the carpeting. The hair on the nape of Mel's neck stood on end. She'd developed a well-honed "weasel alert" over the years, and it was clanging loudly in her head right now. This guy was bad news.

Mel didn't know what to do. She couldn't exactly drag Tori away—that would be kidnapping. Or would it be a rescue mission? She could call her cousin, since Amanda and her husband owned the resort. Blake Randall would know how to handle this and would have the authority to do something.

She was reaching for her phone when a rough voice from behind her broke the charged silence.

"Is there a problem here?"

Her first thought was that she was now in a hidden hallway, trapped between two men she didn't know. She took a steadying breath and turned coolly on her heel, as if she was totally in control of the situation. Years walking a runway had taught her that trick—she and Luis called it "body acting." But any sense of control she had, real or faked, evaporated when she took in the stranger who'd walked up behind her. *Very* close behind her.

He was a big man, not only tall but broad-shouldered and rock-solid. He was older than her—probably midthirties. His red hair was just long enough to brush the collar of his white dress shirt. His nose was a little crooked, as if it had been broken, and he definitely looked like the type of guy who might get into a fistfight or two. Even with that flawed nose, he was attractive— in a slightly brutish way. The reddish stubble on his chin completed the "bad boy" look, which was softened only by his striking blue eyes, now narrowed in on Tori. His mouth hardened into a straight line.

"Seriously? You're *still* not dressed? You're killing me, kid. Get moving."

Big Ginger gave Melanie that once-over men were so good at—a quick toe-to-head survey to see if she was worth his interest or not. Considering how she was dressed, and the fact that she still had her hair wrapped in a towel, she was surprised to see a tiny flare of heat in his eyes before he gave her a barely polite nod and turned to Gary.

"I told you to make sure she got ready."

"I'm her golf coach, Shane, not her damned *nanny.*"

Tori's voice was full of dramatic teenaged whine. "*Please*, Shane. I'm so *tired* of being *nice* to people."

The corner of his mouth quirked up briefly. Melanie wondered how often women threw themselves at Shane's feet because of that crooked smile and those eyes. Just because she'd sworn off men didn't mean she couldn't appreciate a hot hunk of man when she saw one.

"I know it's a bore, kid, but we have to be nice to the people who pay money to support your career." He glanced over to Mel, gave her a quick, smooth smile and extended his hand. "Shane Brannigan. And you are…?"

"Melanie. Are you related to Tori?"

"I… What? No. Tori's on the women's golf tour. I'm her agent. Gary Jenkins here is her coach. Is there something I can help you with?"

Ice sliced through her veins. He was an agent. Great.

Look, Mellie, you know I have your best interests at heart. Everyone needs topless shots in their portfolio, so stop fighting Marcello on this.

Mel surprised herself as much as she did Shane when she poked her finger hard into the center of his chest.

"You can 'help' me by explaining why you let her walk to her room alone with this guy! How *old* is she? Where are her parents? Where's her chaperone? Who's watching out for this girl?"

OF ALL THE things Shane could have imagined happening today, being physically assaulted by a lunatic with razor-sharp purple fingernails was not one of them. He wouldn't be surprised if she drew blood with that stab in the chest, and it took all his self-control to keep from checking.

Instead, he stared into her shockingly violet eyes while determining his next move.

He'd spotted her the minute he stepped off the elevator—tall and somehow elegant, even in leggings, a T-shirt and flip-flops. The white towel twisted around her head made her look even taller. From behind, she'd looked like a very sexy space alien.

But when she'd tiptoed closer to the corner, his attention had shifted. The only rooms around that corner were Tori's suite and his suite. What the hell was she up to? She was so busy listening to Tori and Gary she hadn't even known he was approaching. Was she a reporter digging for dirt? Or perhaps a fan crossing the line of acceptable behavior?

Before he could ask, she was gone—leaping around the corner with him hot on her heels. And now here she was, lighting into him like a pit bull about "watching out for Tori." It was his god-damn *job* to watch out for Tori Sutter, and Shane was very good at his job. And he didn't take criticism well. Especially from strangers. Not even strangers who had curves everywhere a man wanted to see curves. Smoky gray makeup surrounded her dark eyes, and glossy lipstick made her full lips inviting. Well, they *would* be inviting if they weren't currently pursed in displeasure. With him. *Yeah, well, tough luck, lady.*

"I'm sorry, Miss...?" He waited.

"Melanie Lowery." She spat the name at him, but he'd gotten her to speak. He was a master negotiator, and he was going to take control of this conversation. He nodded and smiled, but his smile didn't have its usual effect. She folded her arms across her chest and glared at him. Her whole body was tense, and for some reason the word *brittle* came to mind.

"Miss Lowery, I don't know what you think is going on, but my client is in good hands here..." She snorted at his word choice, but he plowed ahead. "Look, we're running late and, frankly, Tori's not your concern." He was hoping she'd take the hint and leave, but no such luck. Indignation rolled off the woman in waves.

"Any time a girl is at risk, it's my concern, Mr. Brannigan. It's also the concern of hotel management and the police. Would you like me to make a call or two? I know the resort owners *very* well."

Shane swallowed the angry words begging to be said. His right temple started to throb. The last thing Tori needed was more negative press. This was what he got for taking on a kid for a client—headaches. Then again, all his clients were giving him headaches these days. That seemed to be his specialty—taking on the clients no one else wanted. Time to turn the Brannigan charm up to full strength. He splayed his hands in surrender. "There's no need for that. I can assure you no one here is at risk. Right, Gary?"

"Of course not! I was just trying to get Tori to dinner on time—right, Tori?" Shane didn't like the way Gary looked everywhere but at him. But the guy was a golf coach. It wasn't exactly a sport prone to shouting and drama.

Tori shrugged in response to Gary's question. *Great. Big help, kid.*

Shane turned to Melanie with his best smile. "See? Everything's fine. Tori, honey, I need you to start getting ready, okay?"

Tori moved closer to the Lowery woman, her eyes wide and suddenly adoring for some reason. "Oh, my God! I know who you are! You're here for the gala, right?" Melanie nodded, the towel bobbing on her head. How did Tori know her? The girl turned back to him, suddenly defiant. God help him, he'd never be able to keep up with her moods. "I'll only go if I can sit with her. I don't want to sit with you guys." She glanced at Gary. Shane caught the look, and so did Miss Busy-Body.

"Tori, two of your sponsors will be at our table. You *have* to sit with us. I'm sure Miss Lowery has other…"

The woman's violet eyes never left his, but she spoke to Tori. "I have some official duties to take care of, but I'll come find you after dinner, okay?"

Shane frowned. He didn't need some stranger inserting herself into Tori's life. "I'm sorry, but our table is full. Tori, go get dressed. Now." He pointed toward her door, and she was smart enough to read his tone, heading into her suite after a quick wave to Melanie. Gary excused himself so quickly he almost left smoke in his wake, leaving Shane and Melanie alone in the hallway.

She rolled her eyes and moved to go past him. He didn't budge, not blocking her exit but forcing her to step to the side to get by. It was a petty power play on his part, but really, it was her own damned fault—she'd attacked him first. He figured she'd fold now that she didn't have an audience.

She didn't fold, but she also didn't engage. She straightened her shoulders and moved to walk by without making eye contact. A retreat, but a strong one. He caught a whiff of her soft, flowery perfume as she brushed by. He wouldn't have expected her to be the floral type, but the scent made his head swim with visions of luxurious flowers on bent stems. She smelled like springtime and rain and...and memories. Something from his childhood? Yes, of course.

"Lilacs."

She'd almost gone past him, but the word, which he hadn't intended to say out loud, brought her to a halt. Her head turned slowly and her eyebrows disappeared into her hairline. "Excuse me?"

Well, he was in it now. "You smell like lilacs. My grandmother had lilacs." Shane Brannigan didn't talk about flowers and childhood memories. Ever. This was not a good power play at *all*, but he couldn't stop the words from coming out. "It reminds me of her cottage on the Cape. There was a big stand of lilac trees loaded with blossoms. After a rain, she'd open the windows and the scent would fill the whole house."

Her eyes softened, and he realized their color could be considered lilac, too. *Nana would have loved that...* Whoa. What the hell was wrong with him? He gave himself a mental shake and shoved Nana and her lilacs out of his head.

"Sorry. Admiring your perfume is a little creepy, isn't it? I...I'm sorry." *Definitely not a power position, Brannigan. Babbling is never a win.* Neither was apologizing. Time to walk away while he still had a shred of dignity. "There's no need for you to join us tonight. Tori's rehabbing from an injury and she's just tired."

"I made her a promise. And I keep my promises."

"That's admirable, but…"

"Her coach put his hands on her."

"He *what*? You *saw* that?" Shane couldn't believe it. Gary seemed like such a mouse.

She hesitated. "No, but…"

"Tori *told* you that?"

"No, but…"

"Then I'd be careful tossing around accusations, Miss Lowery. Gary's reputation is spotless."

She paled, and her gaze went unfocused for a minute, as if she was so far lost in thought that she was barely present. Then she shook her head and looked up at him—but not very far up, since she was close to six feet tall, even in those flipflops.

"You don't see a problem with two grown men acting as chaperones for a teenage girl?"

He frowned. When he'd taken Tori on as a client last month, he'd assumed her family would be around a lot more, but she was the oldest of five kids. They had their hands full with the crowd at home, and were trusting others to look after Tori. They were trusting *him*.

"Yes, two grown men are chaperoning a mature young woman who has an entire suite to herself. She's my responsibility, and I'm handling it."

Melanie gave him a slow once-over, then turned and walked away, her footwear making slapping sounds despite the carpeted floors. It didn't diminish her brittle dignity one ounce. It also did nothing to take the steel out of her words.

"Yeah? Well, you're doing a piss-poor job from what I can see."

CHAPTER TWO

AMANDA WAS THE only one still waiting when Melanie rushed to the ballroom doors ten minutes late, breathlessly apologizing. Amanda just laughed.

"Damn, girl! You look *fierce*."

Melanie glanced at the hallway mirror, still amazed she'd managed to make it down here so quickly after the melodrama upstairs. It was a good thing she'd had plenty of experience changing clothes in a flash. But that color in her cheeks wasn't just from cosmetics or her mad dash to get here. It was the result of her interaction with a certain blue-eyed ginger. Something about the man got under her skin, and it showed. She blew out a breath and assessed her appearance. In her agitated state, she wouldn't be surprised to find she'd put the dress on backward or something.

But no, the pewter metallic gown clung to every curve and swirled like silk. Between the draped neckline and plunging back, Luis's design left little to the imagination. She'd pulled her hair into a low, messy knot—the best she could do with the limited time she'd had. Since the dress was such a showstopper, the only jewelry she wore besides a wide silver cuff on her wrist, were simple diamond studs set in platinum. The earrings had been a gift from the photo shoot where she'd met Luis four years ago, and she'd always felt they brought her luck. After all, Luis had saved her life.

"You're seven freaking feet tall! What are you—oh, no wonder." Amanda glanced down at Mel's shiny black Louboutins. "Thanks for making me look like a shrimp, cuz. Let's go, everyone else is inside."

Silver iridescent walls shimmered softly in the recently remodeled ballroom. Thousands of pink and white fairy lights were strung across the ceiling and wound around the light fixtures. Gallant Lake and the Catskill Mountains surrounding it glowed in the mid-June twilight beyond a wall of windows. Tall glass doors opened onto a large veranda overlooking the lake.

The crowd was an eclectic mix of wealthy businesspeople, celebrities, athletes and military veterans with various disabilities. Some of the vets had obvious injuries, such as missing limbs or burns. Some, like Bree's husband, Cole, had less visible wounds—head trauma or PTSD. The fund-raising event had been a smashing success, and they were on track to raise more than half a million dollars to help injured veterans transition to civilian life.

Her cousins were seated together at a table near the stage, where Bree was already giving her pre-dinner address, thanking everyone for their participation, as Mel slid into a chair next to Luis. Bree explained how the silent fashion show would work, with models wandering among the tables during dinner. A sketch of each design was in the printed program, along with information on how to contact Luis Alvarado Fashions. She asked Luis to stand, along with Amanda, Nora and Melanie, to show off their dresses. Camera flashes went off around the room as enthusiastic applause began, and Luis gave Melanie a wink. Between the press coverage and social media, some of his designs were sure to get attention.

As dinner began, Luis set a glass in front of Melanie. It was clear and sparkling, with a slice of lime. She nodded her thanks. With a full glass in her hand, people were far less likely to offer her a cocktail.

Cole jumped to his feet and pulled out a chair when Bree came back to the table. She beamed at him, kissing him on the cheek before settling her pregnant body with a sigh. Normally soldier-stoic in public, Cole leaned over and kissed the top of Bree's head, whispering something in her ear that made her blush. Mel watched her cousins and their men as they laughed and talked together. Bree had Cole. Nora had her fiancé, Asher, who was clearly appreciating Nora's red cocktail dress. He couldn't keep his eyes, or his hands, off her.

And then there was Amanda and her husband. Blake was tall, with black hair and dark eyes—a stark contrast to Amanda's petite build and blond curls. He'd be intimidating if it wasn't for his easy smile and obvious love for his wife. They were *that* couple. Beautiful, successful and happily building a family in their historic mansion, right next door to their five-star resort. Whenever they looked at each other, the love in their eyes made Melanie's chest tighten.

She was thrilled her cousins were finding happiness and starting families. Really. She was thrilled. *Thrilled.* But that didn't mean it didn't hurt her heart sometimes to watch. Most of her energy was focused on sobriety and finding a place in the world outside of modeling, and that was okay. But once in a while, usually at the darkest point of her often sleepless nights, she longed for what her cousins had found. Loving partners to spend the rest of their lives with. She just couldn't see that happening for her.

Luis's low voice broke through her melancholy. "You and that dress were made for each other, *chica.* You look different tonight—like you're ready for battle. It's a good look on you."

That look of battle-readiness probably came more from her confrontation with Big Ginger than the dress. He'd managed to ignite a fire inside her, and she wasn't sure if that was good or dangerous. She didn't want Luis to worry, so she kept that to herself.

"I have to admit, I feel pretty invincible in this gown. It's going to be the star of your collection."

"*Our* collection, Mel. It's your company, too. Your hand is in every one of these pieces."

She just shrugged in response. For most of her life, she'd received praise for only her looks, which she had no control over, so the compliments meant nothing. She didn't know how to handle praise for something she actually helped create.

Luis frowned. "You doing okay?"

Being dressed up and on display, being in a crowded room, being near an open bar… There were a lot of triggers here tonight, and Luis knew it. She gave him a bright smile. "I'm alright. Maybe a four, but no worse."

"You tell me the minute it climbs above a six, okay?"

"I promise."

Tori and Shane came into the ballroom halfway through dinner, walking to a table on the opposite side of the room. Neither of them looked happy. Tori was wearing a neon-orange dress that was far too tight and short. And…bright green high-top sneakers. Her hair was teased up into some crazy kind of pigtails. This kid's fashion style was stuck somewhere between Miley Cyrus and Bride of Frankenstein. She may as well have been wearing a flashing sign that said Unhappy Teenager.

Shane's expression made him look like he'd been sucking on lemons, and Mel was pretty sure Tori was responsible. He escorted Tori to a seat and rolled his eyes behind her as she sat. Yeah, the two were definitely arguing. She felt a pang of sympathy for Tori.

But she was surprised to feel a touch of concern for Shane, too. He looked down at Tori in confusion and showed a quick glimpse of that vulnerability he'd surprised Mel with upstairs with his talk of lilacs and his grandmother. Those words had hit her heart, since she wore the pricey Amouage scent because it reminded her of her *own* grandmother. She excused herself and headed for their table.

People stopped her along the way, and she accepted their compliments and autograph requests with a practiced smile. A man in uniform stopped her to thank her for being on the cover of *Sports Quarterly*'s swimsuit issue three years ago. He pulled the well-worn folded page from his pocket and asked if she'd autograph it for him. It took every ounce of her strength not to dwell on how awful that Cozumel photo shoot had been. Between the sand fleas and a particularly lecherous photographer, it had been one of the worst jobs she'd ever taken.

By the time she got to their table, Shane was headed toward the bar with a sandy-haired man walking with a barely perceptible limp. Gary was nowhere to be seen. Tori was talking with an older woman. More accurately, the older woman was talking, and Tori was nodding sullenly. The girl's shoulders were rounded, and she was tugging at her dress. But when she saw Melanie, she jumped up to greet her, pigtails bouncing like springs on her head.

"You're here! I told Shane you'd come!"

"Oh, my goodness! You're that model! You did the Coastal Jeans campaign, right?" The woman Tori had been talking to now joined them. "You know Tori?"

Tori nodded, her sulking long forgotten. "Yes, Mrs. Covington, this is Mellie Low. We're…" She hesitated and Melanie jumped in.

"Tori and I are friends. And I go by Melanie Lowery now. Or just Mel."

Mellie Low died a long time ago.

Tori beamed as Melanie extended her hand to

the woman. Susan Covington explained that her
husband was CEO of Covington Golf, and they
were one of Tori's equipment sponsors on the
women's golf tour. She introduced Mel to another
couple at the table, the founders of Winthrop Athletic, a clothing company. Helen Winthrop was
nowhere near as pleasant as Susan and had barely
released Mel's hand when she started in.

"Mellie, you're in the fashion business, so
please, God, can you give Tori some much-needed
fashion advice?" Tori yanked at the hem of her
dress. Mel gritted her teeth. What this girl needed
was *compassion,* not cat claws.

"Please call me Mel. And, actually, Tori's outfit reflects popular urban fashion for teens right
now. She's following a trend."

Tori's shy smile had Mel reaching to squeeze
her hand, which also kept her from fidgeting with
her dress. Helen gave Tori another once-over.

"Hmm. Perhaps it's the 'urban' part I don't get.
We need Tori to reflect our *company's* values, not
those of the Kardashians."

*Melanie, I don't care if it's your favorite shirt
or not, you can't wear it. Nothing is about you
anymore—it's about our clients, and you represent them every waking minute of the day, so
get used to it.*

Helen turned away to say something to Susan,
who rolled her eyes at Mel in sympathy when

Helen wasn't looking. Tori tugged at Mel's hand and whispered to her.

"Everyone's staring at me. I was just trying to get back at Shane for making me come to this dinner, but now I feel like an idiot. I never thought he'd let me wear this."

Melanie could draw only two conclusions. Either that boulder of a man was clueless and thought Tori really wanted to come to dinner in this getup or he'd decided to let her embarrass herself deliberately to teach her a lesson. Either way, the girl was feeling humiliated, and that wasn't going to happen while Mel was around. Phones were already aimed at Tori from around the room. Social media would have a field day with that outfit.

She leaned over and whispered in Tori's ear, "I just happen to know where there's a room full of clothes and accessories that could tone this up or down any way you'd like. If you're interested."

Tori's eager nod was all she needed. Shane was still at the bar with the other guy, paying no attention to his client. She couldn't wait to see his face when Tori turned the tables on him.

"You look like you're ready to kill someone, Shane. Lighten up, will you?" Tim slapped his back a little too hard. "We're here to have a good time, remember? And make money. By being nice to people. Ring any bells?"

Shane nodded absently. He made his living as a sports agent by schmoozing his way through rooms like this one. The Dealmaker. That's what they'd called him in Boston when he'd come out of nowhere and signed a Beantown deal for one of the hottest basketball players in the league. It was a crazy scheme hatched in college, where he'd first met Marquis Jackson. They'd become friends, and Shane, a cocky law student, had sat at Marquis's side once he'd declared himself eligible for the draft. When Marquis got himself arrested for a barroom scuffle and then mouthed off to some reporters afterward, some of those people had backed away. But not Shane. He'd started making calls to NBA teams himself, to Boston specifically, and had ended up working out the deal that had made Marquis a star. The two of them had landed on the cover of a Boston sports magazine.

Nana had loved the headline, where he'd been referred to as "The Dealmaker" for the first time. So much so that she'd framed it and hung it on her wall. He frowned. Weird. That was the second time today his tiny Irish grandmother had come into his thoughts. It was all because of that violet-eyed beauty and her damned perfume. Or was it the way Melanie Lowery had stood up to him to protect Tori? That was something his feisty nana would have done. At his side, his best friend and business partner flagged down the bartender.

"I remember why we came." Shane straightened his shoulders. "I came here to kick your ass in the golf tournament today."

Tim barked out a laugh. "I hate to break it to you, pal, but you failed. I warned you this new stored-energy prosthetic foot has been killer for my golf swing. The rotation unit is kick-ass, and you owe me a hundred bucks, Brannigan."

"Whatever. You only won because you were lucky enough to get paired with the club's pro golfer."

"Lucky. Sure." Tim snorted and stepped away to order. "Drinks are on you."

His buddy being paired with Cody Brooks for the tournament was something Shane had quietly arranged. That was his special talent, making quiet arrangements behind closed doors. He'd also arranged for himself to be partnered with Carter Patterson. A hotshot college quarterback, Carter entered the pros a few years ago in a burst of publicity and attention that proved too much for a kid from Wisconsin. He'd let the pressure get to him and started making ridiculous mistakes on the field. The fans on social media had turned him into a joke. One team after another had cut him, and his agent was doing nothing to help the guy. But Patterson was only twenty-six and had plenty of career left if he could get his head straight. Shane's deal-making had paid off well today—Tim and Cody had won the charity tournament, and Patterson had agreed to set up a meeting with Shane soon.

The only blemish on the day had been the skirmish upstairs before dinner. Then again, confronting the enigmatic Miss Lowery had been the most energizing moment of the whole day, as well.

"Dude, seriously, put away the resting bitch face." Tim handed him a drink. "Come on, look at all the gorgeous women here! If I was into that sort of thing, I could totally score tonight." Tim nodded toward a blonde leaning against the bar. "But you could do alright, man."

Shane smirked. "I already scored today with Patterson. He could be our golden ticket if we can keep him focused. Now, if I can just get Tori to behave herself, we could be in good shape."

At that, Tim put on his business face. Shane was The Dealmaker, but Tim was the money guy. And the resident worrier. "Do we need to be concerned about her reputation? The social media crowd is really going after her partying ways, calling her 'Slutter Sutter.'"

Shane winced. "Yeah, I know. It may have been a mistake to take her on." Tim had tried to tell him as much when Tori's parents had called, begging for help managing her skyrocketing career and the mess she was making of her online presence. "What the hell do I know about teenagers? Especially *girl* ones?"

Her clothing choices were a huge challenge, and one of the reasons she got so much flak online. She was a pretty girl, but one day she'd be photographed shopping in a skirt so short she was at constant risk of exposing herself, and the next day she'd be in baggy jeans drooping around her hips, like Bieber. At last year's ESPYs, she'd shown up in a butt-ugly dress made out of strips of paper, á la early Gaga. He had no clue how he was going to turn her fashion fails around.

"Have you seen the mystery lady who tried to invite herself to our table tonight?" Tim asked.

Smoky eyes immediately came to mind. And long legs. And a sharp tongue.

"The Lowery woman? No. She probably won't show. She was just trying to be a good Samaritan or something when she heard Tori and Gary arguing. And speaking of that…"

"Yeah, I know. Her parents might trust the guy, but he doesn't give me the warm-and-fuzzies."

"The woman said he grabbed Tori."

Tim stiffened. "You think it's true?"

He thought about the way Gary had shuffled around and avoided eye contact. But, no, a guy in his position wouldn't do anything so stupid. At the same time, Shane had been relieved when Gary had begged off from dinner tonight.

"She didn't actually see anything. She was probably overreacting." Melanie's words poked at him. *Who's watching out for this girl?* "I'm going to talk to Gary tomorrow, though. He might be pushing Tori too hard."

Everyone had agreed Gallant Lake was the perfect spot for Tori to heal her bruised ribs out of the larger, national spotlight and away from her parasitic "friends." The new golf course at the resort was a great place for her to work on getting her swing back in shape. In a few weeks, she'd be ready to rejoin the tour. Shane and Tim had been so busy out on the West Coast the past few weeks trying to keep baseball's hottest third baseman's career from imploding—again—that Gary had been left in charge of Tori's schedule. And Shane didn't like anyone being in charge but him.

Tim nodded in agreement, then cocked his head to the side. "That outfit you let her wear tonight isn't helping her reputation any, you know. That hot mess will be all over the internet by midnight."

His grip tightened on the glass he was holding. "Don't remind me. I made her change twice, and each outfit was worse than the last. She was hoping I'd cave and let her stay up in her room, but I called her bluff." No one outsmarts Shane Brannigan, especially some kid. Tori had looked horrified when he'd accepted the glow-in-the-dark dress. She'd tried to backpedal, but he hadn't given her a chance to change. That would teach her a lesson for trying to play games with the king of gamesmanship. He'd regretted it as soon as they'd walked into the ballroom. He'd felt her stiffen at his side, but it had been too late.

Tim nudged him and suggested they spend some time with Tori's sponsors, so they headed back the table. He did his best not to overreact when he didn't see Tori there. Damn it, if that kid sneaked out and went back up to her room... He glanced out to the veranda and realized with a jolt that a better man would be concerned about her safety first. What if she'd followed some creepster out to the now-dark lakeshore? What if someone had followed her up to her room because she was alone? How long had he and Tim been at the bar? *Who's watching out for this girl?* He was starting to feel a sincere sense of panic when Tim made an odd strangled sound. Shane followed his gaze and nearly choked on his whiskey.

Melanie Lowery and Tori Sutter walked into the ballroom, and heads everywhere were turning. Tori's crazy getup had been transformed, and so had she. Her tangled hair had been slicked back and up into a tight twist on top of her head, secured with what looked like chopsticks. Her makeup had been toned down, and her lips were soft peach instead of the nearly black shade she'd been wearing earlier. She still had that crazy orange dress on. At least, he *thought* it was the same dress. The top was visible under a short white jacket, but the bottom was covered with some kind of colorful fabric wrapped and knotted at Tori's hip. It allowed a peek of the short dress beneath where it was tied, but just a peek, as the rest of it fell to sweep the floor. The sneakers were gone, replaced by orange stilettos. The kid suddenly looked like the young woman she kept insisting she was.

Mrs. Covington jumped up and hugged Tori, who was relaxed and smiling. She twirled to show off the outfit. Even cranky old Mrs. Winthrop seemed to approve. Melanie, sipping from the drink in her hand, nodded at something Mrs. Covington said, then raised her head. Her gaze slammed into his before she headed his way.

Her hair had been hidden under a towel earlier, but now he could see it was dark and, although it was knotted together at the back of her head, there were enough strands falling free that he could see it was long and wavy. In those crazy shoes, she was as tall as he was.

Her dress swirled like liquid mercury around

her ankles, and it looked as if polished steel had been poured over her body, hugging every long line of her. It was a dress a kick-ass female superhero would wear. He half expected her to whip out a jeweled sword and strike a battle pose. Instead, she just stopped and looked at him, violet eyes assessing. A slow smile lifted the corners of her mouth, painted to match her eyes, and his breath hitched. So that was her superpower—a smile that could paralyze a man.

Her hand rested on her waist in a challenge, but she was smart enough not to be the first one to speak. In negotiation, everyone knew the first one who talked was the loser. Shane was impressed. He was also not about to say anything.

It was Tim who finally broke the silence.

"I apologize for my friend. I think that dress may have caused him to have a stroke." Tim winked at her as he took her hand. "I'm Tim Monroe, and you are a sorceress based on the transformation of Miss Sutter over there."

She laughed, and Shane discovered superpower number two. Her laugh was deep and husky. It was a whiskey laugh, and it warmed his skin the same way whiskey warmed his throat.

Tim was still holding her hand. "You know, when Shane told me he met a woman named Melanie, it never occurred to me that it could be Mellie Low. It's great to meet you."

Shane frowned. Tori had recognized her upstairs earlier. Was she famous or something? She gave the briefest of glances down toward Tim's artificial leg.

"I go by Melanie Lowery now, and my friends call me Mel. Did you serve?"

"Two and a half tours in Afghanistan, ma'am. Mostly in the western mountains. Army Rangers. Our chopper went down in a storm." Tim wasn't usually chatty about his service time. He'd almost died on some godforsaken Afghan mountain five years ago, and even with good financial resources and the support of family and friends, he'd had a tough time of it when he'd first come home.

But Tim wasn't done sharing. "I'll tell you something, Miss Low...Miss Lowery. The winters were long and cold over there, and more than one guy had that cover shot of you in nothing but paint taped up next to his bunk to keep him warm."

Her laugh now seemed more self-deprecating than pleased. That made sense, since Tim was basically implying soldiers did impure things to themselves in front of her likeness. Not Tim, of course. Tim would have been keeping himself warm to a clandestine picture of Matt Bomer. But it finally clicked where he'd seen Melanie before. She'd been on the cover of that bathing suit issue a few years back in a painted-on bikini. Literally painted on, without a stitch of actual fabric. He hadn't known her name at the time, but the photo was unforgettable. It had been locker-room talk for weeks. He cleared his throat, anxious to take back control of the conversation.

"I appreciate what you did to help Tori with her dress, Melanie, but I was trying to have a teaching moment with her. Tori needs to show a little more maturity." Christ, he sounded pompous to his own ears, so he could only imagine how it sounded to everyone else.

"So you thought it was a good idea to 'teach' a teenage girl by humiliating her in a room full of people and cameras? Brilliant move, Socrates."

"Yeah, brilliant move, Socrates." Tim rolled his eyes at him before turning back to Melanie. "You'll have to forgive him, Melanie, he tends to say really stupid shit in front of pretty women." Shane started to object but stopped when Tim's foot—the *titanium* foot—came down on his toes. Tim pressed on, "He was basically left at the altar by one of you not long ago, so…"

Melanie's eyes went wide.

A low growl came from Shane's throat. Karina had split when Shane "stopped being fun." Funny how the death of a man's father could do that.

"How convenient to blame all women for the actions of your runaway bride rather than looking in the mirror." Her smile was deadly now.

The truth of her words, and the fact that she'd had the guts to say them right to his face, left him silent, torn between rage and admiration. Maybe Melanie was more than a pretty face, after all. Maybe she was a damned flamethrower dressed in steel. Tori joined them before he could come up with a reply.

"Shane, isn't this awesome?" She waved her hand down toward her clothing. "Mel did this in, like, ten minutes! It was like having a fairy god-mother or something. And she said she'll help me find makeup for tournaments that won't melt away in the sun. She lives here in Gallant Lake, right above that coffee shop you love, and I'm going to do yoga with her tomorrow morning. She says it'll be good for my focus."

Shane pressed his lips together and shot a suspicious glance at Melanie. Just because she was famous didn't mean her interest in Tori was healthy. And his experience with models wasn't exactly stellar—they loved to latch onto rich ath-letes. Too many young bucks were happy to hand over their dough just to have a gorgeous woman as arm candy. Was Melanie doing some twisted kind of attention-seeking by attaching herself to Tori? Maybe he'd made one deal too many, but in his world people expected payback for their so-called favors. He just had to figure out what her angle was.

"Tori, I'm sure Melanie has other things to do than be your BFF."

There was a hush, and he knew he'd gone from sounding pompous to sounding like a grumpy old man. Both were unwelcome reminders of his father. Tori looked crestfallen, and Melanie and Tim were glaring at him, so he quickly reversed course. "But we can try to work something out. You look really nice. I...uh...like your hair." Tori beamed, then bounced off to sign some autographs and pose for selfies with some fans at a nearby table.

He aimed his best smile at Melanie, and knew in a heartbeat she saw right through it. Interesting.

"Thank you for helping our girl. And don't worry, I'll make sure she doesn't bother you after tonight. She has a full schedule."

Melanie stiffened. "Tomorrow's *Sunday*, and I'm expecting her to show up. You're pushing her too hard. She needs a break."

There might be some truth in that. Tori *could* burn out if they weren't careful. There was just one problem—Shane didn't take well to lectures. He'd been listening to lectures from his father all his life. He sure as hell wasn't going to listen to one from some fashion model.

"Let me guess—you think posing naked on the cover of a sports magazine makes you a sports expert, right? Why don't you just leave Tori's career to people who know…"

Helen Winthrop walked up, forcing him to shut his mouth in a hurry. That may have been a good thing, since Tim was making a slicing motion across his neck and Melanie had been puffing up in indignation with every word.

"Shane!" Mrs. Winthrop grabbed his hand, her husband, Mark, a step behind her and silent. Mark might run the company, but it was pretty clear who ran Mark. They were paying Tori big money to be the fresh young face of their golf-clothing line. "I was absolutely shocked when Tori came into dinner earlier looking like she did…"

Shane lost track of the woman's complaints when Melanie stepped away to greet a mountain of a guy who'd just walked up. The dark-skinned man had his hair pulled back into a man bun. Dressed in a trim dark suit, he handed Mel a fresh drink and spoke softly in her ear, earning an affectionate smile from her that made Shane's chest go tight. She held up five fingers, making the other guy shake his head, but she patted him on the arm. Was she telling him how many drinks she'd had? The man gave her a gentle kiss on the forehead before walking away. Mrs. Winthrop's voice droned its way back into his brain.

"…and, honestly, after some of Tori's very public misbehavior lately, Mark and I were wondering if we'd made a mistake. But it was brilliant to bring in someone like Mellie Low to mentor Tori, and what a way to demonstrate it! She worked a miracle, and just look at Tori now!"

They turned to watch Tori laughing with a woman and her young daughter, who was clearly a fan. Tori looked like an average kid having fun. He felt a jab of guilt. She *was* just a kid, and he suspected Gary wasn't providing a lot of fun in her schedule. He'd been treating her like a thirty-year-old pro. Maybe Shane had been, too. *Who's watching out for this girl?* Damn it to hell. It wasn't like him to make that kind of mistake.

"I can't thank you enough for hiring Mellie to show us what Tori can be with a little guidance. Very smart move, Shane. And she should be a fabulous influence on Tori's style."

Wait. *What?* Tim was coughing behind him, and he could have sworn he heard laughter in that cough. Shane finally caught up with the conversation. The Covingtons thought he'd *hired* Melanie to work with Tori? He watched Melanie walk over to join Tori's growing audience. She tossed her head back and laughed at something Tori said, and Tori reached out to hold her hand. Here he was working on ways to get the woman *away* from Tori, and his biggest sponsor wanted him to *pay* her to give freakin' beauty tips to his client.

"Um, that's not exactly what I had in mind, Mrs. Winthrop. I'd rather Tori work on her rehab and golf swing."

"Did you know Mellie Low had over half a million followers on Instagram before she dropped out of the public eye? She knows how to use social media to build a brand, and if she can help Tori learn some self-control, it will be good for all of us, don't you think?"

Shane had a feeling the last thing Melanie Lowery was going to be was good for all of them.

Especially him.

CHAPTER THREE

THE RINGING ALARM made Melanie wince and groan at the same time. She'd be fine once she got to her feet, but the moments between alarm and arising were never easy. All those years in modeling had totally screwed up her sleeping patterns, and it wasn't at all unusual for her to end up wide-awake in the middle of the night. But her chronic insomnia hadn't been the problem last night.

No, last night she'd slept. And dreamed. Of ginger and blue. Of a rough voice pushing her and challenging her. In some dreams, Big Ginger had been an adversary, but in some... She stretched and sighed. In some he'd touched her with gentle hands. Held her with strong arms. Kissed her...

Mel sat up abruptly, her pulse racing. Enough of that nonsense! *No more men for a while, remember?* If she was home in Miami, she'd work off some of this agitation at the gym. Maybe take a kickboxing class or a spinning session. She tossed off the sheet and sat on the edge of the bed. Miami wasn't home anymore. After her accountant had squandered most of her earnings, the beachfront condo had been all she'd had left. At twenty-nine, she'd made and lost a fortune. The condo was a stark reminder of the places and people that weren't healthy for her anymore. So she'd sold it and invested in Luis's new fashion line.

She stood and stretched, looking across her cousin's loft and out to Gallant Lake, silver-blue in the soft morning light. Wisps of fog clung to the tops of the mountains. She'd moved into Nora's vacant apartment a month ago. It was supposed to be temporary, of course, until she could find a place in the city, closer to Luis's studio in the fashion district. Gallant Lake was as close to her former stomping grounds as she could handle for now.

Someone rapped on the door downstairs, and it opened, meaning it could only be one person— her landlord. Nora's voice carried easily through the loft apartment. "Rise and shine, sleeping beauty! I bring coffee!"

Her one remaining vice was caffeine, but she'd forgiven herself for that one long ago. That was a good thing, since she now lived directly above Nora's coffee shop, the Gallant Brew. She grabbed a pair of yoga pants, calling over the railing to the room below, "I love you for the coffee. And hate you for the hour."

"Hey, yoga girl, it was *your* idea to teach me this stuff. What's got you in a twist this morning?"

Her cousins were all as close as sisters, but no way was she sharing that she'd dreamed of Shane Brannigan last night. She'd never hear the end of it, and they'd all be playing matchmaker for the only unattached cousin left. Besides, Big Ginger was all wrong for her. She hadn't missed the glass of whiskey in his hand, or his need to be in charge. Two major triggers for her, and she wasn't going down that road. Not again.

She'd barely taken a sip of the double espresso Nora had delivered when there was a light knock on her door. Nora shrugged when their eyes met. "Asher's on his way to Albany to meet with a client, so it's not him. Maybe Becky decided to join us, but I thought she was going to church with the baby and meeting us at the resort later."

It wasn't Nora's daughter who was waiting when Melanie opened the door. Instead, she found Tori Sutter smiling brightly. And standing right next to her was Shane Brannigan, who was *not* smiling. Mel did a quick mental inventory of her appearance—had she even brushed her hair before coming downstairs? Oh, Lord, she was barefoot, wearing leggings and had on a cropped top that barely covered her sports bra. And no makeup. This was not her usual meet-a-handsome-if-annoying-man look. She felt her face warming, but Tori didn't seem to notice.

"I'm not too late, am I? You said around seven for yoga, right?" Tori brushed by Mel, who was still staring at Shane. And he was staring right back. The corner of his mouth rose in a crooked smile.

"You seem surprised to see us, Miss Lowery. You were so adamant last night that Tori honor your invitation. Are you having regrets now that the liquor has burned off?"

She hissed in a sharp breath. He thought she'd been *drunk* last night? Well, if he did, it was her own fault. That's why she drank tonic water with lime at parties. No one ever questioned whether it contained alcohol or not, avoiding awkward explanations, pitying looks or the inevitable person who insisted that "just one drink won't hurt." Apparently her ruse worked, because Shane assumed she'd been pounding back vodka all night. She decided not to set him straight, since it was none of his business.

"I'm not at all surprised to see Tori. But I *am* surprised to see you, since I don't recall extending you an invitation. Are you interested in yoga, Mr. Brannigan?"

He shook his head, looking bemused. "Yesterday you ripped into me for not caring *enough* about my client's well-being, and now you're surprised I want to see where she's going for yoga lessons?" He stepped inside and looked around. She had to concede he made a good point. But before she could say so, he opened his mouth and spoiled it. "I mean, all I know about you is you pose for pictures and like to eavesdrop on conversations."

"I don't 'pose for pictures' anymore. And any time I hear a young girl being pushed around by someone, I'm going to do something about it." His blue eyes went icy, but before he could reply, Tori cut him off.

"He's just grumpy because Mrs. Winthrop thinks he hired you to help me, and he can't figure out how to deal."

Shane glared at Tori, then closed his eyes tightly and sighed.

"You have a big mouth, kid. Do your thing with Melanie and come downstairs when you're done. You've got thirty minutes." He turned to leave, but Mel stopped him with a hand on his arm. His very solid, well-muscled arm that tensed when her fingers touched it. She felt a surprising little zing of attraction zip down her spine but did her best to ignore it. She was in the midst of a very long dry spell, so her physical reactions simply couldn't be trusted.

"Explain that comment about Mrs. Winthrop."

Tori jumped in again. "She thought Shane staged my makeover last night."

"Really? How wonderfully sexist of her to give *him* the credit."

His eyes lit up with amusement as Tori giggled behind her.

"I know, right? She thinks you've been hired to improve my image."

Mel looked at her, ignoring Nora's delighted expression behind her. Her cousin was going to be giving her the third degree later, no doubt.

"And why exactly does your image need improving?"

Tori's bravado faltered, then recovered everywhere but her eyes. "Haven't you heard? I'm golf's 'wild child,' whatever that means. Shane's worried about my sponsors."

He stared at Melanie's hand on his forearm as he spoke. "Shane's worried about your *career*. That's my job." Mel pulled her hand back, and he frowned. "Go do your yoga thing. I need coffee. Scratch that—I need a triple shot of espresso."

After he left, Mel taught Nora and Tori a few basic stress-reducing poses, learning through trial and error which ones Tori could do without causing pain in her bruised ribs. The girl talked about dealing with her new life after winning her first women's tournament last year at fifteen, then defeating several male pros at an invitational "skins" game in Las Vegas. One of those men happened to be one of the top five PGA players worldwide, and the entire sports world had turned their attention to the phenom from Cleveland.

Melanie helped Tori with the extended triangle pose, thinking how similar their stories were. She'd been thrust into the limelight at sixteen after being "discovered" on a Florida beach. The agency rep had told her everything she'd wanted to hear: she was beautiful; she could be famous; she could make a lot of money; she could live a life of glamour and travel to exotic places. And sure enough, she'd found fame. But like Tori, she'd discovered it wasn't all sunshine and roses. A teenager without a good support system could so easily be led astray.

"This apartment is sick." Tori looked from the bright black-and-white kitchen to the living room with two-story windows looking out over Main Street and the lake. The furniture belonged to Nora, who'd left the apartment to live with Asher in the mountain home he'd built.

Mel shrugged. "It's very bricky."

"Hey—I love that brick!" Nora laughed, falling over in the middle of a boat pose. The century-old building's original brick walls were exposed on both sides of the apartment. It was cozy, but it was nothing like Mel's sleek glass-and-chrome condo in Miami.

Tori sat on the carpet next to Nora, and Mel joined them.

"It's like a city loft in the middle of this cute little village," Tori said, looking up at the exposed beams.

"You like Gallant Lake?"

Tori nodded at Mel's question. "It's okay. There's no press hounding me here."

"How'd you hurt your ribs?"

Tori went quiet, staring out the windows for a beat before speaking. "Nothing dramatic. I tripped and fell on some stairs."

Mel and Nora looked at each other. Had Tori injured herself on purpose to avoid competing? She'd seen it happen with models who would intentionally gain weight or change their hair just to avoid a certain fashion shoot or catwalk. Or had something more sinister happened? God, she'd turned into such a cynic.

"How long has Shane been your agent?" As an agent, he was only in this to line his own pockets. He needed Tori healthy, but that didn't mean he was watching out for her the way he should be.

"Shane? Only a few weeks. It was right before the accident. My first agent was a lawyer friend of my parents. She was nice but kinda clueless. Shane said the sponsors I have came to me in spite of her, and he said that's not the way it's supposed to work."

"Do you like him?"

Nora gave her a curious look. Tori thought for a moment before answering.

"I guess. But he's always traveling, so I don't see him much."

Mellie, I can't be here every freaking minute to hold your hand. Grow up, do what people tell you to do and stop asking about when you'll get home. You'll get there when you get there, okay?

"That didn't really answer my question, Tori. Do you like him? And Gary? Do you miss your family? Do they ever visit? When were you home last?" Tori frowned at the burst of personal questions, and Nora jumped in.

"Don't mind her, honey. She doesn't function real well in the morning. I think what she meant to ask was, are you okay?"

Nora gave Mel a hard look. Using the code question wasn't exactly subtle. That was how Luis and her cousins gauged Mel's stress level—their subtle way of asking if she was at a two or an eight. And, yes, even at this hour, her number was in the danger range. Between sexy dreams, arrogant men and a girl in trouble, she was spending too much energy fighting off the past. She took a deep breath and nodded to her cousin. She could step back. She had to.

Tori looked confused and gave another shrug.

That seemed to be the kid's go-to move when she wasn't sure of herself.

"Am I okay? Sure, I guess." She picked at a cuticle on her thumb. "I miss my family."

"They don't visit?"

Another shrug.

"When they can. They're in Cleveland. They try to come every other weekend, but it doesn't always work."

"Why do your rehab so far from home?"

"It was Shane's idea. He says my friends are a bad influence on my career."

Mellie, forget your stupid prom, okay? You're going to be partying in Morocco while those losers listen to canned music in a smelly gymnasium. Seriously, where would you rather be?

Why were Shane and Gary intentionally isolating this girl?

"Hey, Nora, would you mind showing Tori some cool-down stretches for a few minutes? And maybe get her a glass of juice? I have to run downstairs." She stood and turned for the door before remembering her fresh-out-of-bed appearance. She was too angry to waste time going upstairs to change. What she was about to do didn't require anything more than the ability to deliver some very pointed words. She grabbed a loosely woven blue sweater that was draped over a chair. It fell to her thighs. She often wore it at night when she was watching television, because it was so big she could curl her legs up underneath it.

Her bed-head hair was hopeless, so she stuffed it under a Gallant Lake ball cap she kept on hand for late-night walks. Luckily she always kept lipstick by the front door, so she glammed up her look with a splash of matte pink. She flashed the girls a quick smile and was out the door before Nora could ask any of the questions clearly burning her lips.

Shane was alone at a table, which was good. His table was all the way to the front of the busy coffee shop, which was not good. She was going to have to march across the shop looking like a Gallant Lake vagrant. His head came up the minute she stepped out of the back hall and into the café. Hoo-boy, she'd forgotten how intense those blue eyes were. Something warmed deep in her belly, and she almost stumbled when she recognized it as desire. She was not supposed to be feeling desire for anyone, damn it. She narrowed her eyes, but that just made him smile.

By the time she got to his table, she was fuming and he was fighting laughter.

"That's quite a look. Are you entering the witness protection program? Do you need a ride to the bus station?"

"I might need protection with you…" As soon as the words were out, she knew they were a mistake.

"I think it's a little early in our relationship to be discussing protection, don't you?"

"Ha ha." She reached for an empty chair, and Shane leapt to his feet to hold it for her, not releasing it until she was seated. The looks of a bad boy with the manners of a gentleman. It was a heady combination, and her brows furrowed as she tried to remember why she was here. Oh, yeah—Tori.

He'd returned to his own chair, nodding to Cathy working behind the counter. She waved, already filling a mug for Mel. She brought it to the table with a plate of mini scones.

He sat back and waited. He was good at that— waiting for the other person to speak. She was tempted to see how long he'd hold out, but this was too important.

"Why are you isolating Tori from her family and friends?"

His brows shot upward and his mouth dropped open, then he scowled at her.

"Is that what she told you?"

"No, she didn't tell…well, yes, she did in a way, but only in answer to my questions."

He shook his head, looking at the ceiling before meeting her gaze. "Why do you care so much about this kid, Mellie?"

"Don't call me that." Her voice was sharper

than she intended. She'd left Mellie behind when she'd walked away from the make-believe world Mellie existed in, and she didn't need any reminders of that life. "Call me Mel. Or Melanie. And you haven't answered my question."

He scrubbed his hand over his face in frustration.

"Alright, fine. You want to know why? Because her so-called friends at home are little assholes. They put her out there on social media to make themselves look cool, and it makes Tori look like some kind of party animal. Golf is a conservative, wholesome sport, and those cling-ons are dragging her down."

"But her family is there—why keep her away from them?"

"I'm *not*. I thought they'd be visiting every week, but... I don't know. I think they have their hands full with their other kids and figure Tim and I will take care of her. And we are..."

He didn't sound very sure of himself. Mel sat back, sipping her coffee and nibbling on a scone.

"It sounds like Tori's friends acted like typical teenagers. They're girls. They're full of hormones and bad decisions. But they're still her friends. You can't isolate her just because they did some dumb things. Did you try talking to them?"

Shane's eyes went wide. "*Talk* to her friends?

I don't know anything about teenage girls. What the hell would I say?"

"No females at all in your life? Sisters? Cousins? Nieces?"

"I'm an only child. The only women were my mom and my nana. Mom's a proper Boston blue blood. Nana, God rest her soul, was a tough-talking saint of a woman. But girls? No. As a teenage boy, my only contact with teenage girls involved convincing them to let me get past second base."

Mel shook her head. *Men*.

"So how on earth did you end up with a teenage girl as a client?"

"Her parents saw how we handled a situation for a rookie basketball player who got in hot water in Cleveland, and they reached out to us. I didn't want to do it, but they begged, and Tori was on her best behavior the first time we met. I had no idea what I was getting into."

Mel almost felt sorry for the guy.

He looked out the window, where the village of Gallant Lake was beginning to come to life. People were strolling the sidewalks and coming in for their Sunday morning coffee. Shane looked back to Mel, his blue eyes solemn.

"Tori got famous overnight, and her family wasn't ready. They hired some local attorney to manage her career, and the woman knew nothing about sports. Tori's contract with Winthrop Athletic is a joke. She should be sponsored by a much bigger name and making a lot more money." Shane shook his head. "When Gary came along and offered to take over her career by becoming her golf coach, her parents jumped at the chance to hand off responsibility. But he can't control her behavior, and it's really not his job to do that. Tori's laser-focused on the course, but then she'll act out like a two-year-old over something like what to wear to a public event."

Mel thought about the outfit Tori had worn to the gala last night. "She's trying to figure out who she is and how to assert herself so she doesn't get lost."

Trust me, Mellie, I know a lot more about this business than you, and if you'll just stop fighting me and do what I say, you'll be famous. Isn't that what you want?

Tori was tougher than she'd been at that age. The girl was fighting to maintain some kind of control over what her life should look like. Mel had handed over control early on in her modeling career, trusting the adults around her. If she'd maintained her childhood friends—stayed in touch, hung out with them to talk about boys and makeup and music—maybe she wouldn't have been so insecure and easy to manipulate.

Shane scrubbed his face once more, then ran

his fingers through that ginger hair until it was standing on end.

"Tori's a good kid," he said. "I want to do the right thing by her, and not just because it's my job." He tapped his finger against his coffee cup, drumming to some unknown beat in his head. "You say she's trying not to get lost, but *I'm* the one who's lost. I'm used to working with guys who are at least old enough to have graduated high school. I can cuss at them and boss 'em around and bust their balls, and we all laugh it off. If they don't like my decisions, they tell me to go screw myself, we argue and we settle it. Out in the open. No mystery involved. I can handle that. But I have no idea how to handle a young girl dressing like a hooker in some sort of protest against me for some unknown reason. I'm not a damned mind reader, you know?"

Mel didn't respond. Shane Brannigan was a talent agent, and she shouldn't trust a word out of his mouth. But she couldn't help but believe him when he said he was lost. Clueless was more like it. Not intentionally so, but the effects on Tori were the same.

"So what does Mrs. Winthrop think you hired me for?"

"Damned if I know. Mentor? Stylist? Chaperone?" He sat back in his chair and his gaze sharpened on her. "You complained yesterday that Tori didn't have a chaperone. Would you be interested in doing that for the next few weeks? She'll be back on the tour by mid-July, in time to pick up most of the majors. I can put you on the payroll…" He glanced at her baggy sweater and ball cap, his mouth quirking up into a grin. "And it looks like you've fallen on hard times, so…?"

He was a real comedian this morning. Of course, compared to her, *he* looked like he was ready for a *GQ* cover shoot in his pressed trousers and blue linen shirt. It was barely 8:00 a.m. On a Sunday.

"You're one of those annoying morning people, aren't you?"

Shane's smile deepened, causing her heart to stutter again. "Guilty as charged. I don't like wasting daylight. Interested in the job?"

She stared at her plate. If she worked for Shane, she'd have to answer to him. Tori needed a chaperone, but even more important, she needed a *friend* in Gallant Lake. Someone who had her back. No one had ever stepped up to do that for Mel when *she* was sixteen. They'd all just looked the other way and collected their paychecks. Mel wasn't going to let that happen to Tori.

"No." There was a flash of surprise in his eyes. "I won't work for you as her chaperone. I'll do it for free."

"For free? That's not a very good business plan,

Mellie…uh… Mel." His brows knit together, as if she'd just presented him with a puzzle to solve. She had a feeling he didn't like puzzles much.

"Look, that girl needs a friend while she's here. Someone she can relax with, have fun with, talk to. I'll be that person, but not on your payroll. Not on your time clock." She stood, emphasizing her point one last time before walking away.

"I don't charge for friendship."

CHAPTER FOUR

"SO LET ME get this straight." Luis set his coffee mug on the table and leaned back in the chair, staring out the window of the Gallant Brew as he put his thoughts together. The Tuesday morning sidewalks were quiet. "Someone just offered to *pay* you to mentor a girl who reminds you of yourself. And you decided to do it for *free*." He shook his head. "That's not a great career move, *chica*."

"I'm not looking for a new job."

"Aren't you, though?"

She didn't answer. Her bank balance was uncomfortably low. Nearly all the proceeds from selling the Miami condo had been poured into Luis's business for the new collection, leaving her just enough to make a fresh start somewhere. She was confident the investment would pay off, but that was an *investment*, not a job. She loved working on designs with Luis, but did she really want to go back into a world that had already chewed her up and spit her out once?

"I couldn't be more proud to be your business partner, Luis."

His broad shoulders shook with laughter. "Such a nice, safe answer, Mel. But you're too talented to be just an investor. You're a natural at design and accessorizing. I could use you on the team full-time."

"You mean the team that works in the fashion district? In Manhattan?" Mel suppressed the tremor that went through her, but just barely. "I don't think that'll happen."

He frowned at her. "I thought Gallant Lake was temporary?"

Mel shrugged, looking around the café and nodding at Nora, who'd just walked in from the back. "I don't know what my next move will be, but I don't think it will be to the fashion district."

Luis stared at her in silence. He was the one person who knew everything. When they'd first met four years ago, he'd been an associate at a major European design house. He'd contributed several pieces to the collection she'd be modeling, and he was hyper-anxious, micromanaging every aspect of the shoot. The photographer had a fit over Luis's constant "advice" and Mel ended up in the unlikely role of peacemaker between Luis and Nelson.

Even more unlikely, she and Luis became fast friends. She liked his creative process and his sense of humor. She even liked the way he obsessed over his work. It made her wish she had something in her life that mattered that much.

Luis somehow saw through the Mellie Low veneer and saw the real her. He also saw the booze and pills and recognized the danger she was in. He made it his quest to save her, even when she rebuffed every effort. When she finally hit her lowest point, though, it was Luis she'd called. He'd held her for hours without a word of judgment the day she'd come apart two years ago. He'd checked her into rehab and made sure no one else ever had a clue. She owed him her life. But in her heart, she knew she couldn't go back into the dog-eat-dog fashion world without putting all that hard work at risk. Not even for Luis.

"Darling," Luis said. "They have these crazy new things called computers, and you can communicate from *anywhere*. Even Gallant Lake."

"Design doesn't happen in a vacuum. As you said, it's a team thing. And the team is in the city." She took another sip of coffee. "Besides, I don't know that I'm really a *designer*. I like playing with everything once the design work is done. Mixing and matching the textures and colors, picking accessories…stuff like that."

When she and her friends had played dress-up as little girls, she'd been the one who told the others what to wear. She liked helping everyone else look pretty. Her becoming a fashion model was a fluke. If her childhood passions were any indication, she should have been one of the assistants backstage, not the one walking the runway.

Luis sat up and rested his big hand over hers on the table. "I'm not giving up on you yet." He winked. "And in the meantime, you have your mentoring job to help pay the bills." He snapped his fingers dramatically. "Oh, that's right—you turned that job down and offered to do the same work for *free*! Does this little town have a soup kitchen? 'Cuz you might need one at this rate."

Mel laughed so loudly that people waiting at the counter for coffee turned their heads. Impulsively, she leaned over and threw her arms around his neck. "My God, you beast—it's like hugging a bull!"

"Funny, that's exactly what my last date said. I think his name was Frankie." She planted an affectionate kiss on his cheek.

"You're my favorite way to start the day, Luis."

"Hey, Frankie said that, too!"

"Stop it, you dirty boy!"

"Are we interrupting?"

Shane and his friend Tim stood by the table. Shane's expression was stormy, and she wondered what had put him in such a mood. Tim, much like the night of the gala, was wearing a smile bordering on laughter. She had a feeling it reflected his normal approach to life.

Luis stood when Mel did, his arm remaining firmly around her waist. She stepped out of his embrace, surprised at his "papa bear" stance as he glared at Shane.

"Hi, guys. Is Tori with you?"

Tim shook his head. "She had a physical therapy session this morning. We just stopped by for some coffee while we work out our schedule for the next few weeks."

Shane and Luis were still glaring at each other in some weird, silent pissing contest, and Mel realized they hadn't actually been introduced.

"Luis Alvarado, this is Shane Brannigan and Tim Monroe. They're *trying* to manage Tori Sutter's career." Shane took his eyes off Luis long enough to narrow them at her. "Luis and I are business partners." She could have sworn Shane smirked at that. "He designed the gowns we wore at the gala."

Luis extended his hand to Shane. "Every one of those designs had Mel's touch, as well. Why don't you join us?"

When Luis turned to shake hands with Tim, the atmosphere at the table shifted, moving from confrontational to something much different. The two men maintained their grip on each other for a moment longer than necessary, and Tim's light smile deepened. Were they…? No, it couldn't be.

Nora brought over a plate of pastries as they all took their seats. "How about some sugar to wake everyone up?" Nora glanced at Mel in concern, but Mel shook her head. In other circumstances, being flanked by three men might be stressful for her, but not today. Luis was Luis. Tim's smile and laid-back attitude charmed her. And Shane? Well, she'd already discovered she could deal with Shane Brannigan.

Luis and Tim were discussing Gallant Lake and the workout routines they preferred—they were both very fine male specimens—while Shane devoured a maple scone, watching her with hooded eyes. He liked to play this see-who-talks-first game, but she wasn't in the mood for games this morning.

She gave him her sweetest smile. "I guess you could say this is the first meeting of Team Tori."

He returned her smile and upped the ante with a wink. "I thought you didn't want to be an employee?"

She convinced her heart to resume normal operations. Something about this man was both deadly and delicious.

"There are all kinds of teams, Shane. We care about Tori, so that makes us a team." He glanced at Luis, but didn't argue with her.

"Actually, this might be a good time to set some expectations."

"Such as?" She picked up a ginger cookie—Nora knew they were her favorite—and nibbled at it.

"As you've so very bluntly pointed out, I need to be doing a better job of watching out for Tori's best interests." He gestured in her direction. "I'm working on that, and right now, you're the unknown factor in her circle of influence. Being her pal is fine, but I won't allow you to interfere with her career."

Mel rested her chin on her hand and fluttered her eyelashes at him. "Wow. It's hard to believe any woman ever dumped a guy like you at the altar. And I won't allow my new friend to be swallowed up whole by that so-called career."

Shane snorted. "It wasn't exactly at the altar, and I'm over it. As far as Tori's career goes, you don't have any say in that, sweetheart." Her eyes narrowed on him. Shane didn't seem to notice that Luis was now watching him closely. "You chose not to be a paid consultant, so you don't get to be involved in that part of her life."

Mel leaned forward. "You want to set expectations? Fine. You can *expect* to be wearing whatever drink I have in my hand, hot or cold, if you ever refer to me as 'sweetheart' again." Shane's eyes widened. "And you *wanted* me on

your damn team a few days ago. Just because I
didn't want to work for you—which in hindsight
seems like a very wise decision—doesn't mean
I intend to stay quiet." He started to speak, but
she held up her hand to stop him. "You *need* me,
Brannigan. I bring experience to the team that
neither you nor Tim nor, God forbid, Gary, can
possibly offer."

Shane stared at her for a heartbeat, then slowly
smiled, as if against his will. He sat back in
his seat and did everything possible to make it
seem as if he was totally calm and in charge.
But Mel made a living using body language to
fool people into believing something that wasn't
true—whether it was self-confidence or sexual
attraction. She caught the way Shane chewed on
the inside of his cheek. One hand slipped into
his pocket, probably clenched in frustration. His
other hand tapped against the tabletop. She'd
poked the bear, and the bear didn't like it. *Tough
luck, bear.*

Tim cleared his throat. "Mel, I think what
Shane is trying to say…" He shot a dark look at
his business partner. "I think he's trying to say
we appreciate your concern for Tori's well-being,
and we agree she needs advice from someone
who has an understanding of her situation."

Shane's right brow arched sharply, which had
a very odd effect on Melanie's ability to think

clearly. Big Ginger was one hellaciously attractive man. Until he opened his mouth.

"So you're saying that someone who plays dress-up for a living can understand what an actual athlete is dealing with?"

Luis started to say something, but Tim stopped him with a look that both cautioned and sizzled. He didn't even try to hide the swift kick he gave Shane under the table, and Mel was pretty sure it was with his metal prosthetic foot.

"Shane clearly hasn't had time to do his homework. But I have." Tim gave her a warm smile. "You were an overnight superstar at about the same age as Tori. You were away from your family and support group. You were under a lot of pressure from people you didn't know. You ended up with a party-girl reputation you may not have deserved. And you're worried Tori will make some of the same…" He looked chagrined. "No offense, but some of the same…*mistakes*… for lack of a better word, that you did. Is that about right?"

"Thank you, Tim," Luis said with a smile. "I'm glad at least one of you appreciates how much Mel can help Tori."

And Tim Monroe *blushed*. Mel looked from him to Luis and back again. She hadn't been wrong before. They were *flirting* with each other. Could they be any cuter? She grinned at Shane, wondering what his reaction to the two guys would be, but he was too busy staring at her to notice. His expression was a mix of confusion and reluctant acknowledgment. And it took all her body-acting skills not to squirm under the intensity of his blue-eyed gaze. He studied her for a moment longer, then nodded, as if to himself.

"Fine. Be her friend. Be on the team. But every team has a captain, and on Team Tori, that's me." Tim rolled his eyes at Mel from over Shane's shoulder. "Her physical therapy wraps up in another week or so, so that'll give her more time off." He drained his coffee, then tried to intimidate her with an all-business warning. *Big, bad agent man.* "I know you think Gary's up to no good, but Tori never complained until you showed up. That doesn't mean we won't be watching a lot more closely going forward. Tim will be around for a few days, and when he's not here, I'll stay or her parents will be with her." He saw her surprised expression. "What? You wouldn't take the chaperone job so we'll have to handle it." He frowned into his coffee cup for a moment. "If you can help her navigate teen fame, fine. As long as it doesn't involve quitting the sport, I'd support that."

"I appreciate your support and all, but I don't work for you. What Tori and I discuss isn't any of your business." He started to object, but she rushed ahead, holding up a finger to silence him. "Look, I get that she's your client and is *technically* your business. I'm just not sure if you're all that good for her."

"So I'm supposed to prove myself to *you*?"

"No. You're supposed to prove yourself to your client." Mel dropped her warning finger and relaxed her shoulders. Turning Shane into an enemy wouldn't help anyone. "Look, I'm not putting limits on what Tori and I talk about, and our conversations will be private. It's the only way she'll trust me. But I promise to give you a heads-up if there's anything going on that concerns me. Fair enough?"

Tim spoke before Shane could. "That's more than fair, Mel. And we appreciate your friendship with our client. Don't we, Shane?" He gave her a smile. "Tori said something about having dinner with you tonight?"

She smiled back. "Yes. It's Taco Tuesday at the Chalet. It's a townie place. None of the locals will bother her." It was one of Mel's favorite things about Gallant Lake. The residents seldom raised an eyebrow over someone being well-known, whether they were guests at the resort or not. People just went about their lives.

"Athletes need a healthy diet…" Shane started, but Tim shut him down. Judging from the wince on Shane's face, Tim was applying pressure with the metal prosthetic under the table as he spoke.

"But everyone should get a chance to enjoy tacos once in a while, right?"

Mel nodded and tried not to react when Tim winked at her. He was such a charmer. Luis let out a very soft growl of appreciation. Shane just growled before standing and stomping out of the café.

"THE NEXT TIME I need you to be my keeper, I'll let you know, okay?" Shane glared at Tim as they headed back to their car. "Don't ever tell people in a business meeting what I 'really' meant to say or do."

"That wasn't exactly a *business* meeting, but fine. Sink or swim on your own." Tim's prosthetic didn't slow his pace, and Shane had to hustle to keep up with him on the sidewalk along Main Street.

"Why wasn't it a business meeting? Tori's our client. We talked business. It's not our fault we interrupted their little coffee date."

"Why do you say it like that? They're business partners, like us."

Shane barked out a laugh. "Yeah, right. As if that's all they are."

"You've lost me."

"Come on, Tim. You saw them when we walked in. They're obviously a couple."

Tim stopped so abruptly that Shane blew several steps past him.

"You think Luis and Mel are a *couple*?"

It didn't make Shane happy to admit it. He'd been thinking Melanie might be an interesting diversion as long as he had to spend time in this hole-in-the-wall town. They were both successful people, and probably had a lot in common. She was smart and he liked the way he had to stay on his toes around her. He liked a lot of things about her. But he definitely didn't like the intimate coziness that clearly existed between her and her partner.

"She was practically sitting in the guy's damn lap when we walked in. Yeah, they're definitely a couple."

"No." Tim shook his head. "They are definitely not."

Shane threw his hands in the air. "And how the hell do you know that?"

"Because…" Tim stopped and gave Shane an odd look over the roof of the car. "You know what? Never mind. Maybe you're right."

"Of course I'm right! I can't believe you didn't see it." He slid behind the wheel of his low-slung Lincoln and couldn't resist needling his friend.

"Aren't you gay guys supposed to be more in tune with relationships and romance and stuff?"

"Don't start on me with that gay-men-make-the-best-wedding-planners crap. Do I look like a matchmaker to you?" Tim gestured to his chinos and polo shirt. "Have you ever seen me drawing hearts and cupids on my meeting notes?"

Shane pulled the car away from the curb. Tim had a point. He was the least gay gay man Shane had ever met. Of course, Tim had been in the army during the days of "don't ask don't tell," so he'd had years of practice at acting like the most macho guy in the room. He smiled to himself— that wasn't really an act. Tim was the toughest guy Shane knew. As a Ranger, he'd been a natural leader and an inspiration to the men he'd led.

"You are definitely not the hearts-and-flowers type." Shane glanced at him. "But you know it would be okay with me if you were."

"Oh, thanks, Dad. I'm glad you're proud of me now that I'm out of the closet. You gonna march with me during Pride Week, too? I'll get you a T-shirt."

"Christ, what is your problem? When have I ever not been 100 percent behind you?"

"That would be a sentence I'd avoid saying out loud at the parade if I were you." They pulled into the entrance of the resort, driving between two massive stone pillars. "But as long as we're all about my gayness this morning, what makes you think Luis wasn't interested in *me*?"

Shane laughed as he backed the car into a parking spot. "I'm not saying you're not a catch, but, dude, did you see him with Melanie? He was all over her. Hetero all the way, my friend."

When they'd first walked into the café, the two of them had been laughing together, and Mel's arms had been around Luis's neck. And when Luis had seen Shane, he'd jumped into alpha-protective mode. The way he'd stood and kept his arm firmly around her waist. The way he'd given Shane the I-smell-a-rival stink-eye when they were introduced. And at the charity event, Luis and Mel had kissed and whispered together like a couple who knew each other's secrets. Shane envied the guy.

Tim started to get out of the car, then turned back, looking oddly amused.

"Well, you would know that far better than me, Shane."

They headed into the resort lobby with the towering staircase winding up through the center like a giant tree. There were even metal leaves hanging from the ceiling three stories above them. The owners hadn't spared any expense in their efforts to bring the place into the twenty-first century. Tim nudged him with his elbow.

"Why are you so concerned with Luis and

Mel's relationship, anyway? Oh, wait." Tim gave his best Valley girl imitation. "Oh. My. Gawd. You *like* her! You like Mellie Low!" The accent vanished. "Hot damn, man. You're swinging for the fences with that one—a supermodel. She's clever, too. And tough."

"And taken."

Tim's mouth opened, then snapped shut.

"What?"

"Nothing. I'm sure you're right, Shane. But I didn't see any rings."

"What does that mean?"

"Do I really need to spell it out for you? If you want her, go after her."

"First, I don't want her." A little alarm went off in his head. Okay, maybe he wanted her a little, but who wouldn't? "Second, I'm not a guy who makes a move on another guy's girl." Tim raised a finger as if he wanted to interrupt, but Shane ignored him. "And third, she may not work for us, but she is mentoring our client, and it would be unprofessional."

"So…would it be unprofessional of me to go after Luis?"

"No, but it would be a waste of your time. I know a couple when I see one, Tim, and those two have been intimate. Did you see that dress he made for her to wear at the dinner? That he probably fit personally to her every curve?" His heart did something funny at the thought of that dark metallic gown. His heart did something less funny at the thought of Luis touching Mel's skin as he fit the dress. "Did you see the way she kissed his cheek this morning, as if they were husband and wife already? His arm around her waist? And where do you think he's staying? I haven't seen him hanging around the resort, so he must be staying at her place."

Tim folded his arms and stared hard at Shane. "For someone who's not interested, you've spent a lot of time thinking about this. You *sure* you don't have the hots for Mellie Low?"

"Don't call her that. She doesn't like it." She'd made that clear, and he suspected there was a story there. But it wasn't his to know. Luis was her guy. And that was fine. The last thing he needed right now was some warrior princess in his life.

Tim looked at his watch. "I gotta run, man. Conference call with the manager in Baltimore to see how interested they might be in our boy Jimmy. Their closer is out for the season for elbow surgery, so they might be willing to over-look our kid's big mouth and sign him up for their bullpen."

"Is Jimmy done with his anger management sessions?" Jimmy Martinez had a bad habit of mouthing off not only to other players, but also to fans in the stands. Baseball team owners didn't like that much.

Tim nodded. "Yeah. We just need to find a team that'll take him on."

"Someday we won't have to deal with this kind of crap."

"Why not?"

"Instead of getting our *players* into the big leagues, don't you think it's time for *us* to make the jump to the big leagues?" Tim was still confused. "Come on, man. Join forces with a bigger agency? Get that corner office we've been looking for?"

Tim waved his hand in dismissal. "That's your dad talking, Shane. You need to let it go. I like our setup just fine. We call the shots, not anyone else. I'll catch you for dinner?"

Tim turned away, then turned back again with humor in his eyes. "Do you want to see if Luis and Melanie want to double date with us? Maybe I could plan their wedding for them."

"Shut up, you jackass."

"What would you do if you were wrong about them?"

"I'm not."

But if he was, that would mean that Mel, with her mile-long legs and violet eyes, might just be available.

And that might just be trouble.

CHAPTER FIVE

MEL CHECKED THE pocket on her running shorts one last time before allowing the back door to close. The key to the apartment was safely in place, along with her phone. Nora hadn't complained the last time Mel locked herself out and had to call for help. But that had been at dinnertime, not four o'clock on a Saturday morning.

Gallant Lake was completely silent. There was only one light in the parking lot behind the row of downtown buildings that held the coffee shop and other businesses and apartments. That light barely lit the metal fire escape she was quietly descending. The only other resident in this cluster of shops was Carl Wallace a few buildings down. It was unlikely the liquor store owner would hear her at this hour, but she still tiptoed down to the pavement.

She'd been awake for hours, and she knew from experience that sleep wasn't going to find her tonight. Pacing the apartment didn't help, so she was off for a run in the darkness to burn off the restlessness that itched under her skin, begging for relief.

Begging for medication. Or maybe a drink.

She slipped her earpieces in place and selected a running mix on her phone. Gallant Lake was much more accommodating of her predawn runs than Miami or Manhattan had been. There weren't any creepsters or drunks hanging out on corners or in alleyways to worry about. Just the occasional raccoon ransacking someone's trash can, or perhaps a deer lifting its head to watch her go by. And, of course, there was Nessie.

The skinny yellow dog had scared the daylights out of Mel a couple of weeks ago, bounding up out of the darkness as she ran along a path by the lakeshore. Mel had fallen as she'd scrambled to defend herself against what had looked like a giant blond octopus coming out of the water, and the creature had been on her in a heartbeat—licking her face and wiggling all over in delight. Since that night, it seemed like the pup was waiting for her to come by. Mel had dubbed her "Nessie" in honor of the Loch Ness Monster, since she'd risen out of the lake that first night.

Sure enough, as Mel hit the outskirts of town, Nessie sneaked out of the darkness to join her. The skittish dog allowed Mel to give her a quick pat on the head, then moved a safe distance away—just out of arm's reach. She jogged along beside Mel, as if she was also looking for something to do in the middle of the night.

Everything about Nessie was long. And thin. She never wore a collar. No apparent grooming. Mud from yesterday's rain was caked on one hip. She was clearly a homeless stray. Mel had seen her hovering around the back door to Nora's coffee shop a few times, but she always bolted when the door opened. Apparently Mel wasn't the only one wondering if Gallant Lake was *home*, a place where she could belong.

She and Nessie jogged east out of town, uphill toward the resort. She turned back just before coming into range of the security cameras—Blake would definitely report her late-night appearance to his wife, then Amanda would tell the other cousins and they would demand an explanation. Mel ran along the dark lakeshore, Nessie at her side, with only the moon to light the familiar path. She'd slowed to a walk by the time they reached the dimly lit lake walk in town. Nate Thomas at the hardware store was working so hard to make it an attraction.

The narrow boardwalk ran along the water, behind a row of shops on Main Street. Nate was determined that the businesses in town should add lights and flower boxes and make the boardwalk a feature of the town. Gallant Lake was struggling to make a comeback from the decades when the resort had been closed and the financial fate of the town had been thrown into jeopardy. Nate was a sweet, nerdy optimist, and Mel hoped he got his way with this project.

At the end of the lake walk, Mel took the path that ran through the park, and she and Nessie ran another mile or so before she decided to call it quits. Winded and slightly chilled from a breeze off the lake, she no longer felt that annoying itch to reach for alcohol or pills. Well, she felt the itch, but it was no longer overwhelming her. With the help of a glass of warm milk back at the apartment, she might even be able to get a couple hours of sleep.

She and Nessie were at the opposite end of town from the apartment, and had just started the walk back, when she heard a car approaching. The dark woods alongside the road flickered with shadows from the headlights. She didn't see a lot of cars on the road at this hour, but it happened occasionally, especially on weekends. Maybe it was Deputy Sheriff Dan Adams, who'd scolded her twice already for running alone at night. But come on, this was Gallant Lake. What could possibly happen here?

She frowned when she realized the car was slowing behind her. Nessie kept looking nervously over her shoulder, and Mel fought the urge to do the same. Making eye contact would be a mistake if this really was a problem rolling up. If it *was* trouble, her only option would be to run into the woods.

"Melanie? Is that you?"

At the sound of a rough male voice, Nessie glanced up at Mel as if in apology, then tucked her tail and bolted into the trees. Great. She was alone out here with Shane Brannigan. His dark Lincoln came to a stop beside her, passenger window rolled down.

"How could you possibly know it was me in the dark and from behind?"

"You're kidding, right? I'd recognize that fashion model strut anywhere. No one moves the way you do."

She parsed the words, trying to determine if they were a compliment or a dig at her former career. There was something about the way he'd said the last sentence that had sounded appreciative, though, and the thought warmed her unexpectedly. She was so busy trying to understand her reaction that she didn't realize he was still speaking.

"...the hell are you doing out here at four thirty in the morning? Did your car break down? Are you okay?"

"I'm fine, thanks. I'm a night owl, and I went for a run." She walked over and leaned against the car, ducking her head to make eye contact with him. The glow of the high-tech dashboard cast rough shadows across his skin and highlighted that imperfect nose. "What are *you* doing out this late?"

"This *early*, you mean. I was back in Boston for a few days." He gave her a grin. "I guess you could say I'm a night owl, too. I woke up a few hours ago and decided to drive while the roads were quiet." He reached over and unlatched the door. "Come on, I'll give you a ride to your place. You shouldn't be out here alone."

It was too dark for him to see her eyes roll. "Have you been talking to Sheriff Dan?"

Mel didn't *need* a ride. It wasn't that far. And she normally wouldn't consider getting into a car at night with a man she barely knew. But something about Shane Brannigan felt safe. Irritating, but safe. She opened the door and slid inside.

"You *drove* from Boston? That's more than a few hours."

He huffed out a laugh. "Not at this time of night. And not the way I drive." He glanced at the dashboard. "I made it in a little over two hours. Who's Sheriff Dan?"

After a moment's hesitation at the abrupt subject change, Mel replied, "He's a friend of my cousin's fiancé, and he's the law around here. He likes to give me grief about my nighttime strolls."

"What do you mean, he gives you grief?"

Shane had pulled away from the shoulder now, and his fingers tightened on the wheel.

"Easy there, Macho Man, I just meant he politely advises me not to do it. He's concerned for my safety. That's his job, right? But seriously, this is Gallant Lake."

He glanced her way and frowned. "I get what you're saying about this town being sleepy, but that doesn't mean it's safe. What if I'd been some drunk looking for trouble just now?"

"I would have run into the woods. I had it all planned out."

They pulled behind the shops and he parked the car, then turned to stare at her in disbelief.

"Your plan was to…run into the woods? Do you have night-vision goggles on you so you wouldn't run straight into a tree or fall in a ditch? Did it occur to you that maybe the drunk guy would be familiar with those woods and *catch* you? In the woods?"

It rankled her to admit he had a point. She scowled.

"But you *weren't* some drunk, were you? And I'm perfectly fine. So it doesn't matter, does it?" She opened the door, flooding the interior of the car with light. This close, she could see the glints of turquoise in Shane's blue eyes. They reminded her of Caribbean waters. Warm and inviting… She blinked. She needed to remember that Shane

Brannigan was an *agent*. He wanted to be *in charge*. And he was clueless about women. It was time for her to go.

Instead of saying *thank you* or *good night* or *drop dead* or any one of a dozen perfectly sensible things to say, she got out of the car, then leaned over to look at him and said the most ridiculous thing she could imagine.

"Want to come up for a cup of coffee?"

His eyes went wide.

"What about Luis?"

She was as surprised by his question as they'd both been by hers.

"What about him?"

"Isn't he staying here?"

"He's in New York." Why did he care so much about Luis? "Look, if you don't want coffee, just say so. Thanks for the ride."

She turned away, shutting the car door firmly. The invitation had been a mistake. It would be best for everyone if he just left. She'd almost made it to the stairs when she heard his door open behind her.

"Hold up. Coffee sounds good. No sense trying to get any sleep at this hour."

Mel nodded. "Come on, then."

"You use a fire escape to get to your back door?" He followed her up the stairs. "Just when I thought this town couldn't get any weirder."

Mel unlocked her door. "Using the downstairs entrance means disarming and rearming the café alarm system. This is much easier." The door swung open and she flipped on the light. "Nora told me the story behind the fire escapes once. Something about a huge fire decades ago and the town made it law for a while that every level of every building had to have a fire escape."

"It's not the classiest way to come into your home, is it?"

It was odd having him here, in her space. Shane exuded a raw power that made the air in the small loft almost sizzle. Not in a frightening way. But it was still scary because it was so unfamiliar to Mel. She wasn't used to men who excited her without setting off all her alarms.

"I'm sorry if my home isn't up to your Boston blue blood standards."

"First, I don't have blue blood standards." He settled onto one of the bar stools at the kitchen island. "And second, this isn't really your home, is it? Not permanently?"

Mel held up a small pod of Sumatra coffee and, when he gave her a nod of approval, she started the coffee maker. She glanced over her shoulder and smiled. Maybe it was just the crazy hour and the Shane-Effect of him sitting in her kitchen, but she liked the way they could poke at each other like this. His casual disdain for his surroundings made him easy to tease.

"First, you *told* me your mother was a blue blood and you're an insufferable snob about Gallant Lake, so I call BS on your standards. And second, I didn't say it was permanent." She glanced toward the windows, where the faintest of predawn glows had appeared on the other side of Gallant Mountain, turning the flat surface of the lake to a shimmering pinkish gray. "But it's growing on me."

"Come on." He looked around the open space, anchored by the small kitchen, highlighted with a wall of windows and topped with the metal loft that held the master suite. "This has to be a comedown from what you're used to."

"It's functional, and there's a certain beauty in functionality, don't you think?"

He took the coffee mug from her with a nod of thanks. "There's beauty in beauty. And function in functionality. But they're two different things."

"How very simplistic of you."

"Yeah, well, I'm a guy, so…"

SHE CHUCKLED, AND Shane watched as she pulled a small plate from the cupboard, arranged a few muffins on it from a bag he assumed had come from the coffee shop and slid it toward him across the island. She turned away to start a cup of cinnamon coffee for herself. She was dressed in gray leggings that stopped just below her knees and a white top that was long but not oversize. In fact, it left little to the imagination. Her dark hair was pulled back into a ponytail, showing off her long neck. Her movements, even in this small kitchen, were graceful and precise.

Beauty in functionality. *Huh.*

She walked around the island and sat beside him. The scent of her cinnamon coffee was cozy and oddly relaxing. But there was nothing cozy about those violet eyes when they met his gaze. There always seemed to be a simmering intensity there.

"How did a supermodel end up in this place?"

Mel's shoulder lifted just a fraction. "Two of my cousins live in Gallant Lake. The apartment belongs to Nora, so the rent's cheap. It's close enough to New York for Luis and I to meet on business regularly." He did his best to ignore the slow burn he always felt when she mentioned the man in her life. "And it's charming."

"*Charming?* Really? Half the stores in town are boarded up. The rest are in various stages of collapse." She rolled her eyes at his exaggeration, but he wasn't off by much. "You must have lived in some pretty swanky places with your job. Don't you feel like you're slumming here?"

She took a sip from her coffee, a smile playing at her lips.

"How's the view from that ivory tower of yours, Shane? I know this isn't Boston, but it's hardly slumming, either. At the moment, this is the right place for me." She blew on the surface of her coffee, which did something odd to Shane's ability to think clearly. "Gallant Lake is what I need."

Need was an odd word. She'd been a famous cover girl, so he had to assume she'd been paid accordingly. Why would she *need* a little place like this? He had a new and burning curiosity to know everything.

"Why don't you want to be called Mellie Low anymore? Wasn't that your stage name or whatever?"

It wasn't his intention to hurt her, but he clearly had. Her eyes clouded and her body stiffened as if ready for battle. He held up a hand in surrender.

"I'm sorry. It's none of my business."

Mel stared into her coffee, not answering for what seemed like hours.

"Mellie Low is dead." Her voice was so flat and final that he almost shuddered from it. "I guess it's more accurate to say Mellie never existed. She was make-believe. Nothing more than a commodity. A business. A mistake." That last word came out sharply, and he almost reached over for her hand. But he caught himself, knowing it would be a mistake to touch her. "So I left her behind."

"That couldn't have been easy."

She gave him a bittersweet smile. "It wasn't. But it had to be done."

Shane watched her finger as it traced the rim of her coffee mug.

"Didn't you have an agent or agency or whatever models have?"

She looked at him with one brow arched in humor or disbelief—he wasn't sure which.

"My experience with agents hasn't exactly been stellar."

That explained why she'd had so much animosity toward him when they met last weekend. She'd lumped him together with the apparent idiots who'd managed her career so far.

"I'm sorry. That's not how it's supposed to work. If you found the right agency, though, you could get back in the game again." She pulled back, her mouth thinning in displeasure, as he rushed to explain. "People already know who you are, so you'd have all the bargaining power. You could set your own terms. Get a good contract. Before you know it, you'd be right back on top."

Mel seemed horrified at the thought.

"On top of *what*?"

"On top of your business. Your industry. Whatever. I mean, you were already there once. It's not too late to get back there again."

He couldn't understand her reaction. Who doesn't want to be the best at what they do? Wasn't that the whole point?

Mel stood, taking her empty cup and reaching for his.

"It's late." She glanced toward the windows, where the sky was starting to glow pink and orange. "Or early. Or something. You should go."

"Mel, I'm just trying to help fix things. Managing careers is what I do…"

"You don't manage *my* career. And you never will. No one will. Whatever I end up doing next, and wherever I end up doing it, I'll be doing it on my own." She spun on her heel and walked to the sink, dropping the mugs in with a clatter. "And it sure as hell won't be modeling." She started down the hall, talking over her shoulder. "I'm afraid you'll have to go slumming again and use the fire escape to get to your car."

He followed, trying to figure out what he'd said wrong. Her career had been mismanaged. He'd suggested fixing that. She should be *thanking* him, right? She opened the back door and looked at him, tall and defiant, shoulders back and chin high. She'd worked up a temper on the short walk, and her eyes were dark and flashing.

"Let's get one thing straight, Brannigan. You

don't know anything about me, my career or my life, so don't presume you know how to fix it. I fixed it myself by walking away. I did it because I wanted to. Because I *had* to. I lost most of my hard-earned money. I almost lost my soul. But I'm *out*. Let someone else scramble over a pile of bodies to get to the so-called 'top.'" A shadow passed over her expression. "Because I've seen the view from there, and it's not worth it. Good night."

For the life of him, The Dealmaker couldn't think of a single thing to say to that. He dipped his head in farewell as he walked through the door, and flinched when she slammed it shut behind him. Her words echoed around in his head, and he knew there was a story there. Her story. It probably wasn't pretty. But he wanted to know every detail.

CHAPTER SIX

"THAT HIPPIE LADY downstairs is a hoot and a
half." Luis set two coffees and a bag of pastries
on the kitchen counter. His long hair was pulled
back into his usual ponytail. He'd developed
quite an interest in driving up to Gallant Lake
lately. Especially if Tim Monroe was around. Although Mel hadn't seen Shane since early Saturday morning, Luis told her Shane and Tim had
apparently both been in town since the weekend,
and it was now Thursday.

"Are you talking about Cathy down in the coffee shop?" Mel laughed. "God, don't call her a
hippie to her face. She hates it—says it ages her.
She prefers bohemian. Or free spirit. But Carl at
the liquor store teases her about the 'free' part,
because she won't give him a resident discount
anymore now that Nora owns the café… What?"
Luis's face was suddenly grim.

"How exactly do you know 'Carl at the liquor
store'?"

"It's not what it sounds like." Mel reached
out and patted Luis's hand. "Honest! He's a

neighbor—the only other resident in this stretch of shops at the moment. We have coffee together most mornings, usually with Nate from the hardware store across the street. Carl's store is four doors down, but I've never set foot inside it, and yes, he knows why. He's just a friend who happens to own a liquor store."

Luis's expression went from worried to warm. "Cathy. Carl. Nate. You're making friends in this town, aside from your cousins. You're putting down roots someplace for the first time."

She *had* made friends here in Gallant Lake. Business owners. Nora's regular customers, like John and Steve, who played cribbage at the small table against the wall in the café. Some of the staff from the resort, like the golf pro, Cody Brooks, and Julie at the front desk. Did those friendships mean she was putting down roots? Was that what she *wanted*? To settle in Gallant Lake? And do what? At that scary thought, she shook her head.

"Just because I've made a few friends doesn't mean I'm settling down here." She dug into the bag and found the ginger cookies she was hoping for. "What did you want me to look at?"

Luis opened his portfolio and spread sketches out across the kitchen island. He was freaking out about Fashion Week coming up in September, and wanted Mel to take one last look at the collection for her advice on accessories.

"Put a larger leather bag with the pants and jacket. And that scarf is wrong—I'd go with a brighter yellow." Luis got busy with his colored pencils, scratching new designs on the pad, and the image looked amazing. She smiled at him. "This is fun. This is the stuff I love."

"You have a great eye for color and accessories. You know what looks good on a certain type of woman or for a particular event. I get bogged down in those detail decisions." He shrugged. "That's why we're such a good team, Mel. We each bring strengths to the game. I need you to make it work."

"Luis, we've talked about this. You need someone who's going to be full-time, not some consultant you have to drive two hours to get to."

"Why don't you let *me* decide what I need, Mel?"

Tears suddenly burned her eyes.

"And what about what *I* need?" She had no idea where this anger was coming from, but it was burning hot and heavy. "I need more than just sitting around waiting for you to call me for advice. I need a *purpose*. I need a reason to get up in the morning." Her voice was sharp and brittle in her own ears.

Luis leaned back in his chair and started slowly clapping his hands.

"It's about damn time."

"Time for what? My long-awaited nervous breakdown?" She wiped moisture from her cheeks, embarrassed by the show of emotion.

"It's about damn time you started thinking about what *you* need, *chica*. Bra-fucking-vo."

Maybe Luis was right. Maybe she was turning some sort of corner. Her thoughts of the future had been random, worrisome ramblings along the lines of "What will I be when I grow up?" It was a worry for *someday*. A mythical time she hadn't thought about over the past couple of years, as she'd fought to find some sense of balance in a suddenly sober life. She'd figured there'd be time to deal with *someday* later. Apparently *later* had just arrived.

"Oh, I almost forgot." Luis handed Mel a bag. "Try this on, hon. I've been playing with some crushed velvets with all the retro stuff going on, and this skirt has your name all over it. I'm dying to see it on a real model instead of just a dress form."

"You want me to play dress-up for you?" She smiled. He'd basically worked out his new collection right on her body over the past year. It helped him see the movement of the fashions, and it helped her get back on her feet to do something familiar, with an audience of one. She peeked into the bag. "Is there a top in here, too?"

"No. Just use a black T."

She used the downstairs bedroom to change, grabbing a top from the clothes hanging in the laundry room. That was one of the problems with staying in Nora's apartment. Mel's wardrobe wouldn't fit in the small closet upstairs in the loft. In fact, it didn't fit in the small closet, the spare bedroom closet, the hall closet and the laundry room combined.

She pulled on the scoop-neck T and took the butter-soft skirt out of the bag. It was an asymmetrical patchwork of blues and black, blocked on a bias so it swirled around her calves when she moved. The thread was shot through with glints of gold and silver. Mel sauntered out to the kitchen in her best runway walk, stopping and turning in front of Luis.

"It's a little heavy for this weather, but for winter it would be divine." She ran her hands down the fabric and smiled. "I can see this with a long sweater and brown leather boots. It's so comfortable." She met his approving eyes. "This is a winner, Luis."

A rumble of footsteps thundered on the staircase. Luis arched a brow.

"Expecting a party of twelve?"

"I'm not expecting anyone." She was headed toward the door before the first knock sounded.

It was Tori. Tears streaked through a thick layer of overdone makeup. Her hair was pulled up into a ponytail on top of her head, making her look twelve. She wore a bright pink bikini top, a pair of gray sweats and her green high-tops.

"I *hate* him, Mel!" Tori stomped into the apartment.

"Hate who? Gary?"

"No! *Shane!* He's nothing but a bossy asshole."

"Hey—watch the language."

"Oh, sure. Everyone can swear but me, right? Everyone knows better than me. Everyone has an opinion about what Tori should do and what Tori should wear and how Tori should behave, and I've had it. I'm getting a plane ticket out of this dump and I'm going home."

Mel looked down the empty stairway to the coffee shop and closed the door. "How did you get here?"

"I walked. I was so mad that I walked, okay?" Tori's tears started afresh. "And don't tell me I shouldn't have done it. I'm here and I'm fine and I can make decisions for myself! I am tired of being treated like a child!"

Mel's eyes met Luis's, and he mouthed a silent *wow*.

"Okay," Mel said. "Why don't you sit down and tell us what happened."

Tori looked around at the word *us* and saw Luis for the first time. A little of the steam went out of her.

"Oh. Sorry. You're the designer, right? Luis Alvarado? You work for Mel?"

Luis choked back a laugh. "I work *with* Mel. And you're Mel's friend Tori, the famous young golfer."

Tori scowled. "I'm done with the 'famous' part. I'm done with people telling me what to do and making fun of me and not letting me be myself. I quit."

"Tori, what happened?" Mel handed her a bottle of water and she gulped it down. It was a three-mile walk from the resort on a hot summer day. She tried not to think about Tori making that walk in a skimpy bikini top.

"*Shane* happened! He's such a jerk." Tori flopped down on the sofa. "I just want to go home."

Mel sat across from Tori, determined to focus on the issue at hand. "Why don't you give me a clue what the problem is."

"He wanted me to do some publicity shots. Said we needed them to release when I go back on tour in a couple weeks. He and Tim want to show the world I'm healthy and ready to go." None of that sounded unreasonable to Mel, except for the part where the teenage golfer was in a bikini.

Come on, Mellie. Sometimes you have to show a little skin to get noticed...

"Did the photographer want you in a swimsuit?" She hated to think a bikini shoot for a teenager was Shane's idea.

"I never even *saw* the photographer! Shane started yelling at me as soon as I came down to the lobby. He *told* me the pictures would be taken on the lakeshore. He *told* me to look nice. He *told* me to wear something attractive, like a suit. Then he had a shit-fit when I did exactly what he told me to do!" Her voice raised on her last few words. "I'm so sick of men!"

Mel came to the same conclusion Luis obviously had, because he was chuckling to himself behind Tori. But Tori probably wouldn't find it funny that Shane hadn't been suggesting a *bathing* suit. He'd somehow assumed a teenager had an actual *suit*. Like a business suit. And then he'd yelled at Tori for not understanding his ridiculous request. He hadn't been kidding when he'd said he was clueless about girls.

"Where was Tim in all this?" Mel knew Tim was usually the balancing factor between Tori's emotions and Shane's bluntness.

Surprisingly, it was Luis who answered. "He left early this morning for some client emergency."

Tori tugged at her baggy sweats. "I hate Shane."

"You don't hate him. You're *mad* at him, and that's okay. It may have been a misunderstanding. Does he know you walked into town?"

Tori shook her head. "He canceled the photo shoot and told me to go 'scrape the paint' off my face and 'put some clothes on.'" She looked at Mel, tears brimming in her eyes. "My mom bought me this makeup."

"Honey, there's nothing wrong with your makeup." She ignored the faces Luis was making behind Tori. "You just need more practice putting it on. And making yourself up for a photo shoot is totally different than going out with friends. The camera lens changes everything." Shane didn't have female clients, so he probably wouldn't know that, but still. "Now that you've been crying and walking and sweating, it's a bit of a mess. Why don't you go into the bathroom and wipe it off—there's special cream in the cabinet that'll make your skin feel great."

Tori stomped down the hall in a combination of pouting and defiance. "Fine. I hate it all, anyway."

Mel's cell phone buzzed on the table, and Luis tossed it to her. It was Amanda.

"By any chance, do you have a certain teenage girl with you?"

"Yes. Why?"

"Shane Brannigan is threatening to tear the

resort apart to find her. He's convinced someone kidnapped her or that she's done something
awful. He wants Blake to call the police and said
we should drag the lake. He even mentioned
search helicopters." Amanda laughed softly.
"When he said they'd had an argument, I tried
to think how an overly emotional girl might react,
and storming off was the first thing that came
to mind. I thought she might end up with you.
Is she okay?"

As tempting as it was to let Shane stew in guilt
and worry for a while longer, Mel didn't want
him causing a scene at her cousin's resort. "She's
upset, and has a right to be, but she's fine. Tell
him I'll bring her back to the resort after she's
calmed down."

"You got it." Amanda hesitated. "He really is
scared about what could have happened to her. I
don't know what they argued about, but the man
is dripping with guilt."

"He should be. He's an idiot."

She set the phone down and looked at Luis.
"What?"

"Look at you, all involved with this girl and
full of advice. You're loving this."

Before she could reply, her phone chimed with
an incoming message from Amanda.

There was no stopping him. He's on his way to your place, and he's coming in hot.

"Great." She stood and nodded at Luis. "See if Tori will stretch out on the sofa and rest for a bit. Shane's coming, and I need to talk to him before he says anything to her." She headed for the door.

"Well, since I work for you now, I guess I have no choice." Luis leaned back and crossed his legs. "Go get him, girl."

SHANE SPOTTED MEL as soon as he brought the car to an abrupt halt in the parking lot behind the apartment. She was hard to miss, pacing back and forth in a long velvet skirt and low-cut top. Her hair was down and free, swirling around her face every time she changed direction. She watched him park the car, her expression so malevolent he was afraid the paint was going to start peeling off his Lincoln.

It had been a shit morning. One of their clients, Alonzo Griffin, had gotten some bad press overnight, partying a little too hard and a little too loudly at a Vegas resort. The Dallas wide receiver had ended up being photographed with a young woman who was very much *not* his wife. The fact that his wife was at the same party didn't matter. The fact that the woman in the photo was a teammate's kid sister, and Alonzo was just trying to shelter her from the photographers, didn't matter. He was an outspoken activist for civil rights, and some people had made it their life's goal to show him in a negative light every chance they got. They were determined to hang the "thug" label on him, and Shane wasn't going to let that happen.

Tim was on his way to Vegas to handle it, but the whole thing ticked Shane off. Alonzo liked to stir things up in order to bring attention to his causes, but the guy was the real deal. It sucked that people wanted to drag him down.

Right after that, Shane's mother had called. She'd found a box of papers in his father's study and thought Shane might want them. Might want to come to Boston as soon as possible for them. He owed Mom a visit, but it didn't make sense for her to use anything his father owned as bait to get him home. Shane had made a vague promise that he'd stop by the next time he was in town.

That was when Tim had texted to remind him about the photo shoot today. Tim thought they needed a bump of good press before Tori went to her next tournament, and pictures of her looking healthy and happy would go a long way. Shane had called up to Tori's room and told her to get ready and wear something nice.

His foul mood had gotten the best of him when she'd come bouncing down into the lobby half an hour later with clownish makeup caked on her face, wearing a skimpy bathing suit. He figured she was just trying to provoke him again with her silly games, and he was *not* in the mood.

A sharp rap on the driver's window startled him out of his thoughts. Christ, he was losing it—he'd almost forgotten where he was. Melanie Lowery was glowering in at him. If only there was a way to rewind this miserable morning and start over. She stepped back when he opened the door, but not by much. She was bristling for a fight.

He held up his hand. "Whatever you're going to say, you're right. I was in a lousy mood and I took it out on Tory."

"She's sixteen, and you humiliated her in public."

"In public?" He thought back. "You mean the lobby? There was hardly anyone there. And I didn't yell at her out in the open, I pulled her aside." Mel started to speak, but he rushed ahead. "I don't mean it like that. I didn't yell at all. I pulled her aside and yes, I was angry. But did you see her? It's like she *tries* to piss me off. And my fuse was extra short today." He scrubbed his hand down his face. "You should have told me she called you for a ride. I went up to her room to apologize and she was just…gone. It scared ten years off me."

Mel's hand rested defiantly on her hip. "She didn't call me. She *walked*. That's how upset she was—she walked all the way here. Alone."

A chill swept across Shane's skin. "In her bathing suit? Barefoot?"

"Thankfully, not quite. She pulled on a pair of sweats and some sneakers first."

He looked up to the door to Mel's apartment. "She's still here, right?"

She nodded. "Luis is with her."

Of course. *Luis* was here. In Mel's apartment.

"So you came down to run interference and protect her from big, bad me?"

"I wanted to make sure you were calm before the two of you talked. She was hysterical, Shane. Crying. Talking about quitting and going home. What the hell happened?"

Damned if he knew. "She had to know she was going to tick me off coming down to the photo shoot like that. Fortunately it was our own photographer, not some magazine photographer. He never saw her. I told him she was sick and re-scheduled. What was she thinking?"

Mel leaned back against his car, folded her arms, and gave him a long, silent stare.

"Did you tell her to look nice?"

"Duh. Yeah. Call me crazy, but I wanted her to look nice for her publicity photos. Like what *you're* wearing. Something *nice*." The blue velvety skirt seemed dressy for the middle of the day, but what did he know about what women wore? He'd never really noticed dresses at all until Melanie had knocked him off his feet with that silver gown at the gala. The glint of metallic in the long skirt reminded him of that. And the way it swished and swirled as she moved, wrapping around her the same way he wanted to be… He almost didn't hear her next question.

"And you told her to wear a suit?"

Shane frowned. "Not a *swim*suit. A *suit*-suit. You know—something professional. We tell all our clients to look professional in public."

Mel stared at him as if he'd just said the moon was made of cheese.

"Do you know many teenage girls who own a *suit*?"

He still wasn't getting her point, but he had a feeling it wasn't going to reflect well on him.

"I don't know many teenage girls, period. But how could she think…"

Mel threw her arms wide. "You told her the photos were supposed to show the world she was healthy and fit. You told her the pictures would be taken by the water. And you told her to look nice and wear a suit." Mel didn't have to connect the dots any further for him.

"Damn it."

"Yeah."

"But what about all that makeup? She had to have done that on purpose to piss me off."

"Shane, she's a girl. And as you keep telling me, she's an athlete. She hasn't spent any more time practicing her eye shadow skills than she has developing a fashion sense. And you've removed her from the family and the girlfriends who might be able to help her!"

"Those so-called girlfriends weren't helping her, trust me."

"Because one of them posted some pictures online of girls being silly? Give me a break. If Tori's learning to navigate fame, so is everyone around her. Her family and her friends are going to have a learning curve, too. Isolating her was a bad idea. Gary was a bad idea. You being her agent without having a clue how teenage girls work was a bad idea. Shall I continue?"

Shane stared at the ground, watching a bug work its way across the hot pavement. He didn't like making mistakes. He especially didn't like having those mistakes thrown in his face. But Melanie was right. He'd blown it with his youngest client, and it was time to admit it. And fix it.

"So Tori thought she was doing what I wanted and I yelled at her for it." He looked up at the door to her apartment again. "And I hurt her feelings, so I owe her an apology. And...I'm the last person she wants to see right now, aren't I?"

"Pretty much."

"Is there any place to get a drink in this dumpy little town? Maybe some dive biker bar? I've always wanted to try one of those."

He wasn't sure what the first emotion was that flashed across Melanie's face when he mentioned getting a drink, but it was gone as fast as it appeared. The corner of her mouth lifted into a half smile.

"The Chalet is the closest thing to a dive biker bar that you'll find in Gallant Lake, which is far less dumpy than you keep insisting." She brushed a strand of dark hair from her face. "I'll go talk to Tori, and you can come back later and apologize." Her eyes narrowed in warning. "Sober."

"I'm not going on a midday bender. I just need to get my head straight and come up with a better plan for the kid, since everything I've done so far is apparently shit." He opened the passenger door. "And I need your help. Get in."

CHAPTER SEVEN

GET IN?

Mel stared at Shane in confusion.

"I am *not* going drinking with you." The words came out more forcefully than she'd intended.

"Then come eat lunch with me." His usual man-in-charge attitude faded. "I'm asking for your help."

He gestured toward the car.

"I'm a little overdressed." She wondered what he thought of her outfit. Bright red canvas flats she'd thrown on as she headed outside, a sparkly blue velvet skirt and a black T-shirt. She wasn't runway ready, that's for sure. Her hair wasn't even styled. It was probably a mess. His eyes raked over her quickly.

"The Chalet won't know what hit them. That's quite the outfit."

"Isn't it? Luis made the skirt for me and I was just modeling it for him."

"Oh." He sounded oddly disappointed. "That was nice of him. You look fine. It's just a quick lunch."

She hesitated, then nodded. All she'd wanted

since they'd first met at the resort nearly two weeks ago was to have him listen to her concerns about Tori. He was offering to do that.

"Let me call Luis first." Shane got that same sour look he had every time she mentioned Luis. "I need to make sure he'll stay with Tori while we're gone. She shouldn't be alone right now."

Luis had raised his two younger sisters after his mother died, so he knew how to handle a teenager. After a few sarcastic comments about babysitting, he assured her that Tori was happily going through his Fashion Week sketches, and he was video-chatting with Tim while he was between flights. She told Luis she loved him, got into Shane's car and gave him directions to the Chalet.

When they arrived, he moved quickly to open her door for her and extended his hand to help her out of the car. For a guy who could be so clueless about women, he had a deeply ingrained sense of chivalry.

Travis Gentry was behind the bar when they walked in. "Hey, Mel! Where's Tori? Oh…hi." He didn't seem happy to see Shane behind her. Travis ran the place for his cousin, and Mel knew Travis had a bit of a crush on her. He'd already asked her out twice. She'd declined by saying she wasn't looking for a relationship right now. And here she was walking in with big, brawny

Shane Brannigan. Whose hand rested in the small of her back, sending tingles of both desire and alarm. What was it with her body's reaction to this man...this *talent agent*...who was all wrong for her? Meanwhile, a guy like Travis, with his laid-back vibe and sweet smile, couldn't come *close* to making her feel the same spark.

Travis looked at her clothing and whistled. "I might need to break out the white tablecloths and candles for that dress." His smile faded when he glanced at Shane. "Special occasion?"

"No, just a little business luncheon. Can we have the corner booth?"

"Dressed like that? You can have any damn booth you want."

Shane cleared his throat loudly. "Can we just sit, please?"

They walked to a booth by one of the large windows, and his hand remained on her back. She could feel the warmth of him through the thin T. Maybe that delicious tingle was a danger signal. But it felt like an invitation.

Travis brought menus and gave Mel a bright smile. "Sparkling water with lemon?"

Shane looked up, surprised. "You really don't want a drink? I thought that's why we came here."

"She doesn't drink. You don't know that?" Travis puffed up a little, enjoying his advantage over this new guy in town. Mel fought to hold back her smile at Shane's quick scowl.

"I didn't know because she didn't tell me." He looked across the table at her. "Wait—I saw you drinking at the gala."

"Did you?"

"Yeah. I saw…" He leaned back against the seat. "It was just tonic water?"

She shrugged.

"So no booze. What is it, a health kick or something like that?"

"Something like that."

Her sobriety wasn't something she wanted to discuss right now, and it was none of Shane's business.

"Do you mind if *I* drink?"

She waved her hand, eager to move on. "Do whatever you want."

"Do you have a good local dark beer?"

Travis nodded. "We have a dark Belgian ale from a great brewery in Cooperstown."

"I'll try that, with a tonic and lime for the lady, and…what's good for lunch?"

"Today's special is our mushroom and three cheese wood-grilled pizza." Travis gave Mel a wink, bringing back Shane's scowl. "I know it's one of the lady's favorites."

Mel slapped the menus back into Travis's hands while the two men glared at each other.

"Oh, for God's sake," she said. "We'll split a pizza, but go easy on the testosterone, okay? It's a little overwhelming in here today."

Travis laughed and tapped her lightly on the shoulder with the menus before turning away. "You got it, babe."

Shane folded his arms and watched Travis head to the kitchen.

"Babe?"

"Travis is harmless. He just likes to tease."

"He'd like to do more than that."

"Well, he's out of luck. Besides, it's just small-town friendliness."

Shane unrolled his silverware from the paper napkin. "Isn't this the same place you took Tori for Taco Tuesday? And it's a pizza joint? Do they serve sushi on the weekends?"

"Careful, Shane, your snobbery is showing again."

He studied her with those intense blue eyes, then looked out the window. Gallant Lake was visible across the road, beyond a row of water-front homes. The mountains rose around it. He looked at the view for a moment before letting out a long sigh.

"I have a feeling Tori's not the only one I owe an apology to. I'm sorry for the other night. I was only trying to help..." He caught her expression and started to laugh. "I get it—you don't need or want my help. You made that very clear."

Yes, she probably had. And she wasn't going to apologize for it. When she didn't respond, his laughter faded.

"Why are you so invested in Tori? I know she likes you, and Tim tells me you bring some sort of special insight to her situation, but I don't get it. She's an athlete and you…"

"Pose for pretty pictures?" She shouldn't care what he thought, but for some reason, his low opinion of her stung.

He rubbed the back of his neck, scowling at the table. "I know I've said some assholey things about that—sorry. I don't know anything about what models do. I'm just trying to understand the connection. Believe it or not, I want to do better for Tori."

"No offense, but how did her parents choose you to represent her? I know you said something about a basketball player, but how does that translate to golf?"

"He was a problem client. And our agency accidentally developed a reputation for taking on problem clients and getting them on track."

"Accidentally?"

"We started with a bang, getting a huge contract for Marquis Jackson straight out of college. It was a fluke—he and I were friends, I didn't like the contracts he was being offered, so I got him a better one. Boom. The Brannigan Agency was formed. But we were a one-hit wonder. Tim came back from the service and I made him a partner while he finished school, but we didn't have diddly for clients. So we started going after the guys no one else wanted. The low-hanging fruit, you know? The troublemakers."

Travis delivered the pizza and some plates, without any commentary other than asking if they wanted more napkins. Shane bit into a slice and Mel smiled at his reaction. His eyes went wide, then closed in deep appreciation for the intricate flavors Travis managed to weave into a simple pizza. Shane's expression did something funny to the inside of her chest, and for just a fleeting moment, she imagined him looking like that while leaning over her. Naked.

What?

She sat up straight and shook her head sharply. Where the hell had that come from? And how could she erase the image from her head? It was a really nice image, but it was never going to happen. She took another bite of the delicious pizza. Food would distract her. And talking. Lots of talking.

"How did you and Tim end up being partners? Did you know each other before he was in the service?"

Shane smiled warmly. *Not helping.*

"Tim and I met when we were kids. He lived near my nana on Cape Cod, and we spent our summers causing as much trouble there as possible."

"How did he end up in the army?"

"He didn't want to be a fisherman." Shane chuckled at her confusion. "It's a long story. He needed financial help getting his college degree, and the military provided it. Tim turned out to be a natural soldier, and even talked about making a career of it, until he got hurt." He sobered. "I didn't bring him into the company out of pity or anything. He was my best friend, he needed something to focus on and I needed the help. He finished his degree and, honestly, I don't know how I would have done it without him."

"And you two took on all the bad boys."

He made a face. "Most of the time they just need a little guidance and a come-to-Jesus conversation about saving their careers. And sometimes their reputations are entirely undeserved, and we have to educate their teams while negotiating their contracts."

"You and Tim are good problem solvers."

"Out of necessity, yeah. I guess. The goal is to reach a place where we don't have to do so much problem solving."

"But Tori isn't a troublemaker. She's a girl, making mistakes."

He set his pizza crust down on the edge of the plate and looked at her.

"I blew it today. Help me figure out how not to do that again. I know how to boss a twenty-five-year-old basketball player around. But a sixteen-year-old kid? I have no idea how to approach her. What to say. What *not* to say."

Shane didn't seem like the kind of guy who showed his vulnerability easily. He was all about winning. Making it to the top. It was probably killing him to admit there was something he couldn't do.

Mel nodded. "She's not a *kid*. And she's not quite a woman. She's a strong, smart female, and she won't take well to being bossed around or being yelled at. I know men love to rag on each other, but women take those words seriously. And saying you were 'just kidding' afterward doesn't do a thing to make it feel better." She smiled. "Just try thinking before you speak. If there's a way your words could be taken the wrong way, change the words."

"So...tiptoe." He didn't seem like the kind of guy who liked tiptoeing, either.

"Not exactly, but for now, that might be a good place to start." It wouldn't hurt for him to be extra cautious for a while. "Shane, you've had women in your life. You've talked about your mom and your nana. I know you've dated. Tim said you were even engaged. What happened there?"

Mel was suddenly curious about the woman who'd walk away from marrying this man. She'd hit a sore spot, and his expression darkened.

"Karina wanted the end-goal Shane, not the present-life one."

"I have no idea what that means."

"She liked the idea of reaching my goal. Famous athletes, big money, lavish lifestyle. She just wasn't interested in the climb required to get there." He looked out the window. "After my dad died last year, she told me I wasn't a lot of fun to be around and left." He smiled thinly. "With a three-carat engagement ring and the brand-new Jaguar I'd just bought for her."

He tried to sound flippant, but Mel could sense the underlying hurt.

"There's more to life than reaching the top. If she didn't understand that, it was her loss, Shane. Not yours."

"Well, I did lose that car."

She felt an odd relief at seeing the laughter return to his eyes.

"Well, yes, there is that. But a divorce would have cost even more."

"Fair point." He rolled his shoulders. "Okay, that was probably the best pizza I've ever had,

and I'm from Boston, so that's saying something."
He looked around the paneled interior of the bar.
A dance floor and stage lined the back wall. "And
I still say the owner has the hots for you."

Mel laughed. "Travis? I think it's more of a little crush than a full-blown case of the hots. He's
one of the good guys."

"Are you saying you've known some bad
ones?"

She drew in a sharp breath. If he only knew.

"A few."

"What does Luis think when guys like Travis
sniff around?"

"Luis?" Mel smiled. "He said Travis was a
'cute little bumpkin' who wouldn't know what
to do with me."

Shane looked thoughtful. "Luis sounds pretty
sure of himself. You two have been together
awhile."

"We met about four years ago. He saved me."

"From what?"

"From a bad situation."

"And that's how he won you."

"*Won* me? No one wins me, or owns me. I don't
belong to any man, and I never will. I spent too
many years being controlled by men to ever want
to deal with that again." Mel straightened in her
seat. She was starting to believe herself when she
said those words, and that was important.

Shane seemed puzzled. "But...you're together."

Good Lord, he thought she and Luis were *together*. As a couple. How could Shane have missed all the flirting that went on between Luis and Tim? She ducked her head to hide her smile. Wouldn't he be surprised when he found out? And who was she to spoil the fun?

"Luis and I?"

Shane nodded, and Mel was barely able to keep from laughing.

"Let's just say we have an understanding."

AN UNDERSTANDING? WHAT the hell did that mean? Were they in some kind of open relationship? Shane had no idea what her so-called understanding was with Luis, but it could mean she was available. And he couldn't decide if that was a good thing or a bad thing. He liked so many things about Mel. Her looks, sure. But also her grit, her sass and her sly humor. It felt as though she had more depth than any woman he'd known. What had happened to her career? What had happened with the bad guys she said she'd known? What was she doing here in this sad little town when she belonged on the world stage?

"How did Luis save you?"

The light in her eyes dimmed just a bit.

"Luis saw me at my lowest, and didn't walk away like everyone else. He helped me find myself again. The tomboy kid I used to be. The fighter." She smiled up at him through long, dark lashes. "I used to be such a tough kid, and Luis made me see that I still had that in me. He gave me my strength back. Luis, and a lot of therapy."

And there was yet another story Shane wanted to know. What was Mel's lowest point, and how did she get there? Did it have to do with those bad guys she'd known? His fingers curled into a fist under the table. She'd been hurt by someone. Her body language—tense shoulders, fingers clutching at her glass, jaw slowly working back and forth—clearly said she had no interest in discussing it any further. So he'd have to wait to learn more.

"We should probably get back. I owe Tori an apology. You must think I'm a complete idiot, but I'm honestly pretty good at what I do. I may be a snob—" he winked at her "—but I'm a smart snob. This old dog can learn a few new tricks. I'm not good at tiptoeing, but I'll do my best for Tori."

"You're gonna hate this advice, but...stop treating her like a child. And stop treating her like an adult. Especially like one of the guys."

Shane barked out a laugh that caught the attention of "good guy" Travis behind the bar. *Tough luck, Travis. The woman's with me now.*

Mel raised her hands in surrender. "I know, I know. But she's right on the razor's edge between childhood and adulthood, and you're going to have to help her navigate it. You and Tim are problem solvers, so figure it out. Tell her you're sorry. And show her you mean it." She leaned forward, and he found himself leaning toward her, just because. "She wants to go home and see her family."

Shane winced. He couldn't control the girl when she was home with all her girlfriends. But then again, he clearly couldn't control her here in Gallant Lake, either.

"Have you at least talked to her about her social media exposure? And, maybe, what not to wear?"

"We've talked a little. I've shared some of my experiences, and the consequences of my decisions."

Shane bit back a protest. She wouldn't tell *him* her experiences, but she'd told Tori.

"Alright. I'll talk to her about having a long weekend at home, as long as she stays off social media." Mel's arched dark eyebrow made him reconsider. "I mean, I'll *ask* her to be careful about what she shares. And wears." The eyebrow went higher. "I mean, I'll keep my mouth shut about her clothing choices."

Mel's mouth curved into a satisfied smile.

It was a smile he wanted to see a lot more often.

CHAPTER EIGHT

MEL WAS ALONE again and restless the following Wednesday night. Luis was back in New York, panicking over the collection. She'd only seen Shane once before he left on Monday night on business. They'd had dinner with Tori over the weekend, where Mel and Shane had kept up this awkward dance around each other. Almost opening up but not quite. Almost sharing but not. Almost flirting but not. It was unsettling, and she was torn between wanting to know more and wanting to avoid making herself vulnerable to a man again.

She looked at the clock on the microwave. One thirty in the morning, and she was wide-awake. May as well go for a run. At least she didn't have to worry about Shane driving by. Tim was back in town now, arriving the morning after Shane left. She didn't know how those two did it, traveling all the time. She suspected Luis would be heading back to Gallant Lake again now that Tim was here. It was an interesting little chess game the four of them were playing, moving in and out of each other's lives.

She grabbed a couple of dog treats from the box on the counter before leaving the apartment. Sure enough, when Mel walked around to the front of the coffee shop, Nessie was lying under the light by the door. This was their routine now. The dog leapt to her feet when she saw Mel, long tail wagging with joy.

"Yeah, yeah. I know what you want." She pulled the dog biscuit out of her pocket, and Nessie took it gently from her fingers, then devoured it. Yes, she'd started buying dog food and biscuits for a dog she didn't own.

"Come on, mutt. It's a good night for a run." They headed south, away from the resort and away from any streetlights, but this was Gallant Lake. The sidewalks in the little town had rolled up hours ago, and no one was around. She settled into an easy pace, and Nessie seemed happy at her side, keeping up with long, relaxed strides. They took walking breaks every once in a while, mostly for Nessie's sake. Whenever Mel slowed to a walk, the yellow dog started sniffing at every little thing, with the concentration of a detective trying to solve some elaborate mystery. Sometimes she'd stare into the woods along the road, seeing or hearing something Mel couldn't.

They'd just turned back toward town when Mel

felt the first raindrops. Damn it. She'd thought the rain had finally moved out of the area. It got heavier as they started jogging again, then turned into an outright downpour. Nessie was blinking rapidly to keep the rain out of her eyes, but her tail still wagged happily whenever Mel spoke to her.

Yes, she was talking to dogs these days.

She didn't have to keep her guard up with Nessie. It was exhausting at times to remember to keep all those layers of secrets when talking to the people in her life. Luis, of course, knew *everything*, but he also *fretted* about everything, so she had to be careful. She definitely couldn't tell him about her mixed-up feelings toward Shane Brannigan.

She told the dog things she couldn't tell her cousins, because they *didn't* know everything, even though they thought they did. They knew about rehab, of course. They knew—in general—why she'd left modeling behind. But they didn't know how far Mellie Low had fallen. They didn't know about that morning in Monaco. They didn't know the truth about Nelson Timmons. Or Steffie Malcor. They didn't know about her many sleepless nights lost to cravings so strong she felt like punching walls. But Nessie-the-dog did, because Mel told her.

The new friends she'd made in Gallant Lake were just that—new friends. They didn't know her past other than what they may have read online, and they didn't ask. They accepted her for who she was now, or at least who they *thought* she was. That was a good thing. But it left her with no one to talk to other than a stray dog.

Struggling to run through this pounding downpour was pointless, so Mel steered Nessie toward the trees along the road, and they huddled under the relative protection of the branches waiting for it to let up. At least it wasn't storm— BOOM! A flash of light made her jump and the following thunder brought Nessie close to her side with a whimper. Perfect. She was standing under a bunch of trees during a thunderstorm, and no one knew where she was. At least there were a lot of other trees around, too, so maybe hers wouldn't be a target. She was just wondering if she should call Nora or Amanda for a lift back into town when headlights swung around the corner and aimed straight at her for a second before the car made the turn. Could it be Shane? The giddy hope that thought gave her was quickly discarded. He was off to San Diego, a city that suited him a lot more than Gallant Lake did. The vehicle slowed to a stop on the shoulder, and the passenger window went down.

"Damn it, Melanie, didn't I tell you not to run alone in the middle of the night?" Deputy Sheriff Dan Adams gestured to the back seat with his thumb. "Get in."

In the less-than-six-degrees-of-separation that defined small-town living, Sheriff Dan was best friends with Nora's fiancé, Asher. Which meant he was in the coffee shop and Asher's furniture studio daily. So, of course, he knew Mel. He'd given her a lecture a few weeks ago about running in the middle of the night, explaining that "small town" and "safe" didn't always go together. She figured he was just doing his job, because seriously…Gallant Lake had to be the sweetest little town she'd ever seen.

"Come on, Mel!"

A soft growl came from her side. Nessie didn't run away like she had before, but she was watching the car with concern, and her tail was no longer wagging. Mel couldn't leave the dog alone out here in a storm.

"You may want to rethink that offer. I've got company—the kind that has muddy paws."

Dan sat up and looked, his eyes growing wide in surprise.

"Well, if it isn't Pita!"

His words gave Mel a jolt of hope. Maybe Nessie had a home and people who loved her, after all. "You know her name? Where does she live?"

A rumble of thunder made the dog in question lean into Mel's leg, but her endless low growl didn't stop.

"Get in the car and out of the rain, Mel. And bring Pita with you."

The dog didn't want to go anywhere near the police car, but she also didn't want to leave Mel's side. With a little coaxing, she ended up sharing the back seat with Mel. Her brown eyes never left Dan, and the growl rolled on endlessly, like a threat. Dan, shaking his head, tossed Mel a towel to dry off with.

When she looked up to meet Dan's amused eyes in the rearview mirror, they both spoke the same words in unison.

"So tell me about the dog."

Mel laughed. "I don't know anything about her. She showed up a few weeks ago and follows me anytime I'm out after dark. She's a good running companion. Aren't you, girl?" Mel ignored Dan's protest as she rubbed the towel over Nessie's head. Or should she say Pita's head? "So who owns her? And what kind of name is Pita?"

Now it was Dan's turn to laugh. "That's *my* name for her, and it stands for Pain In The Ass. I get nuisance calls about her digging through people's trash a couple times a week, but I can never catch her. Bill over at animal control has been trying, too, but she's cagey. Probably because people are always throwing stuff at her to chase her away. We figure someone dumped her off in town." Dan's eyes met hers again. "Unless she's yours?"

Dan pulled the car into the parking lot behind her apartment in town. The rain had let up some, but it was still dark and wet outside. Dan turned in his seat and waited for her answer.

"And what happens if I say she's not?"

His face sobered. "I think you know. I'll deliver her to animal control, and if she's not claimed…"

Mel looked into Nessie's eyes. The dog was gazing at her with wide-eyed trust and affection. She didn't have Nora's permission to bring a gangly, mud-covered pup into the recently redecorated loft. It would be crazy to claim her.

"She's mine."

Dan choked back a laugh. "Okay. In that case, I'd recommend you get her a collar and a leash and take her to a veterinarian for her shots so she can be registered. And try not to let her wander the village causing any more havoc—we have leash laws in this county. I'll let Bill know you've got her, just in case someone calls looking for her. But I doubt that will happen." Nessie's growling had stopped, and her tail was beginning to wag the more Dan talked. "What's her name? Or is Pita going to stick?"

"Her name is Nessie, like the Loch Ness monster."

He nodded. "That fits—she's been a terror around here. She's gonna be a big girl, you know. You sure about this?"

Mel looked at Nessie's long legs and oversize paws. "How big are we talking?"

"She's only a juvenile. Maybe a few months old. Looks like a mix of yellow Lab and hound of some sort. My guess is she'll top out at eighty-five pounds or so."

Mel swallowed hard. That was a lot of dog to take on. But she wasn't about to send her to the pound and who-knows-what fate. If she ended up leaving Gallant Lake, surely she'd be able to find someone to adopt a sweet dog. She nodded, her words coming out with less conviction than before.

"I'm sure."

"Okay. Good luck, Mel." Dan grew serious again. "And, if you really have to go walking or running at this crazy hour, take her with you. And maybe a can of pepper spray. Even Gallant Lake has some lowlifes, and you never know who might just be driving through. And for Pete's sake, take a flashlight and rain gear!"

"Yes, Dad." Mel winked at Dan and got out of the car with her new dog. Nessie wasn't crazy about climbing the open metal stairs to the second floor walkway, but she finally followed Mel up to the apartment. Mel wondered if she'd balk at coming inside, but Nessie trotted through the door like she'd lived there forever. And shook the water and mud off her coat with a great deal of enthusiasm at the entrance to the kitchen.

"DAMN IT, RILEY, you can't keep doing this shit! The team's only going to give you so many free passes, no matter how good you are." Shane was pacing back and forth in front of the police holding cell. He'd left Gallant Lake a week ago for a succession of meetings in Dallas, Phoenix and San Diego, and now here he was in LA, trying to resolve another pop-up crisis. It was the story of his life.

Their client, one of the best young pitchers in baseball, was sitting inside the holding cell, his head in his hands. He didn't respond, so Shane kept on talking, hoping something would get through to the idiot sitting in front of him.

"Two DUIs, Riley. TWO. We dealt with the last one because it happened when you were in college, but this one's in the middle of the sea-

son! The league will probably suspend you, even
if the team owners don't. They'll probably make
you check into rehab, and frankly, that might be
the best thing. Tim's already had your attorney
on the phone with the DA, trying to work out a
plea deal so we can avoid a media circus." Shane
stopped pacing and waited in silence until Riley
finally raised his head and focused his red and
swollen eyes on him. The kid was a mess.

The arresting officer said he blew a 0.09 on
the breath test. One point over the legal limit and
completely stupid, but at least the kid wasn't stag-
gering and incoherent, despite his bloodshot eyes.
Riley was a hothead and a challenge to manage,
but substance abuse was one of the few mistakes
the Oklahoman hadn't made since he and Tim
had signed him two years ago. Until tonight.

Luckily, Shane had been in nearby San Diego
when Tim had called from Gallant Lake to say
their baseball bad boy was in jail. While Shane
drove to the LA police station, he'd kept hearing his late father's words on a repeating loop
in his head.

*You represent lunkheads who play stupid games
for a living. If you represent losers, then what does
that make you?*

"I'm sorry," Riley croaked. He cleared his
throat and tried again. "I'm really sorry, Shane.
Emma Sue and I had a big blowup. She threw

my college championship ring out the window! I was ready to kill…"

"Shhh!" Shane hissed. "You're in a police station, you idiot." Riley didn't need to know the only reason he was still sitting in that cage was because Shane had asked the arresting officer to leave him in there to scare him sober.

"I didn't mean it."

"Still, don't say it out loud, okay?"

Riley nodded. "She went to a hotel. Said she's moving back to Tulsa. I picked up a bottle of Patron and started drinking. After a while, going after her seemed like a really good idea…"

"Until you ended up passed out on the side of the road with the car running." Shane shook his head. "You're lucky you weren't in an accident, or this could have been a career-ender. You understand that? A. Career. Ender."

"She *left* me, Shane! We've been dating since high school, and she walked out on me. Said she didn't want to be a ballplayer's wife. What the hell, right? She knew I wanted this life, and then she dumps me when I finally get here? What am I going to do?" Riley started to cry.

Shane stared up at the ceiling and swore softly to himself. Someday he and Tim would move on from representing the problem children of the sports world, and they'd have clients who were both talented *and* mature. But that day hadn't arrived yet. So he went into problem-solving mode, pulling a chair over to the holding cell after getting a nod of permission from an officer walking by.

"Riley, you need to pull it together. Emma Sue didn't leave you over baseball." The girl wasn't some trophy wife—she'd gone to college on a softball scholarship. She was more knowledgeable about the game than most players. "What exactly happened?"

Ten hours and one visit to Emma Sue's hotel later, Shane discovered Riley really *had* been spending far too much time away from his young bride. It wasn't because of baseball but because of a secret running poker game with other players on the team. At twenty-one, Riley Chapman was desperate to fit in with his new team, and now he was in so deep with the older players—who were obviously taking advantage of him—that he had no way out. The pressure, and the rising debt, had taken its toll on Riley's mood and affections, and Emma Sue was fed up with his sour attitude. She had no idea he was being punked by a handful of assholes on the team.

Tim and the attorney worked their magic with the DA, and Riley was released with a plea deal agreement promised as long as he agreed to ongoing counseling. Meanwhile, Shane met with the team's general manager and got his promise that the locker-room hijinks would come to an end. The manager swore he had no idea the other guys were giving the young rookie a hard time. Shane found that hard to believe and made a mental note to speak with the team owner. If they weren't going to take care of his client, he'd find a team that would.

Emma Sue was waiting for Riley when Shane brought him home Wednesday afternoon. It turned out she'd thought his long nights were symptoms of an affair, not a card game from hell. Shane endured a hard embrace from Riley and a flood of grateful tears from Emma Sue. Another crisis averted. Another happy client. Another return to an empty hotel room.

It stung to realize he was envious of what Riley and Emma Sue had—a relationship strong enough to weather some bumps in the road and still be rock-solid. His thoughts drifted to Mel and Luis. She'd told him Luis had "saved her," and Shane really wanted to know what that meant. Literally? Like running into a burning building? Or just that he'd gotten her out of modeling? He still had no idea what Mel meant when she'd called it an *understanding*.

Their relationship, like Riley and Emma Sue's, was built on friendship that grew into... something. It was the exact opposite of what he and Karina had tried—a one-night stand that had turned into a tense relationship.

Shane watched Riley and Emma Sue walk up to their house, hand in hand, her head on his shoulder. He wanted that. The realization nearly took his breath away. He *wanted* that. He wanted a woman who'd love him and leave him if he deserved it and forgive him if he deserved that. A woman who knew him. A woman who understood him. And that imaginary woman looked a lot like Melanie Lowery.

CHAPTER NINE

SHANE TURNED AWAY at that thought. A relationship like that had never been part of his big plan. He wanted to find someone, sure, but it had to be someone compatible with his goals. Someone who wanted the same things he did. Not someone settling down to live in some podunk town in the mountains. Shane would never reach his goals from Gallant Lake, and besides, Mel had that *understanding* with Luis.

She would be a distraction, and not the one-night kind. Mel deserved more than that, and Shane didn't have time for it. What mattered was getting into that corner office and becoming a partner just like his dad. Sure, he was in sports law and Dad had done corporate law, but becoming partner in a major firm would have impressed even his father, if he'd been around to see it.

He pulled out his phone to order a ride to that empty hotel room. When was the last time he'd slept in his Boston condo? A month ago? Longer? He rubbed the back of his neck and stretched with a groan. Too long. But this was the life he'd chosen. He and Tim had had a goal from the start, and The Brannigan Agency was finally getting attention from the big dogs in the business.

Three nights ago, in San Diego, Calvin Bolton himself had walked over and greeted Shane in a restaurant. The managing partner of Bolton & Bolton, Calvin ran the largest entertainment talent agency in LA, and they were branching out into the sports world. Calvin had told Shane he wanted to get together sometime to "pick his brain" on how to make that move. Shane was sure that was code for a job interview.

His phone buzzed in his pocket. He pulled it out and glanced at the screen.

"Tim, if you tell me the DA rescinded, I swear to God…"

His partner chuckled. "Nah, he's a loyal team supporter and sympathetic to Riley's adjustment period. We got lucky. Was this mess seriously due to some asinine hazing from the team?"

"Just a couple of veteran idiots picking on a younger idiot. Harrison assures me he'll get his clubhouse under control, but I'm not convinced. We'll need to stay on top of it." Shane scrubbed his hand down his face and swore. "We need to make sure these young guys are on guard for this crap. It's more than providing financial managers for them. They need help making simple grown-up decisions on their own. I'm tired of us having to act like these guys' parents." A dark sedan pulled up with a familiar sticker on the window. "My car's here. I'll call you after I sleep for a week or two."

"Not so fast, man. Our actual child athlete needs attention."

It was a sign of how tired Shane was that it took him a moment to realize who Tim was referring to.

"Tori? What did she do now?" He knew they never should have let her go home on her own.

"Tori's good. The weekend at home helped her attitude a lot. She and Mel have been hanging out and doing yoga or whatever together." Tim hesitated. "But I've been doing some quiet asking around about Gary, and I don't like what I'm hearing."

Shane held up his finger to let the driver know he needed to wait. "Seriously? Her parents are convinced he's one of the top coaches on the tour."

"Yeah—because that's what *he* told them. He has very few even midlevel female golfers, and one of those dropped off the tour. The rumor was she was using growth hormone shots. I don't like it."

"Drugs? Son of a…" Shane slid into the back of the sedan and nodded at the older man behind the wheel. "Let me guess—you've already booked me a flight to New York?"

"I've got you on the red-eye. I'll pick you up at JFK in the morning and we can drive to Gallant Lake together. Sleep's overrated, right?"

"Yeah. Overrated. Right. Catch you tomorrow."

His mind was already cataloging potential replacement coaches, how he was going to handle firing Gary and how Tori might react to the change. If there was one thing he'd learned since becoming her agent, it was that teenage girls were impossible to predict.

Hopefully Mel could help. His pulse jumped just a notch or two at the thought of seeing her again. Those sharp violet eyes had crossed his mind at least once a day since he'd left Gallant Lake.

"I CAN'T BELIEVE you got a dog, Mel!" Tori wrapped her arms around an enthusiastic Nessie, who was doing her best to make morning yoga impossible. Tori didn't care, laughing in delight as the dog pushed her onto her butt and tried to wiggle onto the girl's lap.

"Yeah. I can't believe you got a dog, either."

Nora *wasn't* laughing. And she clearly was not delighted. She was perched on a kitchen stool, watching Nessie through narrowed eyes.

Mel joined her cousin at the island, watching as girl and dog wrestled on the floor. "She hasn't had a single accident inside since last week, Nora. I'm trying to keep her off the furniture, except the bed, of course." Nora arched a brow, and Mel lowered her voice. "Give me a break—it's the first time in ages I've had company in bed I actually enjoy."

Nora gave her a sly grin, then glanced around the room and wrinkled her nose.

"She sheds."

Nessie didn't just shed—she expelled hair like ninja knives. How one thirty-pound puppy could lose so much hair every day and not be bald was beyond comprehension. A new vacuum cleaner was definitely on her shopping list.

"Are you really upset about her being here?"

Nora sighed and shook her head. "Dogs are too much chaos for me. But if she makes you happy, then I'm happy. And she is sweet. Asher said she's going to be the size of a small horse, though. If you're really thinking about staying, this apartment may not be the best place for her." Nora gave her a sharp look. "You're doing okay, right?"

Maybe someday the people closest to her would stop worrying, but it wasn't going to happen anytime soon. Her cousins would have someone watching her around the clock if they knew how dark the darkest hours really were.

"I'm fine." Her voice lowered. "I went to a meeting last night. Everything's fine."

"Can I take her for a walk, Mel?" Tori and Nessie were on their feet, both looking energetic.

She checked her watch. "When is your session with Gary this morning?"

Tori's face fell. "Not until eleven."

Nora and Mel looked at each other. Tori hadn't said much about Gary since she'd returned from visiting her family this past weekend. Tim had been here to welcome her back to Gallant Lake. Naturally, Luis had driven up from the city the same day Tim arrived. The two men were starting to spend a lot of time together. She nodded toward the back door. "Her leash is on the hook. You can take her along the lake walk, but be back by ten so we can get you up to the resort." It was a Thursday morning, and even though it was summertime, the village didn't start really filling with tourists until Friday. No one would bother Tori this morning.

Nora cringed as Nessie skidded down the hallway to follow Tori.

Mel patted her hand. "I'll pay for any damage she does to your floors."

"It's fine." Nora didn't sound any more convincing than Mel had when she'd said those words. "These are the original plank floors— they're already scarred and scraped up. Amanda insisted I leave them that way for 'character.' And since she's a professional at interior design and

I'm not, I did what she told me to do." Nora took a sip of her coffee. "But Asher's right—that dog's going to be huge. I mean, this loft is yours as long as you want it, but have you thought about your next move?"

Mel traced her finger around the top of her coffee mug. "Lots of thoughts with no conclusions. I like Gallant Lake. I feel good here. I've found a good support group that meets at the Methodist church. I'm making friends. But…" She glanced around the apartment, full of Nora's furniture. "All my things are in storage and my life is on hold. I need a job. A purpose. Something."

"I'm looking for part-time help down in the coffee shop."

Mel laughed. "I don't think coffee barista was exactly the career move I was looking for." Mel caught herself. "I mean, you're great at it and I'm happy for you…"

Nora waved her hand. "I get it. But aren't you already working with Luis?"

"I *invested* with Luis. It's not the same. He needed the boost to get his business going, and I had some money from the condo. But it's *his* business, not mine. It's *his* dream. I don't want to be around the shows or photo shoots anymore. It's not healthy for me."

"But you have such an eye for it. Luis brags about you all the time. Why don't you open a little dress shop or something? Share your skills on a smaller level. You have better taste and style than anyone I know." Nora brushed her dark hair back and preened. "As a small business owner and member of the newly formed Gallant Lake Business Chamber, I could give you all kinds of free advice. Let's face it, if I can do it, anyone can."

Nora had bought the coffee shop on a whim last winter, eager to get out of Atlanta and closer to her unwed pregnant daughter. She'd had no clue how to make fancy coffee, much less run a business, but she'd learned. And Asher, the handsome architect and furniture maker next door, had made the deal even sweeter.

"A dress shop in Gallant Lake? I don't know. You sell something everyone needs—coffee. But could this town support a designer boutique?"

"Well, I didn't say anything about it being a designer boutique, but that sounds amazing. What would that look like?"

Mel thought about the old store for sale just down the block. It was dirty and dusty and reminded her of Shane's comment that half the town was falling down. While not exactly true, the former general store looked shabbier than most. But the depressed property values around here, and the building's poor condition, put the asking price within her limited budget. And if the structure wasn't too far gone, she might even have enough left to renovate it. Every time Mel walked by, she thought about how cool the store would look with fresh white paint and polished floors. Maybe a chandelier in the center…

She shook her head. "It *would* be amazing, but in Gallant Lake? Doesn't sound like a solid business plan to me."

Half the storefronts in Gallant Lake were empty. The buildings, a mix of brick and clapboard, were generally looking weary. Even the gazebo across the street had peeling paint and broken gingerbread trim. They were too far from New York to be a bedroom community, and even though the resort was growing, Mel didn't think of Gallant Lake as a tourist mecca.

"Are you kidding?" Nora waved her hand toward the windows overlooking Main Street. "Have you paid any attention to what Blake and Amanda are doing at the resort? It's becoming a wedding destination for a very upscale crowd from Albany, White Plains, Connecticut…even Manhattan. And those crowds want something to do. Amanda said they're thinking of buying one of those cute trolley buses to run back and forth from the resort to downtown, but they need more businesses open to support it." Nora leaned forward, clearly warming up to the idea. "The chamber is talking about encouraging people to open gift shops and touristy stuff like that. A boutique would fit right in!"

"Whoa! Easy, girl. I don't even know if I *want* a business like that. First I need to figure out my living situation. I love this place, but you're right—it's small."

"There's plenty of real estate available if you're serious about staying. I bet Amanda knows some of the Realtors around here—she and Blake have been buying up property like crazy between building the golf course and protecting the resort."

She remembered the story. When Amanda and Blake first met, he'd intended to tear down the dated resort and the historic home beside it to build a casino on the lake. The town had fought him tooth and nail, and then he'd fallen in love with Amanda and decided to make the lakeside mansion their home. His family wasn't happy about the change in plans, and had threatened to build the casino without him, but Blake was one step ahead of them. He'd bought up every scrap of land in the area until they'd finally walked away.

"Asher just remodeled a house on the lake, and he said the owner is going to sell it. It's beautiful—lots of windows and all open concept." Nora nudged Mel's shoulder. "This town is turning around, and you could be a part of it."

It was a tempting thought. With a waterfront

home, she could watch the sunrise over the lake every morning. Go for long walks with Nessie. Start a new business. Start a new life.

"Give it a rest, Nora." Mel stood, dismissing the dream as too good to be possible. "I've got to find Tori and get her back to the resort."

CHAPTER TEN

MEL DROVE BACK to the resort's golf course a few hours after dropping Tori there. They were going to grab an early pizza at the Chalet, and then she was going to introduce Tori to her favorite movie, *The Princess Diaries.* When she heard Tori had never seen it, Mel had vowed to remedy the matter as quickly as possible. She walked around the back of the new clubhouse. Asher had designed the building, and it was pretty spectacular—all stone and timber and glass. It looked modern, but it also looked as if it could have been there, hugging the lakeshore, for a hundred years.

"Look, Tori, you need to loosen up to get more motion in your backswing, and this will help." Gary was apparently just wrapping up Tori's session.

"Gary, I told you before, I don't want to take anything. What if I get tested?"

"Come on, you're sixteen. No one's going to test you."

"I thought these were for pain? What about the other stuff?"

"Sure, for pain. But they also help you relax, kiddo. The other pills are for strength—we need to get more power in that backswing of yours. My clients do it all the time. Trust me on this, okay?"

Mel stopped in the shadow of a tree, listening to the exchange, her pulse racing.

A couple little pills won't hurt you, Mellie. Don't you trust me?

When she realized what was happening, she rushed up the slope to where Tori was staring skeptically at a pill bottle. Tori barely had time to look up before Mel snatched the pill bottle out of her hand.

"Are you taking these?" She shook the bottle at Tori, who stumbled back.

"No! I don't like medicine. I didn't take anything!"

Mel turned back to Gary, whose face had paled considerably. "Were you seriously trying to force her to take these?" She looked at the bottle. "This is *oxy* for God's sake. Are you insane?"

"I wasn't forcing anything." Gary's voice leveled. "Look at the bottle. It's prescription medicine in Tori's name. If anything, you should be yelling at her for refusing doctor's orders!"

Mel hesitated, reading the label in confusion. It did have Tori's name on it. But surely an athlete shouldn't be taking anything so addictive? Mel's fingers tightened on the bottle. She hadn't used a lot of oxy, but she knew other models who'd been seriously hooked on the stuff. She looked to see where the prescription originated. Dr. Elliot Becton from Kenosha, Wisconsin.

Wisconsin?

"Tori, didn't you tell me Gary is from Wisconsin?"

Unsure what was happening, Tori just nodded quickly.

Mel stepped toward Gary, shaking with fury.

"You son of a bitch! You called in a prescription from some doctor friend of yours, didn't you? You think I don't know how that works?" Mel had plenty of experience with magical prescription slips showing up from doctors she'd never heard of. "You're trying to push this crap on a *minor*? On an athlete?"

"Lower your voice!" Gary hissed. "Stop being stupid. Everyone does it these days."

"Really? If everyone does it, why do I need to lower my voice? Why can't I shout to the world that Gary Jenkins endorses the widespread use of illegal drugs to his clients? Maybe I'll take out an ad in one of those fancy golf magazines. Would that work for you? Since *everyone* does it?"

Gary's face went from pale to a very dark shade of red. He stepped up into Mel's face, and it took all of her strength not to back down. She wouldn't let him bully her.

"Shut up! This is none of your business. You're just some rich bitch who thinks she knows everything, and you don't know shit. And if this little brat..." He gestured toward Tori, who was frozen in place. "If she wants to get anywhere on a tour with grown-ups, she'll do whatever the hell I tell her to do." He moved closer, his chest almost brushing Mel's, and it was finally too much. She stepped back. Emboldened, Gary moved forward again, and Mel nearly stumbled in her effort to back away.

"What the ever-loving *fuck* is going on here?"

Mel looked over her shoulder to see Shane Brannigan directly behind her, his voice an angry growl. Tim was a few steps behind him, fists clenched and just as ready to rumble as Shane was.

"Shane!" Gary moved away from Mel, and she could finally breathe again. He gave her a triumphant smile. "Am I glad to see you! These two women are out of their minds."

Mel pointed at Gary. "He's trying to give her drugs!"

Shane's scowl was carved in granite.

Mel's nerves were jumping faster than her heart rate. Shane's voice lowered, but still dripped with danger.

"Tori. Back to your room." Tori started to object but stopped at the sharp shake of his head.

"Now." She started to turn away, but Shane stopped her again. "Wait. I gotta ask—has Gary done anything to you? Has he touched you?"

"What? No!" Tori stepped back, her face screwed up in disgust. "No way."

"You shut up, Brannigan!" Gary stepped forward, and Mel instinctively stepped back, bumping into Shane's hard chest. His fingers wrapped around her upper arm, holding her there. "This bullshit story is completely fabricated. And if anyone says otherwise, I'll sue all your asses so fast you won't know what hit you."

Shane's gaze flickered to Tori. "I need you to go."

Mel knew he was protecting the teenager from what was surely going to be an ugly scene, but Tori didn't know that. She only knew the adults in her life were very angry about something that involved her. She was wide-eyed and anxious, and Mel rushed to reassure her.

"You're not in trouble, Tori. Maybe Tim can take you to the coffee shop. You can take Nessie for another walk for me, okay?"

Shane's fingers tightened briefly on her arm. He didn't like having his orders countered. Well, that was too damned bad, because Tori didn't need to be sitting alone up in her room, fretting that she'd somehow caused this mess. His grip relaxed again as he probably worked around to the same conclusion.

"Fine." His tone sharpened. "No texting, no tweeting, no nothing about this until we talk. Got it?"

Tori nodded. Tim draped his arm around her shoulders and lifted his chin to Mel, silently letting her know he'd take care of her. As they walked away, Shane released her arms and moved to her side. She was glad he wasn't trying to send *her* away.

"Tell me what happened."

Mel shook the pill bottle in Shane's face. "He's been asking Tori to take these pills. It's oxycodone, for God's sake. An opiate. She could have gotten addicted!"

Shane squinted at the label. "They're prescribed to her."

"Exactly!" Gary threw his hands in the air. "That's what I've been trying to tell this nosy bi—"

"Watch it." Shane's voice crackled with warning.

"Yes," Mel said, "they're prescribed to Tori. By a doctor she's never met."

"She's seen a dozen doctors, Miss Lowery." Gary's condescending tone made Mel stiffen. "She can't possibly remember them all, and how the hell would you know, anyway? Shane, why are you letting this washed-up has-been hang around your client?"

Shane stepped forward with a low growl, but she put her hand on his wrist to stop him. She didn't need a savior.

"Dr. Becton's office is in Wisconsin," she pointed out. "That's where you're from, isn't it, Gary? And, since Tori's sixteen, wouldn't he need her parents' or Shane's permission to treat her?" Mel looked at Shane, trying to ignore the anger in his frosty blue eyes. Confrontation was not her thing, and if anyone asked, she'd have to admit she was easily at a level eight right now. "Did you authorize a Dr. Becton to treat your client?"

"I think we all know the answer to that." Shane gave her an almost imperceptible nod of approval before turning to Gary. "You're fired, effective immediately. Tim will draft a statement for you to release to the media. It will be something along the lines of Tori making such great progress in her rehab that you're returning to your busy roster of other clients. We'll back that up, and everyone moves on."

Wait a minute. He was letting Gary just walk away? Shane must have sensed her rising indignation, because he took her hand and gave it a quick squeeze to silence her. That was sweet, but it wasn't going to work.

"You can't let him get away with this! He gave

a minor a controlled substance. He took advantage of a girl who trusted him. I saw it!"

Shane's voice lowered and lost its edge. "We'll talk later, but for *now*, let it go."

His eyes were begging her to trust him.

"You need to promise me *she's* not going to cause trouble." Gary was glaring at Mel.

Shane chuckled, not taking his eyes off Mel. "*She* doesn't answer to me. But I think it's in everyone's best interest to do as I suggested." Mel wasn't sure she agreed, but she lifted her chin to show solidarity with Team Tori as he finally looked back to Gary. "I also think it's in everyone's best interest if you leave Gallant Lake today."

"Today? I can't get a flight out of New York that fast."

Shane was unconcerned. "I'll put you up in a hotel in the city tonight and make sure you get a flight home tomorrow. I'll even arrange a car to take you there. Soon. As in, you should start packing."

Gary's mouth opened and closed a few times, but no words came out. He'd lost and he knew it. Shane released Mel's hand and she ignored a pang of loss. He pulled out his phone and started texting someone, probably Tim. He glanced up at Gary and raised a ginger brow, as if wondering why he was still standing there after he'd been dismissed. Gary muttered a curse under his breath and walked away.

Mel took a deep breath and tried to release the tension from her body. She looked at the pill bottle, still clutched in her hand.

Come on, Mellie. Of course, they're safe! Look, a doctor prescribed them just for you, honey.

Shane scowled at his phone, tapping angrily. She slipped the bottle into her pocket. She'd dump the pills down the toilet as soon as she got back to the apartment. No, that wasn't safe for the environment. Her fingers tightened on the small bottle. Well, she'd figure it out. As long as she kept them away from Tori, that was all that mattered.

It wasn't like Mel was going to use them or anything.

TIM'S TEXTS TO Shane finally started consisting of more than curse words aimed at Gary, and he confirmed that he'd arrange a car, a room and a flight to Wisconsin. He was also drafting a short press release. Shane slid the phone back into his pocket. Odds were the news wouldn't even make a ripple. Tori had been expected to recover quickly, and it was hardly surprising that her coach would return home at some point. Once she got back on tour in a few weeks, they'd quietly release the news that Tori and Gary had mutually agreed not to work together anymore due to scheduling conflicts or whatever, and that the split was amicable.

Another crisis brought under control. He glanced over at Melanie, who seemed to be having an intense conversation with herself. Her right hand was fisted in the pocket of her skin-skimming jeans. She was angry he hadn't gone after Gary harder, but sometimes in this business you had to step back and see the big picture. It wouldn't do Tori any good to be sucked into some melodrama in the middle of the tour. Especially one involving drugs. For one thing, her sponsors wouldn't be happy.

Her social media behavior had been pretty mellow since Melanie had stepped in. He'd been worried about her trip home, but the online photos he saw were of her siblings and a couple of friends at a backyard pool. And her clothing choices, even today, were age-appropriate, if not exactly conservative. Short shorts and a bare midriff would never fly on tour, but she was still rehabbing and there didn't seem to be any press sniffing around this tiny town.

Mel jerked her hand out of her pocket and shook her head sharply. He couldn't help smiling at whatever one-person debate she was having over there. Her presence during the confrontation with Gary had been necessary, since she was the one who knew what was going on, but it had also been distracting. Shane preferred negotiating from a power position, but he seemed to lose his power mojo whenever Mel was around. He'd leapt to her defense, even when she clearly hadn't needed it. There was no way Shane could be Switzerland once Gary had started sneering at her. Shane had shown a point of weakness, but Gary had been too busy scrambling for a dignified exit to notice.

"Do I have something on my face?"

Shane blinked. He'd been caught staring at her. He didn't like being caught at anything. The corner of Mel's mouth lifted into a pretty little dart.

"No. Uh…sorry… I was lost in thought." Or he was just lost, period. "Let's go check on Tori."

They headed to the parking lot. He sent a quick text to Tim to make sure Gary checked out of the resort within the hour, then jogged to catch up with Mel's long strides.

"You can ride with me. I've got a car." He pointed to the Lincoln.

"So do I." She pointed to a sleek white convertible. His phone buzzed in his pocket. He looked at the screen and groaned. This day just kept getting better. He nodded to Mel. "I'll meet you there. I have to take this."

She walked away with a wave of her fingers. He admired the smooth sway of her hips as he answered the call.

"Hi, Mom. Is everything okay?"

"I was going to ask you the same thing, dear. I still haven't seen you." Eleanor Brannigan's disapproval came through the phone in waves. Hopefully she hadn't discovered that he'd been to Boston recently. She'd never let him forget it if she learned he'd been there without letting her know. Boston Irish mothers knew how to throw the guilt around, and his was no exception.

"I'm sorry, Mom. You know this is my busiest time of the year."

She gave a sigh of resignation. "What city and sport is it this week?"

"Right now I'm in a little nowhere town in New York, dealing with a golf client."

"A little nowhere town?" She laughed. "How are you liking *that*?"

He looked back at the clubhouse. The sprawling building was elegant, and the view of the lake and mountains beyond it was impressive. But outside of the resort and a decent pizza/taco place, Gallant Lake might as well be the moon. Shane was a city boy through and through. He'd grown up in a Boston brownstone and had known how to catch a cab by the time he was ten. He thrived on the hustle of crowded city sidewalks, backed up with the honking horns of impatient drivers. The pace of the city was his pace—brisk and task-oriented. He may not have chosen his father's career path, but he was still his father's son.

"It's boring as hell here. But it's where my client is."

"And then you'll be off to another client in another town? Don't you ever go to your own office? Or your home?"

"My office follows me. Tim holds down the fort as needed. And my 'home' is a rented condo that doesn't miss me." She knew all of this, of course. They'd had this conversation on every single call. He bit back a sigh. "Mom, is there something you need?"

"Nothing urgent. I'd just like you to come home once in a while. This big house gets lonely, Shane." He pictured the brownstone, decorated and furnished just the way his father had liked it—conservatively. Brown on beige on white. The only rooms that displayed his mother's more colorful touches were the kitchen and sunporch. The rest of the place was staid and straitlaced, just like Dad.

"Mom, why don't you sell that place and get a nice condo out on the Cape? Or in the city if that's what you want. Something on one level that's easier to take care of, that'll be *yours*." He leaned against the hood of the Lincoln and watched a tangle of seagulls spinning and diving through the air along the water's edge. He waited for an answer, using his negotiating skills on his own mom. Half the shit he'd gotten away with as a kid was because he could outwait his mom's resistance. But on this subject, she could out-stubborn him.

"This is our home, Shane. Our memories are here. I always thought I'd see my grandchildren playing on the same stairs you used to play on."

Grandchildren?

"Mom, have you been day-drinking on a week-day? Grandchildren are a long time off. A *really* long time. And remember what Nana Brannigan used to say—memories don't live in places or things." There was something about being around Melanie Lowery that kept evoking memories of Nana. Must be the lilac perfume. "Don't save that house for me."

"I'm not ready to leave yet. In the mean-time, try to schedule some time in your very busy schedule to come visit your poor widowed mother." Shane rolled his eyes. His attorney father had left his wife a very wealthy woman. He'd left not a dime to his only son, but Shane didn't care. He hadn't been good enough for dear old dad when he was alive, so he didn't want the old man's money now.

"Okay, Mom. I have to stick around Gallant Lake for a while, but I'll try to get to Boston in the next week or two. We'll go to dinner and talk. But *not* about grandchildren. Deal?"

"Ugh, you and your deals. Fine. And in the meantime, you call me, okay? A mother shouldn't have to call her son all the time, begging for someone to talk to." His mother was on the boards of half a dozen charitable foundations and played bridge twice a week, not to mention all her friends at St. Ann's. She wasn't alone, but he knew what she meant. He was her son.

"You got it, Mom. I promise. Talk to you soon."

CHAPTER ELEVEN

"So SHANE JUST showed up out of nowhere and fired the guy?"

Nora set a mug of coffee with a double shot of espresso in front of Mel and joined her at the table by the coffee shop window. Mel took a sip and hoped the caffeine would jolt her frayed nerves back into shape. Coffee was the closest she came these days to the relief the pills used to give her. The fact that she was even thinking about that told her how close to the edge she was. She'd moved the pill bottle from her pocket to her bag to dispose of later, but she could still feel the weight of it pressing on her.

The next support meeting in Gallant Lake wasn't for another five days. Maybe she'd look for one in White Plains. Or maybe she'd be just fine. It was just a bottle of pills.

"Mel?"

"Oh, sorry. Yes, I was yelling at Gary, and suddenly Shane was just *there*."

"Tori was pretty upset when Tim brought her

in here. But that hairy dog of yours made her smile again."

"She's not hairy! The vet said she's mostly Lab, and they have short hair." The vet also said Nessie was younger than they'd all thought, and would probably top out near a hundred pounds. That was a lot more dog than Mel had ever intended to take on.

"Short hair or not, she covers everything around her with the stuff."

"But look at the two of them—she's like a therapy dog for Tori." The girl and the gangly pup were across the street from the coffee shop, running around the gazebo in the tiny park by the water. The dog's joy was contagious.

"And for you?"

Mel shrugged. "I guess. She makes me laugh, even when she digs all my shoes out of the closet and steals my laundry. She gives me something to do…"

The door to the shop swung open and Amanda Randall marched in. She saw Mel and put her hands on her hips. "So do you want to fill me in on why Gary Jenkins is checking out of his long-term suite right this minute? What's going on? Is Tori okay?"

Mel winced. She should have given her cousin a heads-up on Gary's departure. "Sorry about the suite. Will you be able to fill it?"

Amanda pulled up a chair and sat, brushing her blond curls over her shoulder. "During the summer? In a heartbeat. But what happened?"

Nora filled Amanda in on the events with Gary and Tori, and how Shane had shown up to settle the matter. Mel watched Tori and Nessie through the window. They were headed down the opposite side of the street now, and Nessie stopped to drink from one of the many water bowls business owners set out for dogs. Nate Thomas stepped out of his quirky little hardware store and scratched Nessie's ears while he and Tori chatted—Mel had taken Tori to Nate's store two weeks ago to introduce her to Hank, the noisy, and occasionally foul-mouthed, parrot who lived in a large cage at the back of the store. Mrs. Smith came out of her beauty salon to hand Nessie a dog treat.

Tori's head tipped back as she laughed at something Mrs. Smith said, pointing to the dog. There was a sense of community here that Tori had been lacking during her stay at the resort, and it was good for her to be making friends, even if they were older than her. At least they wouldn't take advantage of her.

Just as they wouldn't take advantage of Mel. She traced the rim of her coffee mug with her finger. The sense of community in Gallant Lake was something *she'd* been missing, too. She was another stray, like Nessie or Tori, and people were making her feel at home here.

"What are you smiling about, Mel?" Nora asked.

Amanda snorted. "Maybe she likes the idea of Shane Brannigan hanging around?"

"Please." Mel rolled her eyes. "The last thing I need in my life is a man who already thinks he's king of the world."

"And speaking of his majesty..." Amanda tipped her head toward the window. Shane was standing outside the coffee shop, his hand on the door, watching Tori and her new friends across the street. "He is one good-looking hunk of man, Mel. You could do worse."

She'd already done worse. Much worse. Shane might be pretty to look at, and he had his moments, but he was off-limits. All men were, at least for now.

Shane's head turned and he met her eyes through the glass. He glanced at the other women and his mouth quirked into a crooked grin, as if he knew he was the topic of their conversation. That was another strike against him—he was so arrogant. He pulled the door open and stepped inside.

"Afternoon, ladies."

Nora stood. "Hi, Shane. Would you like a coffee? Espresso? Iced coffee?"

"Thanks. It's Nora, right? Can I get a coffee with a double shot of espresso? That red-eye flight is catching up with me."

Mel did her best to ignore the wide grins her two cousins shared. Shane drank the same caffeine-loaded combo she did. So what? That didn't mean anything. He grabbed a chair from another table and dragged it over, straddling it backward and nodding toward the window.

"Who's Tori talking to over there? And where the hell did she get a *dog*?"

"That's Nate and Mary," Amanda answered. "Nate owns the hardware store and Mary has the hair salon. And that dog-slash-horse belongs to Mel."

"Why does everyone keep picking on my dog?"

Nora returned with Shane's coffee. "Maybe because Nessie is messy and socially inept, which is the exact opposite of you."

"Nessie? What kind of name is that?" Shane took a sip of his coffee and grabbed one of the cookies Nora had brought to the table.

"The first time I saw her she came out of the lake in the dark, so I named her after the Loch Ness monster."

He nodded as if that made perfect sense to him. "She's a stray, then. She looks like a pup. How long have you had her?"

"A week or so."

He choked on the cookie and coughed, looking out the window to see Tori leading Nessie down the sidewalk away from them. "A week? How do you know she's safe to be around?"

"Trust me, Nessie's safe. Unless you're a shoe." Mel appreciated his concern for Tori's safety, but she was also annoyed that he thought her goofy dog might be some foamy-mouthed killer.

Amanda's phone pinged with a message. She looked at it, then back to Shane. "Gary checked out and is on his way to the city."

He nodded and thanked her. He looked out the window again and frowned. Tori was no longer in sight.

"She's on the lake walk, on the other side of the buildings," Amanda said. "Everyone will keep an eye on her." He didn't seem reassured. "Relax. It's Gallant Lake, and it's a Thursday, so there are very few tourists around. The locals take care of their own."

Shane wasn't impressed. "That sounds adorably homespun, but she's a sixteen-year-old girl walking alone. A *famous* sixteen-year-old. Just because this town looks like Mayberry doesn't mean it's safe."

Mel rolled her eyes. "It's not what it looks like that makes it safe. It's the people." Amanda shot her a curious look. "And she's not walking alone—she's got thirty pounds of dog with her."

"And that thirty-pound puppy is going to be so helpful against a two-hundred-pound man, right?" He drained his coffee and stood. "I'm going to check on her."

Amanda piped up. "Mel will go with you!" Shane and Mel both looked at her, and her cheeks flushed pink. "I mean, it's Mel's dog, right?"

Nora nodded in agreement, her native Southern accent getting thicker with every word as she spoke. "Yes, Mel knows everyone in town and can introduce you. And it *is* her dog." She patted Mel's arm. "Y'all should go with him, hon."

Mel glared at them both for being so obvious. But to her surprise, Shane agreed.

"Sure. That way you can take your dog and I'll get Tori back to the resort for some rest."

Outnumbered, Mel stood and followed him out the door.

"You know they were trying to…"

"Hook us up?" Shane put his hand lightly in the small of her back before they crossed the quiet street. "Yeah, I know. I'd have to be pretty dumb to miss it. What does Luis think of that?"

She couldn't stop a laugh from bubbling up. "I told you, Luis and I have an understanding. And they've never played matchmaker before today. I hope they never will again." He gave her a look.

"Just because we ordered the same coffee, they decided it was fate or something ridiculous like that. They know I am not in the market for another man." She waved her hand. "So you're off the hook."

He grinned. "Oh, good, because I have no desire to fight a guy the size of Luis for your honor."

And there it was again. Luis. The image of the two men brawling over her was hilarious, and she laughed even harder. Maybe the stress of the day was catching up to her and inducing hysteria. They'd come to a halt on the sidewalk, facing each other. Shane's smooth smile was something he probably used every day in business to build trust, and it was highly effective. He had a dimple in his right cheek when he smiled and, combined with his red hair, it gave him just enough little-boy charm to weaken a woman's—no, she meant *person's*—resolve. In *business*. She wasn't thinking about that smile in any other context.

His blue eyes darkened, and Mel's face heated. He knew she was standing there admiring him, and he was…what? Amused? Smug? Aroused?

IT WAS THE first time Mel's laughter had been aimed directly at him, and the effect was nothing short of electric. At her first giggle over her cousins' odd matchmaking efforts, Shane's pulse had quickened. But when she'd laughed about him fighting Luis over her, his whole *body* had quickened, from his feet to his scalp. Just like an electric shock, but without the pain. He felt a quick jolt of excitement and danger and a crazy desire for it to happen again.

He'd always known how to make people laugh. It was one of his gifts as an agent, charming people to get their guard down. But getting Melanie Lowery to laugh made him feel like he'd just earned something rare. Something precious. Before he could dismiss the idea, he realized she was looking at him. *Really* looking at him. Her eyes met his and went wide with...something. Color blossomed on her cheeks, and the realization hit him somewhere below his belt. It was raw desire he saw in her eyes.

The woman was usually so guarded, so determined to keep him at a distance and in his place. But that look, with her standing just a few feet away, dark hair blowing softly across her face, lips slightly parted as if caught in a moment of surprise. Yeah, he knew how she felt, because he was surprised, too. He felt like a high school freshman when he realized he was getting hard just thinking about her in his arms. In his bed.

"Are you *sure* I don't have chocolate on my lips or something?"

Shane blinked in confusion. "What?"

"You're staring at me again. More specifically,

at my mouth. I had one of Nora's chocolate eclairs earlier, and I thought maybe I'd been wearing chocolate icing for the past two hours. Or is there something else you're looking at, Shane? Do you see something you like?" She ran her fingers over her lower lip and smiled. Holy sweet mother of...

Shane saw a spark of something in her eyes. The warrior princess was toying with him, like a cat with a mouse. He didn't know if he was angry or thrilled to be her target.

"Nicely played, Melanie. I'll give you credit—it's easy to see how you made a fortune with your looks." As soon as the words were out, he knew they were a mistake. The light dimmed in her eyes and she dropped her hand. "I didn't mean it like that. I mean...you're beautiful." He'd always been a pretty smooth player, but around Mel he was all verbal thumbs and clumsy words. "I'm just saying I understand why people wanted you."

Right now, *he* wanted her.

"No one wanted *me*. They just wanted the *look*. The same one that just left you slack-jawed. You thought it was real. You thought it was me. You fell for my trademark pout, Shane. And yes, that's the one that made me famous. But it's just a pose. A sham. I started acting that part at sixteen, and everyone believed it."

Shane frowned, trying to understand what had

just happened. Was she angry because he admired her? Wasn't that what women wanted?

"I'm trying to compliment you, Mel. You're a gorgeous woman…"

She glared at him, and he shuffled his feet, unsure what to do next. She always seemed to have that effect on him. "I don't know what you want me to say. I'm not going to tell you you're ugly, for God's sake."

She threw her hands in the air. "I don't *care* what you think about my looks, Shane Brannigan!"

"O-*kay*! I'm sorry I think you're beautiful! Christ, you make me crazy."

Her brows gathered together and she opened her mouth to respond.

"Mel! Catch her!" Tori's voice called out behind him, and Shane spun instinctively. She was running up the sidewalk, chasing the big yellow dog with a leash dangling from its collar. Mel reached out and caught the leash, but the dog was still running full-speed. Shane wrapped his arm around Mel's waist to keep her upright, and put his hand over hers to grab the leash.

The sudden contact after the weirdness just before was almost too much for his body to process. *Stop the dog.* Hold the woman. *Stop the dog.* Pull her closer. *Stop the dog.* Her butt was pressed against his pelvis now and… He gave himself a mental shake. *Stop the damn dog*, who was now struggling to get free.

Mel pulled out of his hold and dropped to her knees, right there on the sidewalk in front of him. *Seriously not helping.* The dog ran back to Mel's arms. Tori ran up next to him, breathing heavily.

"I'm so sorry! The trash truck came to pick up the garbage bins behind the shops, and Nessie freaked out when it started backing up right next to us. They started banging the bins on the side of the truck to knock them empty, and I couldn't hold her."

Mel looked up from her position at Shane's feet and smiled. The sight made him weak in the knees.

"It's okay, Tori." Mel gave the dog, now relaxed and happy, a quick hug before standing. "She's not used to being on a leash yet, and she probably panicked when she couldn't get away as fast as she wanted to." She turned and gave him a bright, if tense, smile. "Shane, meet Nessie. Current circumstances aside, she's a very good girl."

Shane's father hadn't believed in having animals in the house. Shane had always wanted a puppy, but had had to be satisfied playing with the revolving collection of mutts at Tim's home when they were kids. He reached down and scratched the side of Nessie's head. She turned to allow easier access, and he grinned. Just like a woman to put herself in position for the best loving. Nessie's tail started to wag.

"Hi, Nessie. Nice to meet you." He cleared his throat, doing his best to focus on the dog. "Try not to kill my favorite client, okay?"

Tori laughed, then grew serious. "Gary...?"

"Gary no longer works for you. We'll talk about it over dinner." He had to get back to thinking about business, not the violet-eyed woman on her knees in front of him. "I think you can finish getting ready for the tour by working with the pro at the country club. What's his name—Cody Brooks? At this point we just want you out on the course and hitting the ball."

"Oh, I really like Cody! He was on the tour for a couple years, then he had to leave. He tells great jokes." Tori was warming to the idea of working with Brooks in equal proportion to Shane cooling to it. He'd heard good things about the guy, but he hadn't heard Cody *had* to leave the tour. And he hadn't known Tori liked him quite this much. He didn't need any more complications. As if reading his mind, Mel stepped in.

"I got to know Cody when we were getting ready for the charity tournament. He left the tour after he was hurt in an accident. By the time he was better, Cody said he didn't have the hunger for competition anymore." Mel looked him straight in the eye to make her point. "He's a good guy, Shane. He and Tori love the same stupid movies, but he's a complete professional."

Mel seemed to organize the men in her life into "good guys" and "bad guys." He wanted to know who the bad guys were that had hurt her. And he wanted to know which category she thought he fell into.

"Hey! Superhero movies aren't stupid!"

Shane didn't respond. He took his job damned seriously, but with Tori, he was relying on a woman he barely knew to tell him who Tori was hanging out with and how safe—or not—they were. He watched a sheriff's car drive slowly through town. The uniformed driver waved to Mel and she waved back.

He didn't like small towns, with everyone in everyone's business. But he could suffer through this one in order to keep an eye on an important client. If that meant he also got to keep an eye on the beautiful and mysterious woman in front of him…well, that was just an added bonus.

CHAPTER TWELVE

NESSIE SMACKED MEL with her paw three times before Mel finally groaned and pulled down the covers. The dog stood over her, impatiently cocking her head from one side to the other. *Smack.*

"Okay, dog. I get it. I'm getting up."

It had been a more restless night than usual, with yesterday's conversations spinning through her dreams. The pill bottle sitting in her purse. The look on Shane's face when she'd given him a "babydoll" pose on the sidewalk. Seeing the heat in his eyes had done something to her insides. Something warm and exciting and newly curious. It had taken all her strength not to keep up the charade, but she didn't want anyone falling at her feet because of her looks. Not even Shane.

The apartment was quiet. Considering Luis was very much a morning person, it was too quiet. Mel followed Nessie down to the main floor and found a note on the counter. *Downstairs having coffee—L.* Mel took Nessie for a quick walk out back, then showered and changed. There was going to be a meeting of Team Tori in an hour, to figure out how to move forward after the Gary debacle. She pulled on a pair of skin-tight white capris with a long purple top that brushed the top of her thighs. The canvas skimmers kept the look casual. It wasn't like she was dressing with a certain blue-eyed ginger in mind. This was *totally* casual. She pulled her hair up and twisted it into a knot, securing it with an antique French hairpin. Totally. Casual.

There were definite advantages to living above a coffee shop, and breakfast was one of them. She headed down to meet Luis. But there wasn't room for her at his table for two. Tim Monroe sat across from him, and the two men were deep in conversation. Mel had come in from the back, and she stood in the little hallway behind the counter and watched. Tim was sitting back in his chair, arm perched on the back of it, confident and relaxed. Luis was leaning forward as he talked, eyes bright and hands animated. Mel felt a pang of worry that he was trying too hard, but Tim's expression was warm. At one point, he reached over and briefly touched Luis's hand, and Mel just about melted at Luis's blushing smile.

"Who are you spying on?" Nora came up to Mel's side and nudged her with her elbow.

"I've never seen Luis this infatuated with anyone before. I'm beginning to think Tim feels the same way."

Nora turned and watched as Tim sat back again, laughing at something Luis had said. "A sports agent and a fashion designer. Sounds like a good match to me." Nora's wink made it clear she wasn't talking about Tim and Luis.

"Oh, my God, stop with the matchmaking already. Shane is not…"

The front door opened and the man in question walked in, stealing the words from Mel's lips. He looked at Tim and Luis, still deep in conversation, and frowned in irritation. Neither man noticed. He looked up and straight into Mel's eyes, and his frown faded. He crossed the café to join her and Nora.

"Morning, ladies. Looks like the gang's all here, but we'll need a bigger table."

Nora nodded. "There are plenty to choose from. Black coffee with a double shot?"

His mouth quirked into a crooked smile when he looked at Mel's empty hands. "Sure. Make it two."

He remembered. Something about that sent a weird little thrill through Mel.

Tim laughed again. Shane glanced at the two men and muttered, "I can't believe they got a table for two."

Mel shrugged. "I think it's sweet."

"I was thinking more like 'rude.' Where are *we* supposed to sit?"

"The Team Tori meeting isn't supposed to start for another hour. They're just getting to know each other. It's *sweet*."

"What's 'sweet' about two grown men sitting at a tiny table who have absolutely nothing in common?"

"Well, they do say opposites attract."

Shane scoffed. "Yeah, in romance, maybe. But they're not..." He looked at the men and his eyes went wide, color draining from his face. Tim had pulled his chair closer to Luis's, and was leaning in to say something with his hand on Luis's arm.

Nora brought two steaming mugs of coffee and set them on the end of the counter. "Do I need to bring a table into the hall for you two skulkers, or are you going to come sit out in the open?"

Shane was staring slack-jawed at Tim and Luis.

"Shane?" Mel touched his forearm and quickly pulled away. He was rock-solid and every time they touched, she felt a zip of energy she couldn't understand. "Are you okay? You look like you've seen a ghost."

Nora chuckled. "Cathy tried to tell me this place was haunted, but I think Amanda is the only one of us with a haunted house." Her smile faded. "Shane?"

"Are they...?" He gestured toward Tim and Luis, acting as if two unicorns were sitting at the table instead of two men he knew.

She knew he thought *Luis* was straight, but Shane and Tim were supposed to be best friends. How could he not know *Tim* was gay? Was Tim in the closet around Shane? She supposed it was possible that he'd managed to hide this side of him from his business partner and friend. But it wasn't hidden now. Tim's fingers were stroking Luis's arm, and Luis's eyes were dark with naked desire. If Tim *had* been in the closet with Shane, he wasn't anymore.

"Shane, I don't know how to tell you this, or even if it's my place to tell you, but...Tim is... attracted to men." Shane's head spun to look at her in some kind of shock. Oh, boy. This was awkward. "And he's especially attracted to Luis. And that's nice, don't you think? I don't know how you feel about homosexuality, but..." Nora was watching the conversation, on the verge of laughter. Mel tried to keep her voice as level as possible. "If Tim is really your best friend, then you should be happy for him. Look how happy he is with Luis..." Her voice trailed off at the thunderous look on Shane's face.

When he spoke, his voice was so loud that it echoed around the coffee shop.

"I *know* Tim is gay, goddamn it. What I did *not* know was that *Luis* was gay!"

Thankfully, there were only a few other customers in the shop this early, and they seemed more amused than shocked. Nora sighed. "Not the first time they've seen family drama in this place." She called out to John and Steve, who were just setting up their cribbage board. "Refills are on the house this morning, boys."

Tim and Luis were staring at Shane. Then Tim started to grin with that sideways smile of his, but his eyes didn't have the usual twinkle. He stood, his hand resting on Luis's shoulder.

"That's a hell of way to out two fellas just minding their own business over coffee, Shane. Any other announcements of obvious facts you want to share?" Tim turned to the cribbage players. "Here's one—Tim's got an artificial leg!" He swept his hand down toward the high-tech metal prosthesis clearly evident below his khaki shorts. "Or maybe you'd like to tell everyone I'm a natural blond?" He ran his fingers through his brush-thick sandy hair. "No? Nothing else to shout out to the world this morning?"

His smile faded, and he stared hard at Shane. Mel cringed as she followed him over to the table. Was it possible Shane was just as clueless about men as he was about women? How did the man navigate through the world like that?

He took a deep breath and lowered his eyes, conceding to Tim's rant.

"I'm sorry, man. I didn't mean to just blurt that out, but she thought I didn't know." He looked at her in hurt surprise. "He's my best friend. Of course I knew his sexual preferences. But I thought you and Luis…"

Luis started to laugh. "You thought she and I were sleeping together? Oh, honey, I don't even deserve her, much less want her. That way." His laughter halted and he gave Shane a hard look. "Just to be clear, *you* don't deserve her, either."

Shane's hands went up. "I don't want her!"

Nice.

"I mean, not that way. She's beautiful…" He glanced her way and couldn't miss her glower. "Sorry, I didn't mean to say that word. You're… great. I guess. I just thought you were…"

Mel narrowed her eyes at him. "Okay, you really need to stop talking now. Maybe forever."

Nora giggled behind her as three women walked into the café. "I'll second that. Can we wrap up this floor show and get you four to take a table and use your indoor voices?"

Shane rested his hand in the small of Mel's back and gestured toward a large table along the wall. Tim and Luis joined them with their coffees, which Nora quickly refilled before heading back to the counter to serve the new customers.

"Is our meeting starting early, then?"

"Looks like it already did." Shane gave him a pointed look. Tim was unperturbed.

"*Our* meeting was strictly personal." Luis's

cheeks flushed again at Tim's words. Her partner was totally smitten.

Shane shook his head. "You could have told me, you know."

"What? That I'm queer? I've been out for years."

"Not that, you idiot. That you were seeing Luis. That Luis was gay. We had a whole conversation about whether they were a couple…"

Mel sat up. "You did?"

His eyes narrowed on her. "Actually, you and I had a conversation about it, too. You told me you and Luis had that mysterious *understanding*. Why didn't you just tell me then that Luis was gay? Not that I care, but I thought you were together and Tim insisted you weren't and…" He looked at Tim. "And that's why you were so sure they weren't. You knew Luis was into guys."

Tim shrugged. "I knew he was into *me*. And the feeling was mutual. It's not my fault you doubted a gay man's gay-dar, Shane. I tried to tell you, but you were so determined to make Mel unavail…" He quickly corrected himself. "To make me think they were more than business partners. I decided to let you live with your little fantasy for a while."

Mel turned to Shane in surprise. "You seriously didn't notice all the flirting that was going on that first morning?"

"I had my mind on other things." Tim snorted, and Shane shot him a dirty look. "On *Tori*. Which is what we should be discussing right now. Can we move on from who's sleeping with who?"

Luis winked at Tim. "No one's sleeping with anyone. Yet."

Shane's eyes widened. "Didn't really need to know that."

"Wait. Where is Tori?" Mel looked outside, wondering if she'd gone over to the lakeshore gazebo.

"I can answer that one." Nora set a plate of pastries on the table, bringing extra plates and napkins. "She's hanging out with my daughter and her fiancé today. She might babysit baby Charlie later so Becky and Michael can go have a grown-up lunch."

Becky was only nineteen, so she and Tori had bonded quickly when they'd met. It was good for Tori to have someone close to her own age to hang out with. And even better for her to see someone like Becky, who was light-years ahead of her age when it came to maturity. Mel had been shocked to hear about Becky's unexpected pregnancy over the holidays, but the girl was handling parenthood with grace and humor. And she was madly in love with Michael, whose father was Nora's fiancé. It was a delightfully tangled small-town romance with happily-ever-afters for everyone.

Shane nodded. "I dropped her off at their place on my way here." He glanced at Nora. "You're sure she's okay to watch such a little baby?"

Nora rested her hand on his shoulder. "You're forgetting Tori has four younger siblings. If there's one thing that girl knows even better than golf, it's babies. She'll be fine. She has my number and yours, and Becky's, and Mel's, all plugged into her phone." She turned away. "And she'll be watching the world's most perfect baby, so it should be a cakewalk."

Shane rolled his eyes, but he was grinning into his coffee mug all the same. "It was good timing, actually. After yesterday's drama, it'll be good for her to have a day away from all of us. Which brings us to why we're here."

The discussion moved along without a hitch. They all wanted what was best for Tori and her career. Shane's usual king-of-the-world attitude was gone. He couldn't stop looking back and forth between Luis and Tim.

"One of your biggest issues with Tori is her public style, right?" Luis asked. "She's sixteen and from the Midwest, and you…" He looked at Shane, who didn't blink, but also didn't argue. "You want her to look like a polished adult. That look doesn't happen in a vacuum. You can't just tell her to 'look nice' and assume she knows what that means to you. You've arranged physical therapy for her injury and golf coaches for her game, so you obviously think she's teachable. But are *you* going to teach her style?" Luis gave Shane's appearance a once-over, causing Tim to snicker, but that snicker vanished when Luis gave him the same perusal.

"Hey! This is an expensive shirt! I wore it special because you..."

Shane gave a snort of laughter. "You're dressing for Luis?"

Mel set her mug on the table and waved her hand dismissively. "As charming as I find that— and I really do—we're getting off track. Tori has three weeks before her first game..."

"Tournament. It's not a game—it's a tournament." Shane's lips twitched.

"Whatever. She needs a new wardrobe, and not just Winthrop Athletic stuff. Does she have a budget for clothing?"

He nodded.

"Fine. I'll set up a girls' day in the city next week and take her to the fashion district. There are some good trunk sales coming up. I'll make a hair appointment, too, and give her a fresh look." She looked across the table at Tim. "Would next Friday be too late for the publicity shots you wanted?"

"No. I can make that work."

"Okay. It's a plan then. Shane?"

He nodded. "Lord knows I can't do it. So, yeah, it's good with me. Just a reminder—keep her off social media while she's there. I don't want the press following you guys in New York."

"Just a reminder—I don't work for you."

"I know that. I'm asking."

Mel managed not to laugh as Tim made a face at the back of Shane's head, holding his hands up as if to strangle his business partner.

"Are you?"

"Come on, Mel." He broke eye contact, her only warning of what was to come. "She'll listen to you. I finally did my homework. You were only a year older than Tori when that photo came out of you at some party…"

A chill crawled down Mel's spine. "The one where I was snorting cocaine from a photographer's coffee table? Yes, I'm aware of the photo you're talking about." She slumped back into her chair. The cocaine had belonged to a fellow model, Steffie Malcor. At the time, Steffie was everything Mel wanted to be. Cool and confident, wildly successful, popular on the party circuit and with a devoted following in the tabloids. Mel hadn't yet discovered that Steffie was also a jealous, manipulative attention-seeker who didn't care who she destroyed as long as she got good press and the best jobs.

Luis's growl brought Mel out of the memory.

"Do you have a point to make, Brannigan?"

"Luis…" Tim put his hand on Luis's arm, but he shook it off. Shane pushed back the shock of red hair that fell across his brow.

"Look, I'm not passing judgment. I don't care what you did recreationally, as long as you don't do it anymore."

Recreationally? There was nothing recreational about the path cocaine and pills led to, especially when combined with booze.

"I would *never*…"

"She would *never*…"

Luis and she spoke in unison. Shane raised his hands in surrender.

"I'm just saying, now I understand that you know what bad publicity feels like. Everyone went after you for being a party girl after that photo, and Tori's been flirting with that reputation already." He looked her straight in the eye. "I didn't mean to bring up a bad situation."

Mel blew out a long breath. "That picture was just the beginning of my bad situation."

"Mel…" Luis sounded worried.

"I'll be okay." He sat back at the use of the code word, but she could tell he wasn't fully convinced. Neither was she.

Especially since she still had a full bottle of pills in her purse.

SHANE FELT LIKE this whole morning had been a weird dream or alternate reality that he was going to wake from at any moment. Tim and Luis were *together*. Which meant Luis and Melanie *weren't* together. Which meant *she* was available. Which meant *he* was in trouble.

After her outburst about not wanting to be called beautiful, he'd finally sat down last night to do some research on her career to see if he could figure out what had happened. And yeah, maybe he'd wanted to see a bunch of pictures of the woman who was basically living in his head, anyway. Was it creepy? No. It was research. It wasn't like he was obsessed with her or anything.

That photo wasn't Mel's finest moment, but it had been years ago. She obviously wasn't some druggie now. Maybe he shouldn't have mentioned seeing it, but he couldn't get that image out of his head. It had jumped right off the screen when he found it, eclipsing the glossy modeling shots.

It wasn't the low-cut, open blouse or the barely there skirt she wore. It wasn't the wild tangle of dark brown waves falling around her thin face. It was her eyes. Those violet eyes were wide and over-dilated, staring up into the camera, rimmed with heavy eyeliner and weighed down with lashes so long and glittery he knew they had to be fake. The girl in that photo looked lost. Lonely. Frightened. Exposed.

His first thought had been that he never wanted Tori to look like that. But now, watching Mel frown as she swirled the last of the dark coffee around the bottom of the mug, he wasn't thinking of Tori at all.

Mel was clutching the leather bag in her lap with one hand as if she thought someone might steal it from her here in the Gallant Brew. Tension radiated from every inch of her. Luis watched her with obvious concern. Shane chewed his bottom lip. Maybe it *had* been a dick move to mention that old picture of a teenaged Mellie Low.

How had this strong warrior princess sitting in front of him ever been in that position? Who had failed to protect her? How had she made it out? Shane's grip tightened dangerously on his mug. What had happened to her while she was there? Was that what she'd meant when she'd said Luis had saved her life?

"I'm sorry." His words caught in his throat, but she heard him and looked up in surprise. Shane cleared his throat. "I'm sorry I mentioned that photo. I… It just…stuck with me. You were a kid then. It sounds like you had your share of people taking advantage of you. You didn't need me doing it today."

Luis mumbled a "Damn straight." Shane acknowledged him with a nod. If Luis had saved her from that circus, Shane was grateful. Last night, he'd seen dozens of photos of her as an adult with rock stars and sports stars, drink in hand, smiling into the camera but looking empty.

Mel studied him for a long minute before answering. "Apology accepted. But you're right—I can share experiences with Tori that no one else can. Hopefully help her avoid my...mistakes."

"You see yourself in her. Your teenage self."

Mel looked quickly at Luis, who was still tense and on guard, then nodded.

"Yes. But this isn't about me, it's about Tori."

This was important for Mel in some way he still couldn't quite see. But it mattered to him. It mattered far more than it should. *Tori* was his client, not the pretty brunette tracing her fingertip around the top of her coffee mug. Who was now surprisingly available. He got lost for a moment, watching that manicured finger go round and round. Tim leaned forward and spoke lowly so no one else would hear.

"Breathe, dude."

Shane blinked and looked at Tim in confusion, then realized he had, indeed, been holding his breath watching that finger go round and round...and there he went again. *Shit. Snap out of it!* He cleared his throat so loudly that Mel and Luis both jumped a little, and Tim snorted out a laugh. Shane glared at him, but that just made Tim laugh harder as he stood and raised his hand, touching the brim of an imaginary hat.

"This *is* about Tori, but we have other clients, too. I have to go call our socially conscious wide receiver and make sure he's okay. Alonzo's still steamed about that Vegas story, but I'm working on giving an exclusive to one of the sports magazines about the inner city foundation he's setting up." His gaze settled on Luis. "Dinner tonight?"

Luis glanced at Mel. "Do you mind a houseguest for another day?"

Her lips twitched with amusement. "Do I need to set a curfew for you boys?"

Luis stood. "How about I just text you if I'm not coming home, Mom?"

Tim blushed. Like…actually *blushed.* Shane had seen Tim in relationships before, but none of those guys had made him act like this.

Shane shook his head. "I'm just glad we're not sharing a suite. Be careful, boys."

The two men laughed and headed outside together, then split in different directions after a quick conversation on the sidewalk.

"Luis has never hesitated to go after what he wants." Mel was watching them, too.

"Tim's an Army Ranger. He might prove more challenging than Luis thinks."

Mel laughed. "Uh, have you *seen* the way Tim looks at Luis? I can't believe you've missed it this entire time. Tim looks at him like he's a giant chocolate bar just waiting to be unwrapped."

Shane winced. "Yeah, I didn't really need *that* image in my head all day."

Mel got up from the table and Shane scrambled to stand and hold her chair. She looked at him and smiled.

"Who taught you all those good manners, Shane?"

"My mother encouraged them, but it was my Irish nana who beat them into me with a wooden spoon." Mel's perfume danced on his nose.

A light laugh fell from her lips, and Shane's chest swelled. He had a million things to get done today, and he hated small towns, but he found himself extending an invitation to the beautiful woman who was *not* seeing Luis Alvarado.

"Would you like to go for a walk?"

Mel looked as surprised as he felt. She hesitated, narrowing her eyes, looking for some ulterior motive and thankfully finding none. She shrugged. "Nessie needs a walk, so if you want to come along…"

"I do." The way he blurted out those two words

made him sound as eager as Tim and Luis. But this was just business, of course. If she was going to be working this closely with his client on sensitive issues, he should get to know her better. Professionally. Totally business.

"I'll meet you down on the corner. Nora has a fit if I try to bring Nessie through the café, so I have to take her around back." Mel gave him a once-over, taking in his blue linen shirt, khakis and Ferragamo loafers. "We'll keep it to the short loop, since I don't think those shoes will do very well on the nature trail."

Nature trail? Was that really a thing? He glanced out the window to the mountains around the lake. Of course it was, in a place like this. His brows knit together. There had been informal trails near the water in Chatham, near Nana's Cape house. He and Tim had clambered all over them as boys, collecting pinecones and seashells and memories. His father used to throw a fit over the sand they'd tracked indoors, but Nana would shush him and wink at the boys.

They'll have a lot o' years t' be men, Jimmy, but only a few t' be boys.

"Shane?" Mel snapped her fingers near his face, making him jerk back in surprise. "Are you okay? I lost you for a minute there."

"I'm fine. I'll meet you outside." He slapped

some cash on the table and bolted out the door before he embarrassed himself any further.

Hopefully the fresh air would bring him some self-control.

CHAPTER THIRTEEN

MEL DROPPED HER bag on the kitchen counter and
called out to Nessie. Before she snapped on the
leash, she dug the pill bottle out of the bag and
tucked it into her front pocket. It didn't show
under her long top, but she could feel it hard
against her hip. She hadn't let those pills out of
her reach since she'd taken them from Tori. It
was just her way of making sure they stayed safe.
That was all. She wouldn't want them to fall into
the wrong hands, and she knew she was strong
enough to resist them. At least she hoped she
was. She patted the small cylinder. She had to
be strong enough. Otherwise the past two years
had been wasted.

Nessie was thrilled to finally be headed out for
her *real* morning walk. The dog had a bottom-
less well of curiosity, and she sniffed and watched
everything until something new caught her attention, which generally happened every five sec-
onds or so. She barked with joy when she spotted
Shane standing on the corner. Mel looked up and
almost forgot to make Nessie heel.

He was leaning against the lamppost with one hand in his pocket. The sun made his hair look like polished copper. At Nessie's bark, his head lifted and he gave a little wave, then looked at his hand as if he couldn't believe what it had done. Mel tried not to smile.

Shane was like an awkward little boy around her sometimes, and she wasn't sure what to make of it. She'd never liked it when men had fawned over her in the modeling world. But Shane's emotions were so jumbled that she didn't know how to read them. It was fun to watch the confusion flash across his face, though. His hand dropped, and he cleared his throat.

"Where to?"

"Let's go toward the resort first." She glanced at his shoes again. "There's a trail by the lake that's pretty level. It's where I found Nessie." They headed past the closed-up bakery on the corner, then Asher's custom furniture studio and Nora's coffeehouse. She told Shane how Nora and Asher had met when Nora's daughter and Asher's son fell in love and found themselves expecting a child. Neither Nora nor Asher had wanted to be grandparents, for very different reasons, but there they were. Neighboring businesses. Neighboring apartments. A baby on the way. And love in the air.

He nodded. "I still say small-town life must feel suffocating after the life you've led."

She knew what he meant. She'd modeled clothing in actual palaces. She'd done a photo shoot on top of a skyscraper high above the city of Dubai. If Shane had really done the research he'd claimed, he knew she'd been a big part of the very metropolitan Miami club scene while she'd lived there. So, yes, Gallant Lake was a major change of pace. But it didn't feel suffocating at all.

"Actually, it feels liberating. I can let my guard down here and just be me." Or at least try. Most days she wasn't sure who that really was.

They strolled past a few other businesses—insurance office, pet shop, florist. Small-town staples run by good small-town people. Well, except the florist. The owner, Thea Winters, was a cranky old biddy who hated everyone. It was an odd personality for someone who worked with beautiful flowers for a living, but it wasn't like she had any competition. The next building was empty. The faded painted sign spanning the width of the three-story brick store declared it the "Gallant Lake Five & Dime." A plastic For Sale sign rested inside the window with the number to a realty office. Mel walked to the vacant windows and stared inside. Shane joined her.

"What are we looking at, other than cobwebs and dust?"

"I don't know. This old store intrigues me. It's as if time never touched it. Look at those high tin ceilings. And the old oak counter with that huge cash register. All those cubbyholes on the back wall." Mel thought those squares would be perfect for displaying shoes and bags. If someone ever wanted to open a dress shop there, that is.

Shane wasn't impressed. "Look at the exposed wiring on those lights. And the water stain in the middle of the floor. And the staircase with three missing steps."

"I love that staircase!" It wrapped around in a grand curve. The steps—and yes, a few were missing—were wide at the bottom, then narrowed as they reached the second floor. "This place has character."

Shane turned his head just enough to lift a brow in her direction. "This place has dry rot. What would you do with it?"

"Well, *I* wouldn't do anything, but *someone* could turn it into a nice boutique. With the resort bringing more and more people here, I bet someone could do a good business." She looked through the window again, thinking about her conversation with Nora. She could see it all— whitewashed walls and ceiling, racks of clothes, tufted sofas and chairs in the center, tables loaded with accessories.

"Excuse me, are you two casing this joint?"

Nessie nearly pulled the leash out of Mel's hands trying to leap on Dan Adams. In uniform, with his dark glasses pushed down on his nose so he could make eye contact over the top of them, Dan was a fine-looking man. The other fine-looking man at her side straightened and extended his hand formally.

"Shane Brannigan, Officer. Sorry, my friend here was daydreaming about fixing up this place. We're not looking to cause any trouble." Did Shane really think Dan was serious? But, then again, why wouldn't he? He didn't know anything about small towns, or Gallant Lake in particular.

Dan flashed Mel a quick, devilish grin. Oh, this was going to be fun. He stuck his thumbs in his belt loops and put on his best swaggering voice. "You must be new around here. Miss Lowery is nothing *but* trouble, mister. Before you know it, she'll be conning you out of your hardearned money to fund her illegal schemes. I'd be careful if I were you."

Mel started to laugh, but there was something about the way Shane bristled in her defense that stole her voice away. He took a step toward Dan, nudging his shoulder in front of her, as if to protect her.

"There's nothing illegal about looking at a building that's clearly for sale. And I don't know where you got those ideas about Miss Lowery, but I can assure you this woman…"

And finally the laughter fought its way to the surface. Shane's head snapped toward her as she started laughing so hard tears sprang to her eyes. Dan joined her, shaking his head as he removed the sunglasses.

"Stop!" Mel said, putting her hand on Shane's arm. "If either one of you calls me 'Miss Lowery' in that serious tone again, I'm going to lose it! Shane, this is Deputy Sheriff Dan Adams, locally known as Sheriff Dan. He and Asher are best friends, and he's one of Nora's best customers at the café. He rescued me and Nessie the night I decided to claim her officially."

Shane scowled briefly, then shook his head. "Small-town humor. Hilarious."

Dan was still chuckling, then he looked at Mel. "You're really thinking about buying the five-and-dime?"

"Me? No. I was just saying *someone* could fix it up and make it a showplace."

Dan looked through the windows, then at Shane. "Is she looking at the same store we're looking at?"

Shane lifted his hands and shrugged. "I think her crystal ball is broken."

"You're Tori's agent, right? Red Lincoln?"

"That's right." Shane frowned. "Why?"

"Relax, man. I just like knowing who's a regular and who's not. Tori's a good kid. And Mel's part of the best family in town. So I'm assuming I don't need to worry about you."

Dan moved on, and Shane stared at his retreating back. "Was that a compliment or a threat?"

Nessie had grown impatient, so Mel headed down the sidewalk with her.

"I'm not sure, so I'd be on my best behavior if I were you."

"Why do I feel like I just landed in an episode of *Longmire*?"

"Dan's really good people. And he takes protecting this town and the people in it very seriously. He and Asher have a poker game on Thursday nights with Nate and Carl and sometimes Blake. You could probably join them next week if you play."

Shane fell in step at her side. "I don't know who any of those people are."

"Well, I already told you Asher is Nora's fiancé. You just met Dan. Blake owns the resort and is married to my cousin Amanda. Nate owns the hardware store over there, and Carl owns this store right here." She waved her hand toward Carl's Liquors.

"Oh, perfect—I need some whiskey. Does he carry anything decent?" He reached for the door and held it open for her. Mel lifted her chin and smiled.

"I'm not a whiskey drinker, and I can't take

Nessie in, so we'll wait out here." Mel nodded ahead. "Meet you across the street?"

"That's right." Oblivious to her tension, he gave her a wink. "I forgot you stay away from the devil alcohol. I'll stop later."

Mel turned away and crossed the road with Nessie, forcing Shane to jog to catch up. Desperate to change the subject from booze, she pointed toward the water. "Look! The sailboats are out!"

Shane thankfully dropped the whiskey talk and looked out at the lake. A cluster of small catamarans were scooting across the surface of the water, taking advantage of the warm morning breeze. He watched them in silence, then a slow smile curved his lips.

"Tim and I used to sail on the Cape when we were kids."

"Really?" Mel leaned over and unhooked Nessie's leash, letting the dog run into the water. "I thought you were a city boy."

"I grew up in Boston, but my nana had a house in Chatham, near the water. That's where Tim and I met. On the water. His dad was a fisherman. And Tim used to man the lobster traps. I'd go out and help with the traps when I could. If the wind was up and the work was done, we'd take his dad's sailboat out and fly across the waves." He grinned at her. "Scared the crap out of me at first, but Tim was a great teacher."

She tried to imagine Shane on the bow of a

sailboat, wind in his hair, blue eyes squinting into the sun. Just as quickly, she tried to unimagine it, because holy good God. But it was too late. The image was burned into her brain, and it was delicious. He watched the boats, and she watched him. Neither of them saw Nessie running up on shore until she shook herself right in front of them. Mel squealed and jumped back, tripping over a rock and sitting down with a grunt. Shane was immediately at her side, pulling her to her feet.

"You okay?" She nodded, rubbing her tailbone and making a face as Nessie danced around them. He tried to look concerned, but she could tell he was amused.

"Yeah. Nothing bruised but my ego." She pointed at Nessie. "Bad dog!" But apparently scolding was ineffective when both humans were laughing. With a sigh of surrender, she clipped the leash back on Nessie's collar and headed to the lake walk in town.

"So what about you?"

She looked at him in confusion.

"What about me?"

"You know about my childhood. What was yours like?"

Her voice dropped, thinking of the photo he'd mentioned earlier. "I think you know."

"I don't think you popped out of the womb and

into modeling at sixteen. You were a kid once. What kind of kid were you?"

"The normal kind. I grew up outside Miami. We didn't have a lot of money, but I didn't know that then. Average student. Rode my bike everywhere. I was a tomboy."

"How did modeling happen?"

"It's pretty here, isn't it?"

"Mel…"

"Okay. I was 'discovered' on a Florida beach by an agency scout. He promised me the world, and the rest is history." She turned and leaned against the wooden railing by the water, striking a classic pose with a pretend flute of champagne in her hand. "Fame and fortune for everyone."

"You said it was a bad situation."

She *really* didn't want to have this conversation. Her hand slid into her pocket and around the pill bottle. "Sometimes it was fun. Sometimes not so much." She turned and tugged on Nessie's leash, walking away.

They were almost through town before Shane broke the silence.

"What do I need to watch for?"

"I don't understand."

"With Tori. You want to protect her from whatever happened to you. What do I need to be on guard for?"

Well, wasn't he clever? If she answered the

question, he'd learn more about *her*. If she didn't answer, he wouldn't be able to protect Tori. They stepped off the boardwalk and walked along the trail leading out of town. Trees offered shade from the sun climbing higher in the sky. Nessie, having burned off some of her puppy energy, was walking between Mel and Shane, occasionally stopping to sniff a random blade of grass.

"You manage famous athletes, Shane. You know fame attracts leeches. You'll need to be on guard for that more with Tori, because she's a young girl." Mel could still feel the shock remembering the first time she'd caught her "friend" Steffie stealing from her closet. Next, Steffie was stealing her boyfriend. And then it was jobs. "She won't see it coming. She won't *want* to see it. It hurts. A lot. She'll doubt herself, and start leaning on other people who will *gladly* tell her what to do." She looked up at the sun sparkling through the green leaves overhead and blinked a few times to clear the memories, trying to ignore the sudden weight of the pill bottle in her pocket. "But those people might not care about Tori at all."

CHAPTER FOURTEEN

SHANE QUIETLY ADMIRED Mel's profile. Stray tendrils of dark hair fell from the loose knot in soft waves, exposing her long neck as she stood staring up at the sky. Her floaty, flowy grape-colored top accented her ivory skin. Shane winced. He was becoming obsessed with women's clothing all of a sudden. Or maybe it was just the way clothes looked on a certain woman.

He decided her neck might just be his favorite part of Mel's body, other than her unique violet eyes. Sure, her legs were fantastic. Her waist was slender. Her breasts appeared to be pretty awesome, and he guessed they'd fit perfectly in his hands. But that neck was sexy as hell—graceful and elegant.

He'd seen it countless times last night looking at her pictures online. Fashion photographers clearly liked her neck as much as he did. And why not? It was a work of art. He idly wondered what it would be like to kiss his way from her raised chin down to her shoulder and…

Whoa. What the hell was he thinking? He

was supposed to be paying attention to her advice about Tori, not having wet daydreams about her. He gave himself a mental shake and tried to focus. She still hadn't moved, seemingly mesmerized by the shifting leaves overhead. To his horror, a single tear moved slowly down her cheek.

She flinched when he touched her arm, looking at him as if she'd forgotten he was there.

"Mel, what is it?" He quickly ran through what she'd been saying earlier. Keep leeches away from Tori. False friends. Betrayal. Bad choices.

Mel blinked and turned away from him to scratch the dog's ears, still wrapped up in her thoughts and not answering. He put his fingers under her chin, lifting her face to meet his.

"Tell me what's happening."

She chewed on her lip, then ran her tongue along it. He gently brushed the tear from her soft cheek with his fingers, unable to watch its sad journey any longer.

Her voice was thick. "You're right—I see myself in Tori. And sometimes it's not a pretty picture."

"Do you want to talk about it?"

"No."

Neither of them moved. His fingers slid to the side of her face and tucked a strand of silky hair behind her ear. Her nostrils flared when he ran a fingertip along the edge of that ear. So he did it again. His thumb rubbed across her lower lip, and her breathing hitched.

It was fascinating. He was watching his fingers move across her skin without any sensation of directing them. They just seemed to know what to do. His other hand skimmed up her arm and slid along the curve of that beautiful neck. He could smell her cologne, but it didn't make him think about Nana anymore. This was Mel's scent now, and he'd never get it out of his head.

She wasn't with Luis. She wasn't with anyone. Sure, Travis at the pizza shop wanted her, but she wasn't *with* him. Shane thought of the way Deputy Sheriff Dan Adams watched her over his glasses. She said he'd rescued her and Nessie one night. No, Dan had had his chance and hadn't made a move. Shane was the one standing here, with his hands on Mel's perfect skin, her lips just inches from his.

He wasn't the possessive type. He'd never been a chest-thumper, proclaiming any woman "belonged" to him. Women came and went from his life, and none of them really left a ripple, except maybe in his wallet. But Mel, this woman, staring at him with those wide eyes, trembling just a little at his touch, barely breathing. This woman was going to leave a lot more than a ripple. He had no doubt that this woman might tear his life, and his heart, apart if he let her. And still…he wanted her. He wanted her to be *his*.

A furrow appeared between her brows.

"Shane…" His name was a whisper on her lips.

"Say that again."

Her eyes darkened, and the furrow faded as a smile teased her lips. Her voice was stronger this time.

"Shane. What are we doing?"

"Damned if I know, but I'm not stopping unless you tell me to."

He waited, and she didn't say a word. His head dropped until his lips touched hers. He waited again, until she tipped her head up to meet him. Her lips parted for him with a sigh, and still, he hesitated. Was he afraid for her? Or for himself? This moment…this moment felt big. She murmured his name against his lips, her arms wrapping around his neck. And he was a goner.

He held her face in his hands, holding her still while his mouth took control. A soft moan rose from her throat, and his heart started banging in his chest. He had to hold back or they'd be naked on the ground in a heartbeat. She wasn't making it easy.

One of his hands slid down her neck, his fingers wrapping around the back of her head, his thumb tipping her jaw up. She tilted her face just enough to let his tongue reach places he hadn't managed to explore yet. His chest vibrated with a low growl and he pulled her closer.

He didn't know how long it lasted. He didn't care. He had no intention of stopping.

Until the dog barked. And barked. And barked. The two of them reluctantly pulled apart. As soon as there were a few inches between them—as soon as Shane's fingers left her skin—he saw the horror on Melanie's face, and it sent icy fingers through his veins.

"What are we *doing*?" Her hand covered her mouth. She took another step back, almost stumbling over Nessie as the dog continued to bark at something in the trees. Her hands shook. Her feet continued to shuffle as if she was looking for footing. She couldn't stay still. He, on the other hand, was completely immobile. He didn't want to spook her any more than he already had.

"Mel… It's okay." His voice was steady, as if he was calming a child. "It was just a kiss."

"Not to boost your ego or anything, but that was more than 'just' a kiss, and you know it."

He grinned, glad she was as affected by it as he was. "Fair enough. But I don't want you freaking out over this."

"Why did you *do* that? Why did you just *kiss* me like that, out of nowhere!"

He reached for her arm but she jerked away from him.

"Don't make it sound like I assaulted you or something, Mel. You were just as committed to that kiss as I was."

MEL OPENED HER mouth to argue, but no words came. Because Shane was right. She had very definitely participated in that shocking kiss. Her lips were still warm from it, and so were other parts of her body. Shane Brannigan might be clueless about how to speak to women, but the man sure as hell knew how to kiss one.

"Okay." She blew out a breath. "Okay. I was swept up in it for a moment, but…I mean, one minute we were talking, and…what the hell happened? And why?"

His brows furrowed in confusion. "*Why?* I don't think I've ever been asked that by a woman I've kissed. I don't know. You were standing there crying, and you looked so damn beautiful that I just…"

Mel held up her hand. "Wait. You kissed me like that because I was *crying*? And you thought crying made me beautiful?"

"Not *because* you were crying. I mean—I didn't like seeing you cry, but…" Shane rubbed the back of his neck. "Do we really have to analyze this? It was a *moment* and I kissed you and you kissed me back. People do it all the time. I was attracted to you. You're a beautiful woman and..."

She flinched. "Stop *saying* that!"

He flung his arms open wide. "I don't even know what we're *talking* about right now!" He stepped closer. "I don't get it, Mel. You might not want to hear it, but you *are* beautiful. I can't be the first one who's ever said that. You look in the mirror every day—you have to know how gorgeous you are. Do you really not see that?" He thought she didn't know? That she was reacting out of some sense of insecurity or low self-esteem? Why couldn't he see it? "So, yeah. I kissed you because you were standing there looking like a fucking goddess, and I couldn't *not* kiss you in that moment. Mel, I don't know who told you otherwise, but you're the most beautiful woman..."

"You think I don't know I was born with high cheekbones and Liz Taylor eyes?" She took a step toward him, and he wisely stepped back. "You think I don't know every inch of this body of mine and how to use it to its best advantage? As you like to point out, I made my living with this body and this face!"

He gestured toward her, from head to toe. "Then what the hell is the problem? *I* think you're pretty. *You* think you're pretty! And we kissed! Christ, I've never been so sorry that I kissed someone."

A moment of silence fell on the little clearing just off the hiking trail. Even Nessie was sitting still and quiet, leaning against Mel's leg as if she knew she was needed. He scrubbed both hands down his face.

"Damn it, I didn't mean that. I just don't understand what we're arguing about."

"No one ever, *ever* sees ME. They see a one-dimensional cutout figure with a pretty face. And that's all they want—the pretty girl, not Mel." She tugged on Nessie's leash, brushing past him, but she didn't get far. His hand closed firmly on her upper arm and he turned her around.

"That's not true. Not with me." His voice softened, and there was something in his eyes she hadn't noticed before. Was it pity? She didn't want that. Or was it heat? Had she missed the embers glowing so fiercely there? "You don't want me to kiss you because you're pretty? Fine. I'll kiss you because you need to be kissed right now. I'll kiss you because nothing about what I'm feeling is skin deep. I'll kiss you because I want more of you. *You*, Mel. Not your pretty face. *You*."

His mouth was on hers again. She should have pulled away. She should have slapped his face. But she didn't do either of those things. Instead, she slid her arms around his waist and leaned into the kiss, hungering for more. This kiss was much more aggressive than the first—less about comforting and more about lust. And Mel was surprisingly okay with that. She pressed her body against his and groaned when his hand slid down to cup her buttocks hard against his obvious erection. It was the middle of the day. They were on a public walking trail. She still had Nessie's leash looped over one wrist. And all she could think about was how far they could go without being arrested.

Her back came in contact with the rough bark of a tree, and their kiss never broke. Okay. Shane was on the same page she was. His fingers slid beneath the waistline of her shorts, rough and urgent against soft skin. Her hand moved to grip the hard ridge beneath the zipper of his chinos, and he nipped at her lower lip. This was crazy. This was insane. This was unlike any other high she'd ever known.

It was only the laughter of children approaching, and Nessie's answering bark, that stopped them from getting it on right there on the walking trail. They both jumped back, breathing harshly and staring at each other in surprise and—she had to admit it—stark desire. Her skin burned everywhere his eyes touched, and she was seriously reconsidering her moratorium on sex.

Three bicycles came around the corner on the

trail. A mom and two young children, talking to each other and laughing. When the woman, her short blond hair fluttering in the wind, saw them, she stopped. She looked back and forth between Shane and Mel, her eyes narrowing in suspicion.

"Is everything okay here?"

Mel's face flamed. Her hand went to her hair, which was a mess from Shane's fingers. Her shirt was pulled halfway up her midriff. The waist of her shorts was tugged down on one side where Shane had slid his hand against her hip. Between the crying and the kissing, her makeup had to be a blurry mess. Shane straightened and tucked his own shirt back into his pants. Had she done that?

"Mel, now would be a good time to tell the nice lady that you're not the victim of a crime." He spoke the words under his breath, but the urgency was clear. The young mom was pulling her phone from her pocket.

"We're fine!" Mel rushed to say it before the woman dialed. "We just…uh…haven't seen each other in a while…and…uh…got…carried away."

The woman studied them another moment, then smiled knowingly, nodding back at the two little girls on bikes behind her. "The oldest was when my husband got back from his first deployment, and the youngest was after his second. But as eager as we were, we still didn't do it outdoors in broad daylight." She looked at Nessie, who was lying at Mel's side, her long tail sweeping the grass. "Or bring a dog."

"Sorry." Shane was trying not to laugh. "We'll take it inside. Have a nice day."

As she pedaled past them, she tossed her response over her shoulder. "My day won't be as good as yours, I'm guessing!"

They watched her leave, then looked at each other in a combination of amusement and horror. Of all the men in the world, why did she have to be turned on by an opinionated talent agent?

"Okay." Shane tipped his head. "So we have some chemistry." He looked at her mouth and his eyes darkened. "A *lot* of chemistry. The first kiss was great. But that second one? You and I have something going on, Mel…"

"No, we don't. We can't. I have sworn off men, and I've sworn off agents, and I've sworn off relationships, and…"

"I'm not relationship material, so you're safe on that count, and I'm definitely not a fashion agent. What I do is different. My life is too crazy for anything serious, and let's face it, you and I have nothing in common. You're here in Gallant Lake, and I'll be outta here as soon as Tori is. But, princess, if we can ignite like that with clothes on, imagine what we could do…"

Mel had already imagined, and it had cost her more than one sleepless night. And that was before she'd known how the man could kiss. That kind of rush might just quench her desire to get high. And that was the problem. You couldn't replace one drug with another. Her hand rubbed the front of her pocket, over the bottle still safely inside. She knew how to control one high. She had no idea how she'd control Shane Brannigan.

"No. You'll have to be satisfied with imagining. That can't happen again."

He stared at her so long she almost surrendered and moved into his arms, but he finally nodded.

"Okay. If that's what you want, Mel."

The ringtone of his phone made them both blink and turn away from each other, probably just in time. He looked at the screen and frowned.

"What is it, Tim?"

Mel watched as he walked away.

"We have trouble, huh? Funny, I was just thinking the same thing." He looked over his shoulder and winked at her. She rolled her eyes and reached down to scratch Nessie's head.

Shane's body tensed. He wasn't getting good news, and Mel worried it was about Tori. "God *damn* it! I told Mark not to drink in public. Ever. I don't care how innocent it was." Okay, so not about Tori. "Get me a flight to Tampa. Call the team owner and beg him not to release a statement until we know for sure what happened."

He dropped the phone into his pocket, cursing softly to himself.

"Trouble?" Mel walked up behind him, resting her hand on his arm.

Shane grunted. "Always."

"Sounds like you're going to handle it, though." She tilted her head to the side. "You like solving problems, don't you?"

They started walking back toward town.

"What I'd *really* like is not having these problems at all. It would be nice to have clients who don't constantly push the envelope. Maybe my father was right."

"But isn't that what makes them good athletes?"

His brow furrowed. "Causing problems?"

"Pushing the envelope. Isn't that the definition of an athlete? I get that it's not good to do in their personal life, but it makes sense that the attitude spills over once in a while." Nessie tugged hard on the leash, and Mel gave a sharp command that brought the dog back to heel. "When you're in the spotlight like that, it's hard to turn it off. You become what people expect to see."

"That's pretty deep. Talking from experience?"

She cast a glance at him out of the corner of her eye. If he only knew.

"Have you already forgotten about that girl you saw in the picture?"

Shane frowned. "You're saying you were doing what was expected?"

Mel shrugged. "Pretty much. I was away from home, surrounded by people who didn't give a damn about me once the cameras turned off. A lot of the shoots were one big pill-popping party. So it felt natural for the party to continue afterward."

"Drugs on photo shoots? Why didn't the photographers or your chaperones say anything?"

They'd reached the village and sidewalks again.

"Who do you think supplied the pills?"

"Christ, no wonder you were so upset when I told you I was an agent. And then with the pills. But you're not doing that anymore, right? Is that why you don't drink?"

She hesitated, then raised her chin. He wasn't wrong. "Yes."

"Because you're afraid you'll lose your ability to control it."

"Something like that."

Just because he'd kissed her silly, it didn't mean she was ready to share her deepest secrets with him. He stopped and reached out to take her hand.

"I will *never* let that happen to Tori. I don't tolerate substance abuse with any of my clients—they know illegal drug use is cause for immediate termination of our contract. In her case, it's my job to keep that shit away from her."

Mel thought about the pill bottle in her pocket.

"How many clients have you lost because of that policy?"

"A few. They all know where I stand when they sign with me. No drugs—performance enhancing or otherwise—or I cut 'em loose."

She wondered how he felt about addicts. Even clean ones. Even struggling ones. His phone chirped with an incoming text. He read it, then looked at her with regret.

"I gotta run. But, Mel, I need you to believe me. I won't tolerate drug use. No exceptions."

He clearly meant that to be good news. Reassurance of some kind. And it was, but it also placed a weight of pressure on her that she couldn't define. He looked at her expectantly, and she forced a smile, squeezing his hand quickly before releasing it.

"Good. That's good."

CHAPTER FIFTEEN

"THIS CITY IS INSANE!" Tori was walking, laughing, talking, spinning and pointing at the same time. It was a common reaction for first-time tourists in Manhattan, so the New Yorkers passing by just rolled their eyes and kept most of their curses under their breaths. The perpetual backdrop of multiple languages being spoken at once, along with constant car horns and drivers yelling out their open windows, just added to the adrenaline rush that was New York City on a hot summer day.

It had been two weeks since Gary had been fired. Tori had gone home to Cleveland to spend the Independence Day weekend with her family, and now they were on their much-anticipated shopping trip to New York to celebrate both the end of her physical therapy sessions and her upcoming return to the golf tour.

Yesterday, Mel and Tori had played tourist. They'd taken the Circle Line cruise, sailing past the Statue of Liberty. They'd lunched at the Freedom Tower, but Tori had hardly eaten a bite. She'd been too busy taking in the views of the city. They'd gone to the top of the Empire State Building because Tori's mom loved *Sleepless in Seattle* and had made Tori promise to get a picture of herself up there. And they'd taken in the hottest Broadway musical last night, courtesy of Luis calling in a favor from an ex-boyfriend in the theater business.

Amanda had arranged for Tori and Mel to share a two-bedroom suite at Blake's midtown hotel, and the views were just as breathtaking from their fortieth-floor room as anywhere else they'd been, especially after the show, when they'd stayed up late to talk.

Mel had turned off the lights in the room and ordered milkshakes from room service. They'd pushed two chairs to face the windows and talked into the wee hours of the morning. Tori had talked about the other women and girls on the golf tour. Some were nice. Some not so much. Many resented her sudden jump into the limelight, and she felt intense pressure to prove herself to them. She was also feeling the heat from her sponsors, her parents, the media and Shane. She said it felt as though everyone had a different set of expectations for her to meet.

Mel's advice to "just be yourself" earned her a well-deserved eye roll. They sat in silence for a while, until Mel started sharing more stories of her past. How she'd let herself be pulled around by other people instead of thinking for herself. How she'd let herself be conned into thinking she "needed" a few pills to wake up and a few more to sleep at odd hours and, hey, why not wash them all down with booze?

The numbness she'd felt had only made her judgment worse, and pretty soon she'd been handing her money over to strangers who'd promised to make her investments grow until she wouldn't have to work anymore. The pills and booze had helped her believe their lies.

Tori had given her a solemn look, with a backdrop of city lights. "You got hooked on the pills? Is that why you freaked at Gary?"

That's when Mel had shared the story she'd only shared with a handful of people. The drugs. The alcohol. The morning she'd woken up in a rock star's bed with no memory of how she'd gotten there or what had happened. Her frantic call to Luis for help. The rehab center in Switzerland. The slow and difficult walk away from modeling and toward...who knew what. When she'd finished, Tori had simply held her hand and they'd watched the city that never sleeps, each lost in their own thoughts. Mel's had swirled around the pill bottle tucked in her bag.

"Can we go to Rockefeller Center today?" Tori jumped in Mel's path, forcing an abrupt halt that elicited sharp curses from the people behind her. Knowing the city well, she didn't bother apologizing. No one would wait long enough to hear it, anyway.

She shook her head. "Sorry, kiddo. Today's a work day. We're going to some sample sales to get you a new wardrobe. Then we're going to have lunch with Luis, and you're going to one of the most exclusive hair salons in New York."

The sample sales were crazy, as usual. Women on the hunt for bargains are a lot like hyenas following the scent of blood. They travel in packs until the target is found, then it's everyone for themselves as they devour the sale items. Tori was intimidated at the first sale, but she watched how Mel pawed through the items, scanning for size first, then quickly assessing each piece to see if she wanted it.

They'd already discussed their goals for Tori's new look. Youthful. Comfortable. Mature without being too sexy. More trendsetting than trendy. Bright, solid colors interspersed with the occasional funky pattern. She promised Tori three vetoes of the things Mel picked for her, and Tori had three free passes to keep things Mel didn't like. By the third sale, they were working like a well-oiled machine. They'd head to different racks and, since they were both tall, they'd make eye contact above the crowd and hold things up in the air. No discussion was needed, just a nod or a quick shake of the head on either side.

They walked into Luis's studio so loaded down with shopping bags that he burst into laughter. "You ladies don't mess around, do you? Are there any clothes left in New York?" They set the packages aside and nibbled on falafels and tabbouleh from the local Lebanese deli, giving Tori an introduction to Middle Eastern cuisine. Luis promised to have the bags delivered to the hotel before he headed to the airport. He was on his way to London to meet with the city's premier department store to finish talks about offering the new Alvarado collection there in the spring. He gave Mel a wink while Tori was looking at the fabrics stacked on the tables.

"Guess who stayed at my place last night, and is taking me to the airport today?"

"Tim?" Mel gave him a quick hug. "So things are…?"

"Good. Things are *very* good. It doesn't make sense really, but it feels like we've known each other forever." He leaned back against a design table and gave her a curious look. "Shane's in the city, too, for some meeting. We could have had a Team Tori lunch, but I can't figure out what's going on with you two."

She sipped her sparkling water. "I don't know what you mean." Mel had all she could do to keep from closing her eyes and imagining herself back in Shane's strong arms, being kissed senseless in Gallant Lake.

"See, you say that, but those red cheeks and dreamy eyes tell me you know exactly what I mean. There's something between you, isn't there?"

Fortunately Tori joined them and saved Mel from having to answer. Yes, there was definitely something, but she had no idea how to describe it. Other than heat. They had lots and lots of heat.

Mel was tired by the time she and Tori got to the hair salon, but she felt good. The fashion district usually put her sharply on edge, but seeing everything through the wide eyes of a teenager made it feel fresh and exciting again. Maybe Luis was right—maybe she *should* come to work with him at the studio. Maybe she *was* ready. But every time that thought crossed her mind, she pictured the Gallant Lake five-and-dime store.

Tori told the stylist she wanted her hair left long enough to pull into a ponytail at tournaments, but she also wanted it to be "edgy." Justine was up for the challenge. Tori ended up with a blunt asymmetrical cut that barely brushed her shoulder on the left and was inches longer on the right. Mel reluctantly allowed them to add a dark pink streak on the long side. She wasn't sure what Shane would think of it, but it wasn't like Tori had shaved her head or anything. It was age-appropriate, and Tori's mom had approved via a video call.

Tori was having her nails done when Mel heard a dreadfully familiar voice behind her.

"Well, well, well. I never thought I'd see Mellie Low back at Justine's again." Mel steeled herself before turning to face Steffie Malcor. "Aren't you a little long in the tooth to be trying a comeback?"

Memories came back in a rush, and none of them were pretty. Of all the false friends of the fashion world, Steffie had been the worst. She never cared who she trampled to get the job or man she wanted. It was Steffie who'd taken Mel to the "best" parties. Steffie who introduced Mel to drugs. Steffie who'd left Mel alone with a predatory photographer who stole her innocence. She took another deep breath and pulled her shoulders back. She wasn't that naive girl anymore. Mel gave Steffie a dismissive up and down glance—something else she'd learned from her "friend."

Mel managed a tight smile. It might even pass as genuine to someone not paying attention. "That's rich coming from someone four years older than I am. Or is it six?"

Steffie hadn't changed much since they'd last seen each other. Her skin seemed a little tight, as if she'd recently had a chemical peel. Her super-short black hair was artfully styled, held in spiky place with some kind of cement-like styling gel. Her makeup, as usual, was flawless, if a bit heavy-handed for midday. She was wearing her usual brilliant green contact lenses, disguising her natural brown eyes. She was a stunning beauty on the outside, if you ignored all the hard edges. But she was a hard-core competitor, willing to do just about anything to get every job she could.

Steffie's eyes narrowed, and she looked at Mel's outfit. Mel might be out of the business, but she damned well knew how a fashion icon needed to dress in New York. She was in Luis's skintight denim pencil skirt, artfully torn and threadbare in just the right spots, with a low-cut black lace tank top and cropped jacket, paired with the orange stilettos Tori had worn just a few weeks ago.

Steffie snickered. "I must have missed the denim memo. Is the hayseed look making a comeback?"

It wasn't the words that hurt. Steffie had never been known for her sharp wit or for her personal fashion choices. And Mel couldn't care less what Steffie thought about her.

No, it was the cutting, competitive edge to her voice that sent a shudder through Mel. It was the look in those artificially green eyes. There was disdain there, yes. But that wasn't what cut into Mel's heart.

It was the terror she saw in Steffie's face. She'd lived with that fear herself for years, but had assumed Steffie was immune. The constant pressure to be thinner and younger, to be invited to more movie premiers, date more wealthy men, get on more magazine covers, have more social media followers, walk the hottest runways…

Mel's hand automatically went to the leather bag slung over her shoulder. The bag with the pills. Maybe it was stupid to carry them around, but she'd convinced herself it was a way to test her resolve. A way to prove to herself that she could resist the temptation. But what if she couldn't?

Steffie waved her hand dramatically. "Well, you've turned into a bore. Have you lost your voice as well as your style? Is that why you dropped off the face of the earth? Everyone wondered what happened."

Mel's hand tightened on the bottom of her bag. She could feel the pill bottle there.

"Why? Did you miss me? Or did you find another young girl to push off on Nelson in return for getting all the best jobs? Or was it his endless supply of coke you were doing it for?" Mel gestured toward Steffie's face. "You've got a little 'diet powder' there by your nose."

Steffie's quick reaction, reaching up to rub under her nose, told Mel she'd guessed right. She was still using. Steffie checked her fingers, then glared at Mel.

"I saw the story about you and Luis working together. You know he's just using your money. It's not like you have any real design talent, and you've packed on too many pounds to make modeling work, unless you're going for the plus-size business."

She kept talking, but the mean words blurred together into a meaningless dull roar in Mel's head. She could have come up with plenty of snappy comebacks, but what was the point? The woman reminded her of a cornered animal, lashing out at anyone who might possibly be a threat. Instead of seeing a rival in Steffie, she only saw her old self—afraid and raw.

"Oh, wow—you're Steffie Malcor!" Tori was at Mel's side. "I forgot you two were friends. Steffie and Mellie. That's so cool." She extended her hand. "I'm Tori Sutter. I follow you on Instagram. Mel brought me here for a makeover—what do you think?" Tori twirled and waggled her bejeweled neon pink nails. Behind her, customers were discreetly aiming their phones at the women.

Steffie changed personas in a heartbeat, smoothly morphing into the smiling, charming celebrity the world thought she was.

"It's wonderful to meet a fan, Tori. Thanks for following me." She gave a sideways glance to Mel. "And how nice of Mellie to take time from her busy schedule to help you. Did you win a contest or something? Or did she just pluck you off the street?"

Tori's brows puckered, but Mel answered for her.

"Tori's on the women's golf tour, Steffie. She's a talented athlete. We're having a girls' day together because *that's* what friends do. Friends don't leave friends alone with rock stars twice their age. And now we have to go." She wanted Tori as far away from this sad, desperate woman as possible. But Steffie wasn't done.

"An athlete?" She gave Tori a critical glance and leaned toward Mel, but didn't bother lowering her voice. "Honey, you might want to share some of your diet powder with the kid. She could lose a few, you know?"

The words made a direct hit on Tori, but Steffie was gone before Mel could hit back. Instead, she put her arm around Tori's shoulder. "Ignore her. She was trying to hurt me, not you. You look strong and beautiful just the way you are. And with that hairstyle? Girl, you are fierce."

Tori followed Mel out the door and onto the hectic sidewalks. They walked a few blocks in silence before she spoke.

"Why did she want to hurt you? I thought you were friends?"

"I thought we were, too. Until I learned differently. After that, it was just good business for us to show up places together and pretend. Take it as a lesson not to believe everything you see on the internet. Pictures don't always tell the truth."

"What's diet powder?"

Mel slowed. "That's what Steffie and a lot of models call cocaine. They tell themselves they have to use it to control their weight."

"You use cocaine?" Tori tried to stop, but the crowds wouldn't let her. Mel grabbed her arm and steered her toward the building front and out of the foot traffic.

"It would be awesome if you didn't yell that out loud on the city sidewalk, okay? And no, I don't use anything. Not anymore." But she wanted to. *Really* wanted to.

Mel's tension level was higher than the skyscrapers around them. If any of her cousins had been around to ask the magic question, she was at a solid level nine. Seeing Steffie. Talking about drugs. Not good. She needed to calm down before she went over the edge. Maybe just one little pill. They were right there in her bag. Just to settle her nerves so she didn't fall apart in front of a teenage girl. Just to protect Tori. She really should have gone to this week's meeting in Gallant Lake.

She'd missed two meetings now, and she wasn't thinking clearly. Of *course* the oxy would make her feel better, but it would be *wrong*.

"Mellie? Is that really you? When I saw Steffie's SnapLife post about seeing you, I didn't believe it. I scooted right out of the studio to see for myself, and here you are."

No, no, no. This couldn't be happening. She couldn't be dealing with Steffie *and* Nelson on the same day. She turned to face the photographer who'd derailed first her childhood, then her career and very nearly her life.

"Nelson. I'd say 'nice to see you' but it isn't. So excuse us." She grabbed Tori's hand and tried to push past him, but Nelson Timmons was tall and broad and he planted himself firmly in their path. Mel's heart rate went from pounding to fluttering and skipping, and it wasn't a good feeling. Sweat prickled at her scalp.

"Oh, honey, don't rush away. Let me look at you!" He frowned. "Are you wearing any makeup at all? Mellie, darling, you really need it at your age. And you definitely need to knock off the donuts or whatever it is you're eating." He winked at Tori. "Your friend used to be one of the most beautiful women in the world, and a goddess in front of the camera. A *goddess*. The things she'd do in the studio…"

Mel could feel Nelson's hands on her, pulling

her clothes away, murmuring soft words as he convinced her it was all part of the job. Bile rose in her throat.

"Nelson…please…" She tried to be strong. She tried to body-act her way through the conversation, but she couldn't pull her shoulders back or lift her chin. She was shaking too much.

He reached out and took her arm. "Mellie-baby, I can see you're in trouble. I can help you." She wanted to pull away, but she was frozen in place, overwhelmed with memories.

Mellie-baby, grab some of those orange pills. They'll put a smile on your face.

Mellie-baby, there's going to be a big party at Mick's tonight, and I got you an invite. All you have to do is smile and be nice to everyone, okay?

Mellie-baby, take a snort before you go, so you won't eat anything. Good girl.

Mellie-baby, rub a little ice on those nipples to make them pop, okay?

Here, Mellie-baby, have another glass of champagne and loosen up. I've got someone I want you to meet.

"Get your hands off her." Tori pushed Nelson's hand away and tugged on Mel's arm to pull her away from him. "She didn't '*used* to be beautiful,' she *is* beautiful. And she clearly doesn't want to talk to you, so get lost."

Nelson's eyes narrowed on Tori. "You don't

know her like I do, sweetie. She may think she doesn't want to talk to me, but she *needs* what I can provide." He leaned toward Mel. "I've got a pocket full of candy if you want some. For old times' sake."

She was there, but not really. She was more of a spectator, watching as Nelson tempted her with the poison apple—so tempting. But Tori yanked her back and started yelling curses at him. People paused around them, then moved on with their day when Nelson didn't respond. He just laughed and walked away, tapping away on his phone, probably to Steffie.

Mel didn't remember how they got back to their suite, but she started to cry the minute the door closed behind them. She was shaking so badly she could barely open her bag, and she panicked for a moment when she couldn't find the pill bottle. No, there it was. She was safe.

"What is that? Are those the pills Gary tried to give me? Mel, no…"

"It's okay, Tori. I know what I'm doing. Why don't you go lie down for a while, and then we'll get dinner, okay? I just need to settle my nerves, and this will help." She already had the bottle open. She was so close to relief. To an escape from the pain.

"No!"

Tori grabbed for the bottle, and it flew out of

Mel's hand, sending pills bouncing across the floor. Mel immediately dropped to her knees and started gathering them up, tears falling on the pills as she grabbed at them.

"Mel, please! You're scaring me!"

Time stopped.

Mel looked at her shaking hands clutching the pills, then up at Tori. She must look unhinged. And she was. Terror filled her. She couldn't do this. But she had to. But she couldn't. She sat back on her heels and covered her face with her hands, tiny pills falling to the floor through her open fingers. This wasn't the way.

But her pain. The flashbacks. The look back into a world that had tried to kill her.

She took a deep, ragged breath.

And she screamed at the demons trying to pull her down.

CHAPTER SIXTEEN

SHANE SPRINTED INTO the elevator from the hotel
lobby, frantic and out of breath. The three people
already inside took one look at him and quickly
exited. Tim's call had had him on his feet and
dashing out of the meeting at the baseball league's
headquarters on Park Avenue with barely a word
of apology. He knew where Blake's hotel was,
and it had been easier to run there than deal with
flagging down a cab.

Tori had called Shane first, but he'd let it go to
voice mail because of the meeting. He'd figured
she just wanted to talk about her shopping trip,
like she'd wanted to talk about her day seeing the
sights last night. He was glad she and Mel were
having fun, but he was busy trying to get a client's
suspension reduced.

Tori had called Luis next, but he'd been board-
ing an overseas flight. Luis called Tim, who,
much to Shane's surprise, was in New York. Tim
had rushed to the hotel, and was with Tori now.
Shane had no clue what had happened, but Tim

had said Mel was in trouble, and that was all he'd needed to hear.

The elevator doors finally chimed and opened, and he hurried to the room. Tim was waiting in the doorway, looking grim.

"Tori's fine. I put her in a limo to Gallant Lake, and Amanda is expecting her. They'll keep her at the house. She's rattled, but she did good."

"And Mel?"

"She's in her room and won't come out. I got it unlocked, but she was yelling at me to stay out, so I did. Tori was pretty sure she got all the pills away from Mel, but she thought she took some bottles from the minibar."

"Pills? What pills?"

"Apparently she kept the pills Gary tried to give Tori."

Oxy. *Shit.* He raked his fingers through his hair.

"What the hell happened?"

"I only got bits and pieces from Tori. Some model from Mel's past gave her shit at the beauty salon. Then some 'creep,' as Tori described him, confronted Mel on the sidewalk and played some head games with her. It sounds like Mel had a panic attack." Tim frowned. "To be honest, what Tori described sounded like a PTSD episode, and I've seen my share of them. Something triggered her, and that was all she wrote."

"What does that have to do with her hanging on to those damn pills?"

Tim nodded toward Mel's door. "She's an alcoholic, Shane. Luis told me today when he called from the airport. She spent four months in rehab. She's in the program, goes to meetings, the whole deal. Only Luis and her cousins know."

His blood ran so cold it was a wonder his heart was still pumping. "She told me she didn't drink. She told me she wasn't taking pills. She said that was all behind her." Or had he just assumed that?

"She's been clean and sober for two years. But Luis says she's been under a lot of stress lately. Her accountant lost a bundle. She's not modeling anymore. She had to sell her home." Tim lowered his voice, even though there was no way Mel could hear them. "He thinks being around Tori so much might have brought back memories Mel couldn't handle. Like I said—a trigger for PTSD."

Shane's hands curled into fists. He was ready to fight, but fight what? Damn it to hell, she'd *told* him she saw herself in Tori. She'd told him to protect Tori from false friends and people who would steer her wrong. He thought about the tear that had tracked down her cheek the afternoon they'd kissed. She'd told him more than once that he was an idiot about women, and apparently she was right. If only he'd paid attention, maybe he could have prevented this.

Without another word, he turned away from Tim and went to Mel's room. He tapped on the door, but no response. He tested the doorknob.

"Melanie? It's Shane. I'm coming into your room, okay?"

Silence. He pushed the door open and stepped into the dark room. The curtains were drawn and no lights were on. As his eyes adjusted, he realized the bed was empty. He stepped to the open bathroom door, but she wasn't there. Fighting panic, he scanned the room again.

She was sitting on the floor in the corner, arms wrapped tightly around her knees, head down.

"Mel?" He approached her cautiously, having no idea what condition she might be in or how she might react. "Are you hurt? Are you okay?" He dropped to one knee in front of her and saw the slightest of tremors run through her. "Talk to me, princess." She drew in a shaky breath, and he could hear the tears that clogged her throat.

Shane sat on the floor and wrapped his arms around her, pulling her against his chest, where she cried silently. Every tear and every shudder burned scars into his heart he knew would never heal completely. She was terrified, and he felt helpless. He dropped soft kisses on the top of her head and murmured random words of comfort. She had to fight her way through this…this panic attack, or PTSD episode, or whatever the hell it was. She had to find her way out of it, and he wasn't going to move until she did.

He didn't know how long they sat there on the floor. He must have dozed off, because it was *really* dark in the room now. The tension was finally gone from Mel's body. She was asleep. One leg stretched out between his, and one arm was loosely wrapped around his waist. His shirt was still damp from her tears. He brushed her dark hair back to look at her face, and something inside his heart shifted.

Her lashes were damp from crying, her makeup blurred and stained. Her lips, usually busy throwing sharp barbs his way, were soft and gently parted as she breathed slowly in and out. This woman, curled up in his arms and intertwined with his body, was the same regal warrior princess he'd seen in that metallic gown in Gallant Lake. But right now she looked broken, and he hated it. His fingertips gently circled her temple, and she sighed in her sleep. Guilt curled its way through his veins.

He'd made fun of her. He'd mocked her career as simply "posing for pictures" when clearly that "easy" career had almost killed her. He'd resisted her advice for Tori, even after she admitted she saw herself in the girl, because he'd been clueless as to exactly what that meant. She rubbed her cheek against his shirt and mumbled something he couldn't decipher, then settled back against him. A glint of reflected light from the floor caught his eye.

It was a tiny bottle of vodka. There were several more small bottles scattered around them that he hadn't noticed before. He picked one up, and breathed a sigh of relief when he saw it was full. They all were. Mel had come in here alone and frantic after emptying the minibar, but she hadn't tasted a drop. She *was* still the warrior princess, and she'd won this battle, even if it had cost her. He placed his lips on her hair and left them there in a long kiss full of…what? Compassion? Admiration? Comfort? Support? Affection? He closed his eyes. It was more than all of that, but he couldn't put a name to it.

He shifted and moved her into his arms, slowly standing. She mumbled something again, and wrapped her arms around his neck without waking. Which was just as well, because her trusting, if unconscious, hug woke yet another new, indefinable feeling in Shane's chest. And this was one he *really* didn't want to examine.

He lowered her onto the bed and drew the comforter up to her shoulders. A ray of light came into the room from the doorway, and Tim nodded at him. His voice was just above a whisper.

"I thought I heard movement in here. How is she?"

Shane shook his head. He wanted so badly to bend over and kiss her cheek, but Tim was watching. Oh, screw it. He placed a kiss on her soft skin, then went to the door. "She's tough as nails, Tim. She'll be okay."

He hoped it was true.

MEL WAS AWAKE, but she couldn't open her eyes. She tried, but they were so crusty from her tears that they refused to budge. She rubbed them gently with her fingertips and finally managed to get them open. It was dark, but she could see the silhouette of skyscrapers against a pale sky through a slit in the curtains. She was in her Manhattan hotel room, tucked tightly under the comforter, but still fully dressed. She struggled to piece together everything that had happened yesterday…or was it today? Some of the memories were incomplete, just jagged collections of images and words in random order.

Manhattan. Tori. Luis. Steffie. Nelson. The pills. Oh, God, she'd tried to take pills in front of Tori.

"No…" She wanted to deny it to herself, even though she knew the truth.

"You're okay, Mel."

The deep voice froze her in place. It sounded like Shane, but it couldn't be. First, this voice was gentle and soft, not clipped and businesslike. And second, what would Shane Brannigan be doing in her hotel suite? Tori—where was Tori?

"Tori?"

The bedside lamp came on, making her blink. A large hand wrapped around hers. "She's fine. She's in Gallant Lake with your cousin Amanda."

"You'll never let me see her again, will you?" She plucked up the courage to turn her head and look straight into those ice-blue eyes. He was sitting in a chair next to the bed. His shirt was rumpled and smudged with...was that her makeup? His ginger hair was rumpled, too—standing on end in places as if he'd been raking it with his fingers. His brows drew together.

"What are you talking about?"

"Tori. You sent her away to protect her from me." It made sense, but the thought made her incredibly sad.

He reached out to gently push a strand of hair from her face. It was such an intimate thing to do. His voice kept its new, velvety texture. She liked it. A lot. Even if she didn't deserve it. "Of course not. We just didn't want to keep her here where she'd worry. When you're ready to go back to Gallant Lake, I'm sure she'll *demand* to see you." His teasing tone made her giggle. It was a short burst of laughter that stopped as soon as it started, surprising both of them. Shane's eyes went wide, and the corner of his mouth lifted.

"There's my princess." She had no idea what he meant, but the words made things flutter in places that hadn't fluttered in a long time. She moved to sit up, and frowned.

"I don't remember coming to bed."

"You fell asleep on the floor." His eyes darkened. "In my arms."

"Excuse me?" She remembered the humiliation of finding herself on her hands and knees in front of Tori, scrambling for the pills skittering across the floor like a desperate junkie. She'd made some really bad decisions in the past, and been in far more dangerous places, but never had she felt so pathetic. And all because Nelson and Steffie had bullied her a little. How could she have been so weak?

"You were hiding in the corner, crying." Something caught in Shane's voice, but his face remained stoic. A small vein jumping in his neck was the only sign of emotion. "You don't remember?"

She swung her legs over the side of the bed, facing him and shaking her head.

"No. It's like the lights just went out after I dropped the pills." Her cheeks burned at the admission. "How did you get here?"

"Tori called Luis. Luis called Tim. Tim came here and called me." He cleared his throat roughly. "You scared the hell out of everyone, Mel."

"I'm sorry." She hated how small her voice sounded, and so did Shane.

"Don't do that. Don't shrink and apologize for something you had no control over. I wasn't accusing you of anything. I was just saying we were scared...worried." She welcomed the return of Shane's sharpness, because it made her sharper, too.

Her foot bumped against something. It was a bottle from the minibar. Half a dozen more were scattered around the corner of the room. She took a quick inventory—they were all unopened. Shane followed her eyes.

"You didn't drink any."

"I wouldn't have pulled them out of the bar unless I intended to."

He tipped his head to the side, considering. "I'm not so sure about that. You carried the pills around all this time and didn't take any. You emptied the bar and didn't drink any of it. Maybe you were just testing yourself. If so, you passed."

"It was stupid. All of it. Stupid."

"Tim thought you might be having some sort of PTSD episode. Maybe a flashback?"

"I honestly don't know. Nothing like that has ever happened before. After Nelson...I remember being so focused on getting Tori back to the hotel safely." Mel had no idea how she'd managed to do that, considering the volcano of emotions boiling inside. "I don't remember doing it, but I remember knowing I had to. Tori tried to take the pill bottle and I grabbed for it. It spilled. And I dropped to the floor like a madwoman, trying to scoop them up. Like they were diamonds or something." She'd never forget herself in that pathetic position. "When I realized what I was doing, I just...snapped. After that, I don't know what happened."

Again, she looked at the front of his smudged and wrinkled shirt. If that was from her makeup, she must look like a clown right now. Her hands came up to her face, but Shane gently stopped her with smile.

"You might want to keep the lights off in the bathroom until you wash your face. You were crying pretty hard." He shrugged one shoulder. "You left most of your war paint on my shirt."

"Tell me what happened." He started to shake his head, but she insisted. "I need to know everything."

He stared at her for a moment before answering. "You were almost catatonic when I came in. Just curled up in a ball over there, surrounded by full bottles of booze. I sat next to you and you ended up in my arms. Crying." Mel closed her eyes tightly. What a nightmare. "We sat there so long we both dozed off. I woke up and you didn't. So I put you to bed."

Snippets of memory drifted through her mind. A big, solid embrace that anchored her to the ground when it felt like she was going to explode. Soft words in a deep voice. Were there... were there *kisses*?

"Did you kiss me?"

She could have sworn his cheeks reddened for just a second, but then it was gone. He straightened his shoulders and gave her a cocky grin. Another glimpse of the Shane she knew.

"Honey, when I kiss you again, you'll damn well remember it."

When? She liked the sound of that. A lot. Maybe that was what she needed right now—a distraction from everything else falling apart in her world.

"So what do we do now?"

"First, I'll get us some breakfast and we'll figure it out from there."

"I need to clean up. And change. I'm not ready to face anybody." The thought made her heart feel like lead in her chest. She stood and he rose with her, keeping a hand on her waist as if afraid she'd fall.

"We won't go anywhere until you're ready to. You should probably get some more sleep."

He turned to leave, and she panicked. "No! Stay here with me. Please. I just want to wash my face and...get fresh. But I don't want to be alone." Shame and fear burned hot in her veins. And Shane was so solid and strong, right there in front of her. She stepped closer, looking to soak up his strength, and his eyes narrowed.

"Mel...what are you doing?"

"You don't want to be near me?"

"What? No. I just don't...I don't want to take advantage of you."

"Poor, frail Mellie Low." The words came out in a singsong whisper.

"Stop it. Mellie Low is dead, remember?" His voice was hard and insistent. Who was he trying to convince? Her or himself? She thought of the sunny afternoon under the trees, when he'd kissed her pain away for a moment.

"Kiss me, Shane."

"What?"

"Kiss me. Please. I need you to kiss me." She stood on the balls of her feet and pressed her body against his. He gripped her arms with his hands. He didn't push her away, but he didn't pull her closer, either.

"Don't do this. You're upset, you're not thinking straight. It wouldn't be right..."

She shut him up with a kiss. He resisted for a heartbeat, then relented and opened his mouth for her with a growl. His fingers tightened on her arms, holding her still while the kiss deepened into a dance between them. A tango, with a drumbeat banging steadily in her chest. This. This she could feel. This she could handle. His arms wrapped around her, and she pressed her leg between his, rubbing against him and making him moan her name against her mouth. Yes. This was the painkiller she needed. Not vodka. Not pills. Just Shane.

And then he was gone. He held her arms again, but he was keeping her at arm's length. The emptiness she felt at the loss of his touch was searing. The look in his eyes, anger and lust and confusion, was enough to finally snap her out of it. What was she doing?

She pulled free and stepped farther away.

"I'm sorry, Mel, but one more second of that and I was going to let us make a big mistake. I want you so damn much, but not like this. Not when you're just looking for an escape. For any escape."

Her hand went to her pocket, but the pills were gone. She was on her own. She nodded sharply.

"Right. Of course. You're right. I'm sorry." He started to object, but she held up her hand. "No. I started that, and I'm allowed to apologize for it. I'm going to take a shower and change. I can't sleep anymore. I probably slept more tonight than I normally do. I never sleep, Shane. I never do anything normal people do." He watched her anxiously. "I'm not going to do anything crazy,

I promise. Kissing you was my crazy peak for today, okay? But I'm done sleeping. You can go. I'll be fine."

He didn't move, not even when she walked to the bathroom and closed the door on him. She looked in the mirror and almost laughed out loud. Her makeup was a dark mess across her face. No wonder he didn't want to kiss her! She turned the shower on hot, peeled off her clothes and stepped in, soaking up the steam and trying to let the warmth seep into her tired, aching body.

But all she felt was cold.

CHAPTER SEVENTEEN

SHANE COULDN'T GET his shower cold enough. He stood there, shivering, willing his body to come to its senses. Having distraction sex with an alcoholic coming off a panic episode that had nearly knocked her off the wagon would be a really sleazy thing to do. Having sex with Melanie Lowery seemed like his every dream come true, but he *had* to keep the two separate. His head was on board. His body was not.

After about fifteen minutes of ice-cold therapy, he stepped out and got dressed. Before Tim had left for Gallant Lake during the night, he'd retrieved Shane's bag from the other hotel and left it here, so he had a clean shirt with no evidence of Mel's meltdown last night. But the clean shirt didn't do anything for the places on his skin that had soaked up her tears. Those stains would be there forever.

She was curled up on the sofa sipping coffee when he walked into the living area. There was another cup on the table. She nodded at it and gave him a thin smile.

"It's not Nora's double espresso, but it's the best I could do in a pinch. I used both packets of coffee to make it extra strong."

He took a sip of the bitter brew. "Well, it's definitely strong. I ordered breakfast with two espressos, so we should survive."

"Shane...I'm so sorry about...this morning. I panicked. I wanted to forget what happened, and you were there, and I know the chemistry we have would be enough to make my problems disappear for a little while..."

"More than a little while, princess." He sat on the opposite end of the sofa. She looked confused, then started to smile.

"Are you seriously bragging about your sexual prowess right now?"

"I'm just saying what we have going on between us shouldn't be rushed." He took another sip of the coffee. "And it also shouldn't be some kind of distraction. When we do give in, it's going to be with 100 percent focus on each other, okay?"

She looked at him seriously. "You talk like it's a done deal."

"You don't think it's inevitable?"

She pursed her lips. "I don't know if I'd go that far, but yeah, the chemistry is definitely there." She tipped her head. "Why do you keep calling me 'princess'?"

He rested his arm on the back of the sofa. "Do you remember that sparkly dress you wore that first night? At the gala? The silver one?"

"It was metallic, not sparkly, and it was pewter, not silver, but yeah."

He snorted. "Pewter. Silver. Sparkly. Metallic. Whatever it was, it made you look like a warrior princess ready for battle. I kept waiting for you to whip out a sword or something. You looked invincible. Like Wonder Woman. You were all pissed off at me, and I'll tell you what—I still wanted you, Mel. Even then, there was something between us." He reached out and touched the tips of her fingers with his on the back of the seat cushions. "But this morning wasn't the time. You talk about wanting me to see the real you." He tapped her hand playfully. "Well, I want you to see me, not just some hot dude who can make your troubles go away for hours on end."

She grinned. "Such an ego. Just remember you're going to have to live up to all these promises if we do...you know. But not today. Not right now. Because right now, I'm *starving*." She grimaced at her coffee cup. "And this is awful coffee."

They didn't head home to Gallant Lake until evening, and Shane was fine with that. Mel was embarrassed and afraid of crying if she saw anyone, which would just make her feel worse. Shane

had almost suggested they spend an extra day—
or week, or month—in that hotel suite. It had
been that good of a day.

Mel had dived enthusiastically into the straw-
berry-covered waffles he'd had delivered to the
suite. After breakfast, she'd spent over an hour
on the phone, trying to make everyone else in her
life feel better.

Luis's was the first call that had come in, but
Shane hadn't heard much of that, since he'd been
busy talking to Tim. Then Mel's cousins had
started to call. Amanda and Nora from Gallant
Lake, and the pregnant one in North Carolina.
That last call had gone even longer than the others,
and Mel's face had been wet with tears afterward.

She had joined Shane on the sofa, curling up at
his side with her head on his shoulder and his arm
around her tight. He'd been worried about what
her cousin might have said to her, but Mel had
told him she'd actually spoken with her cousin's
husband. He was ex-military, a Ranger like Tim,
and he'd had some heavy-duty PTSD issues.
The kind of issues that had put him in rehab for
weeks, with ongoing counseling. He'd gotten on
the phone and talked to Mel at length about how
to work through the panic attacks, and had encouraged her to find someone she could reach
out to in emergencies.

She'd told Shane about what had triggered her

episode the day before. The Malcor woman and Nelson on the street. The words. The pressure. How she'd already been on edge from spending time with Tori. How Nelson had offered her goddamn cocaine right in front of the kid. It had taken all of Shane's strength not to lose it at that point, but he'd just listened and held her tight.

Deciding they needed a distraction that didn't include sex or him beating the crap out of her enemies, he'd turned on the television and they'd binge-watched episodes of *The Office* all afternoon. They'd laughed and talked about favorite shows and movies and music. With every passing hour, he could see the tension leaving her body, until she was up dancing to "Life is a Highway" along with the cast on the road trip episode. Mel had sung half the words wrong, and Shane had laughed until tears ran down his face. He hadn't laughed like that in years, and it had felt good. The whole day, despite its terrible start, had felt good.

And now he was driving up Rt. 87 toward Gallant Lake and back to reality.

Mel shifted in her seat and glanced his way, catching him staring at her.

"What?"

"Nothing." He looked back to the road. "I just… it sounds weird to say, but…it's been a good day."

"That's funny—I was just thinking the same thing."

He swung out into the passing lane to speed by a tractor trailer grinding its way up a long hill. They were well out of the city now, and the mountains ahead were glowing in the last light of day. Country living may not be his thing, but he had to admit it was beautiful.

But there was an elephant in the car that had to be dealt with.

"Yesterday was *not* a good day, though. How do we make sure that doesn't ever happen again?"

She stared out the side window and another ten miles went by before she answered.

"I'm an alcoholic. An addict. I went too long without going to meetings. I got wrapped up in helping Tori and taking care of Nessie and trying to figure out what I was doing with my life, and…it was stupid. The stress has been building, and I should have talked to someone."

"Don't you have a sponsor or something?"

"It doesn't always work like that, but yeah, I could find one if I tried. I went to rehab in Switzerland. It wasn't exactly a twelve-step program, and they were more into personal responsibility than leaning on a mentor." She looked at him. "I wasn't a…I wasn't an ugly drunk. I was a quiet, desperate drunk. I didn't drink to get drunk. I didn't take drugs to get high. I just needed something to dull the pain. To perk me up. To get me to sleep. To fit in with the cool crowd. I drank to survive." She looked down to where her fingers were twisting on her lap. "Or at least that's what I told myself. I called it my painkiller."

Shane thought about the girl in that photo he'd found online, wide-eyed and lost. His chest tightened.

"And the people you ran into yesterday caused you pain."

Her laugh was humorless. "Yeah, you could say that."

The urge to pound on someone nearly overwhelmed him. That's how Shane operated. Face the problem and beat the shit out of it. But there was a tender spot in his heart whispering that wasn't what Mel needed. Which left him frustrated. The car went silent for twenty miles or so as they both withdrew into their heads. He thought of the Waterford tumbler his father would fill with Irish whiskey every night.

"My father was an ugly drunk."

OF ALL THE things Mel was expecting Shane to say, that was so far down the list she hadn't even considered it. His father drank. That's why he didn't tolerate substance abuse in his clients. Because he'd seen it firsthand. And now he knew she was an alcoholic. She fought back the wave of panic—he must have hated what he saw the previous night. But he'd sat with her and held her and, even when she'd humiliated herself by throwing herself at him this morning, he'd *stayed*. He'd laughed with her and made sure she was okay. And, all the time, he was dealing with the memory of a father who was an ugly drunk.

His hands were clutching the wheel so hard his knuckles were white.

"I'm sorry." She rested her hand on his thigh. "Was he…abusive?"

Shane had to think about that for a moment. "Not in the way you're thinking. He was just an asshole, and the booze made him a bigger, louder asshole. He was never satisfied with anything or anyone. Especially me." He shrugged, but it was unconvincing. "It was no big deal. I'm just saying, I know what an ugly drunk looks like, and you're definitely not that."

"Your dad passed away, right?" He'd mentioned it, but she couldn't remember the details or if he'd shared any.

"Last year. Just as disappointed in me as always."

"I'm sure he wasn't really, Shane. I mean, you've built a business. You're very successful— you represent famous athletes and you do it well."

He shrugged again, almost as if he wanted to

shake off the memories. Shake off the conversation.

"Dad had different standards for success. A steady paycheck. A nine-to-five job. A respectable law firm. A title. A fancy office. Quiet clients who didn't get their names in the tabloids and drag my name with them." Shane glanced at her. "He thought I wasted the law degree he paid for. I offered to pay him back when I signed Marquis, but he refused. He didn't want 'that kind of money.' You see, dear old Dad was also a racist, privileged bastard. He thought my clients were losers, and repping them meant I was a loser, too."

Mel couldn't imagine how this man next to her, this man who was so honorable and so dedicated to helping his clients, had come from *that* man.

Shane kept talking, almost to himself. "James Patrick Brannigan made it crystal clear that my career choice wasn't worthy of the Brannigan name." He huffed out a short laugh. "That was pretty funny, considering his mother had been as shanty Irish as they come, working herself ragged in an Irish hotel out on the Cape to put Dad through law school. Once he made partner at a 'very respectable' law firm..." Shane shook his head. "He always said it like that, as if he had to constantly remind me that what he did was 'very respectable.' Meaning, of course, that what I did was not. Once he made partner, it was as if our entire family history was rewritten to match his newfound status."

"And your mom?"

Some of the tension faded from Shane's face. "Mom wasn't like that. She was publicly loyal to the man she'd married, because that's what proper Beacon Hill wives do, but she quietly worked behind his back to make sure I didn't turn out like him. She sent me to his mother's house on the Cape as often as possible."

"Wait. She sent you to your *dad's* mother's house? The nana with the lilacs was *his* mom?"

And now there was an actual grin on his face. "Nana was as different from her son as I was. Like I said, she'd worked her ass off to put him through college, and whatever happened to change him there…she couldn't bring him back. She blamed it on what she called the 'fancy-dancy bratty frat boys' he hung out with. Threatened to beat me with that wooden spoon of hers if I joined a fraternity. It wasn't easy, but I managed to get through school without being in one." He gave her a quick wink. "Drove my father absolutely bonkers when I spent more time tutoring college athletes than hanging out with the frat crowd."

"And that's how you got into being an agent." She remembered his story about signing a college buddy. How sad that his success had never been recognized by his own father before his death. "Shane, you and Tim care about your clients. You're doing something special, and you're good at it."

The corner of his mouth lifted. "That's not what you said when we first met. Or a week later. Or a week after that." He glanced at her. "Shall I go on?"

"I was talking about Tori specifically then, and let's face it, you had no idea what to do with a teenage phenom for a client. But it wasn't from lack of caring. It was just a lack of…ability."

"Ouch." He exited the highway and turned onto the road to Gallant Lake. The sun had set, and the sky was a glorious display of pink and orange and blue. "But yeah, that's true. I couldn't have figured it out without you." He reached over and took her hand. "For some crazy reason, you and I make a good team." They drove the rest of the way to her apartment in easy silence, hand in hand.

CHAPTER EIGHTEEN

SHANE CARRIED MEL'S suitcase up to the apartment, watching her hips move as she climbed the metal stairs ahead of him. She unlocked the back door and gestured for him to follow her in, turning on lights as she went.

"Where's that thing you call a dog?"

"It's quiet without her, isn't it? Of course, the way she sheds, she's always here in some form. She's staying with Nora's daughter, Becky. Do you want anything to drink?" She caught herself and gave a little laugh. "Non-alcoholic, of course."

There was a weird vibe in the air, and Shane couldn't put his finger on it. It had been a long, strange day of soul baring, and he felt more… exposed…than usual. He wasn't sure if that was a good thing or not. Staying here any longer with her was probably a bad idea.

"Sure. I'll have a ginger ale."

Mel smiled so brightly that he couldn't take back the words now. He sat at the kitchen island and watched with appreciation as she opened the refrigerator and bent low to pull two sodas from the bottom shelf. The woman had a really remarkable butt. She caught him staring when she turned.

"Taking in the view?"

"Just thinking about all that chemistry going to waste right now." His brain was no longer filtering his thoughts from becoming words. He was just blurting out stuff he had no intention of saying. And he couldn't stop. "Someday, we're going to set this place on fire with it." He finally reined himself in. "But not tonight. That would be wrong."

She walked around the island and handed him his soda with a smile that held some emotion he couldn't define.

"That *would* be wrong, wouldn't it?"

That sounded more like an invitation than an agreement. Or maybe he was just hearing what he wanted to hear. What *did* he want to hear? Those last twenty miles or so in the dark car, winding through the dark mountain roads, with her hand warm in his, had clearly done something to his resolve. They hadn't spoken a word, but he'd felt a rare sense of peace in that silence. As stupid as it sounded, he'd had a flash vision of the future, of the two of them driving that same road thirty years from now, holding hands and feeling content.

Large DANGER! signs started flashing in his brain. Her hand stroked his thigh.

"Mel…" Was it a warning or a plea? What the hell was happening?

"I'm not looking for a distraction, Shane. I'm looking for…chemistry. What if 'someday' turns out to be tonight?"

His hands rested lightly on her hips. It took all his strength not to draw her in closer. He had to think this through. He had to make the right choice here. For her. And for him.

"This is a bad idea. It's been a crazy day. This might not be the best time…"

She leaned in and brushed her lips against his, silencing his voice and his brain. His hands lifted and his fingers twisted in her long hair. He kissed her. Hard. Unrelenting. Like he was mining for gold. Like he'd found it. Her soft moan just propelled him onward. His hands moved to the hem of her shirt and slid beneath it. So soft. So smooth. So fragile. He pulled away from the kiss, but not from her. Because that would have been impossible.

"We need to talk first."

"Do we?" But she settled back on her heels, staying comfortably in his arms.

"There's no going back if this happens, Mel. I don't want to take advantage of you. I don't want you to regret this. *I* don't want to regret this. And it's going to change things. Even if it's just one night, it changes everything. We'll have to deal with the fallout. I need to know you're ready for that."

"Shane, I've *been* vulnerable. I've had men take advantage of me. I've had plenty of regrets." A shadow crossed her face. "I've made mistakes. Some I could blame on being drunk, but sometimes I was just stupid. A guy would tell me what I wanted to hear, and I'd believe it. I thought all those guys wanted *me*, but they only wanted Mellie Low."

Shane's throat grew thick with emotion. The last thing he wanted to talk about while his fingers traced slow circles on Mel's back was a long list of men she'd been with before tonight. And he *really* didn't want to know about the men who had hurt her at this particular moment. But that history was a part of who she was, and he had to understand it.

"I don't want Mellie Low. I want the strong woman standing in front of me right this minute. I want *you*." He leaned forward and kissed her softly. "I want *you*. If we do this tonight, we forget the past. We forget mistakes. We forget hurts. We only care about Mel and Shane, not the baggage we both carry. Is that a deal?"

She smiled slowly. "There's that Brannigan

ego again. You're setting the bar awfully high for yourself."

"Princess, I don't make promises I can't keep." He gave her one last chance to reconsider. "So are we doing this? Tonight? No regrets?"

Mel lowered her head and ran her tongue up the side of his neck, sending off an electric shock right to his groin. She pulled back and gave him a long, steady look.

"Tonight. No regrets."

Thank Christ.

He tugged her close for another kiss and quickly unhooked her bra. She laughed against his lips. "In a hurry?"

Yes, of course he was. But no. No, he shouldn't rush this. But he couldn't help wanting his hands on her skin. Everywhere. With one smooth move, he stood and lifted her onto the marble kitchen island. He pulled her top up and over her head, taking her bra with it. He paused, momentarily stunned at the beauty of her sitting there, waiting for him. For *him*. She was *his*. At least for tonight.

He dropped his head to her breast, sliding his tongue around it until she was squirming and clutching at his shoulders with her nails. When he took the rosy tip into his mouth, she fell back and he had to grab her to keep her where he wanted her. He lifted her long skirt and ran his hand up her leg, tracing his fingers across her ankle, her calf, her thigh. He moved to her other breast and pulled at it with his lips as he slid his fingers past her lace panties. She moved in rhythm with his slow, steady strokes, murmuring his name and other, unintelligible words. He was too busy enjoying the taste of her, the feel of her warm and trembling on his fingers, to care.

She shifted, and he removed the panties with one hard pull. They were both beyond caring now. He released her and she dropped back on the stone surface, her back arched in ecstasy. He stopped for a moment, trying to memorize every inch of her, just like this.

"So beautiful." He bent to kiss between her breasts, then traced kisses down her stomach as she gasped and twisted in his hands. His mouth fell on her at the same moment his fingers entered her, and she cried out and fell apart for him, right there on the kitchen island under the bright overhead lights. It took a few minutes before her eyes focused on him again. He kissed each breast and grinned at her.

"Still think my ego is larger than my ability?"

Her laugh was rich and genuine.

"That was a pretty awesome start."

"Start?" Shane scowled playfully.

She sat up and rubbed against the hardness of him as she answered.

"I think we're forgetting someone."

He dropped his head to her shoulder and nipped her. "If you keep doing that, it'll be all over before I even get my pants off."

"Then I guess we should get ourselves up to the bed. Because as fun as that was, I'm not spending the night on this cold slab of marble." He pulled her off the edge and set her on her feet, letting her skirt swirl free around her legs.

"Let's get up those stairs while I can still walk." His pants were straining as it was.

"You? My legs are gelatin." She pointed at the island, and bright spots of color appeared on her cheeks. "I can't believe I just had the best orgasm ever on my cousin's kitchen island." She looked at him, humor and satisfaction glowing in her eyes. "Don't you ever tell a soul we did that!"

Shane turned her shoulders and pointed her toward the stairs. "Wait until you see what I can do on that staircase, with you bent over in front of me, gripping that railing…"

Mel looked over her shoulder playfully. "Big talk again, Shane. But let's try the bed first." She dashed across the room topless and slapped a switch on the wall. A motor whirred softly and the blinds closed on the windows. He was both shocked and turned on that neither of them had thought to do that before he'd laid her out on the kitchen counter.

MELANIE HURRIED ACROSS the bedroom loft, unzipping her skirt as she ran. She jumped onto the bed and turned to watch Shane following her up the steps. His every move was slow and deliberate, weighted with the significance of this moment. She sat back and tried to slow her racing heart.

She'd just had sex with Shane Brannigan. In the *kitchen*. She'd never been the adventurous type when it came to sex. It was generally something she *did*, not necessarily *enjoyed*. She was a missionary girl all the way, and she resisted any suggestions to try anything else. She'd often felt used as it was and usually just wanted it over with as quickly as possible. But it wasn't like that with Shane. He was at the top of the stairs now, shedding his shirt and smiling in a way that turned her lower regions into hot, clenching desire. Whatever he wanted, he could have. At least for tonight.

He dropped his pants at the side of the bed, but not before reaching into his wallet for several silver foil packets.

"Feeling confident, are we?"

He laughed, tossing a trio of condoms on the nightstand as he joined her on the bed. "Feeling hopeful, at least."

He cupped her face with his hands and kissed her lazily, taking his time and exploring her mouth before sliding his lips down her neck to nibble lightly at her throat.

"I've had dreams about kissing this neck." He traced kisses up to her chin and back down again, tickling and teasing and tasting her. He started exploring her with his mouth, sending trails of fire everywhere he went. She was twisting and turning in his arms, so full of need and lust and frustration that she thought she'd burst. He was hard and heavy against her, and she started to move her hand up and down his length.

"Shit. Stop. Wait." The words came out in pants of breath. He rolled on a condom and lifted her hips, entering her with one long, slow glide of pure pleasure. Then he stopped, looking down at her with dark, troubled eyes.

"What's wrong?" What could possibly be wrong when she felt so damned good?

"Nothing." He sounded confused. Maybe surprised. "It's just… You're just…perfect." He kissed her and started moving, slow at first, and then more demanding. She went with him, rising in rhythm with his motions, until she fell over the edge and stars burst beneath her tightly closed eyes. She didn't fight the wave of blissful exhaustion that washed over her, clutching tightly to Shane as he groaned out her name through clenched teeth, shuddering with his own release.

His head dropped next to hers, his solid body

weighing her down, but she didn't care. She wanted to feel every inch of him against her. She never wanted him to leave. Her eyes snapped open. Shane's deep breathing told her he was sleeping, or temporarily rendered unconscious. So she had time to freak out in the darkness alone.

They both knew they had "chemistry," whatever that was. They'd known it from that first kiss in the woods. Or maybe even from their first meeting. They'd certainly felt it downstairs in that wild, uninhibited dance on the kitchen island. But she suspected neither of them had expected *this*.

Once they'd gotten to the bed—once they were both fully naked—there'd been a dramatic shift between them. It wasn't lust, although there was plenty of that, too. No, this was different. It wasn't just chemistry. It was a *connection*. Their bodies, their fingers, their lips, their words, their heartbeats—everything connected in a way she'd never felt before. Shane felt it, too. And he was right.

They were perfect.

CHAPTER NINETEEN

SHANE WOKE UP wrapped in the sweet scent of Melanie mixed with the musky scent of sex. Best smell ever. He reached out, but the bed was empty. Fully awake now, he sat up and looked around, trying to understand what was happening. Had last night been real? Apparently so, because he was naked in Mel's bed. And the night wasn't over yet, because it was still pitch dark outside. A light glowed downstairs. He washed up, pulled on his pants and went down the stairs.

Mel was curled up at the end of the flowered sofa, wearing a long, white robe and cradling a large mug of something in her hands. She didn't look up at him until he sat in the chair next to her.

"What's going on, princess?" A little smile danced across her lips at the nickname.

"I just needed a little time. And space. And cocoa."

"Do you want me to leave you alone? Do we need to talk? Tell me what's happening, Mel."

She swallowed hard, then met his gaze. "I was hoping you could tell *me* that. Because I don't

know what to think about…what happened tonight. What now?"

"Do you always spend this much time analyzing your kisses and your…adventures?"

"Is that what tonight was? An adventure?"

"No. Tonight was…" Tonight was life-altering,
but he didn't want to freak her out, especially
when he didn't understand the feeling himself
yet. "Tonight was amazing. But come on, we both
knew it would be. We're great together."

"Shane, I've made so many mistakes. I don't
want you and me to be another one."

He frowned, not liking where this was going.
"Do you think tonight was a mistake?"

"No! But that's the point. How would I know?
I have no idea how to navigate the feelings I'm
having right now."

He moved closer, taking the empty mug from
her hands and setting it aside. "Okay, let's talk
this out. You and I have had something going on
since the minute we met. Sometimes it felt like
hate, and sometimes it felt like something completely different. But it was always there. Why
is it freaking you out *now*? Why are you so worried about it being a mistake?"

"Because mistakes are my specialty, Shane.
You have no idea…"

"So help me understand."

"You want me to write you a list?"

She tried to move away from him, but he tugged her into his side. "A list of your former lovers? No, thanks."

"That's just it. I didn't *do* 'lovers.' Men always assumed they had the right to put their hands on me. At parties. In the photo studio. After a while, it didn't mean anything. There were always plenty of men ready to have sex with me, whether I wanted it or not, but lovers? The whole boyfriend-girlfriend thing? No."

"Wait. Let's rewind. What do you mean by 'whether I wanted it or not'? Were you forced into...?" A chill settled on him. He'd been worried about taking advantage of a woman dealing with addiction, but was she also a victim of sexual assault? Maybe she was right. Maybe tonight had been a mistake. Maybe he'd pushed her too hard.

"Was I forcibly raped? No. Probably not."

"What the hell does 'probably not' mean?" He didn't want her to think he was angry with her, but his voice was shaking.

She stared down at her hands twisting in her lap.

"There are nights I just don't remember, Shane. One night I was pressured to go to a party in Monaco. They paid us to do that, you know. Fashion models make a nice backdrop. There was a very famous rock star there, and he was pretty handsy all night, or at least as much of the night as I can remember." She looked up at him through those long eyelashes, her eyes dark and troubled. "I woke up alone the next morning, naked in a hotel suite I didn't recognize. I had no idea how I got there or what had happened. Luis was in town for the same photo shoot, and I called him, hysterical. He took me straight from the hotel to rehab." She gave a short laugh. "He told me afterward he didn't want to give me a chance to change my mind about getting sober."

Shane pulled her onto his lap and held tight, the same way he had the night before in the hotel. She rested her head on his shoulder. "So when I say I've made mistakes…"

They were both silent for several minutes.

"Mel, I meant what I said earlier. Tonight is a night of no regrets. No baggage. Just you and me." He kissed her forehead. "I don't assume I have the right to do anything with you. I hope you don't…"

She placed her fingers on his lips. "Tonight was *nothing* like any of what happened to me before. That's what's so confusing. I don't know how to process what I'm feeling right now."

He let out a silent sigh of relief. "So maybe you need to stop trying to process it. Maybe you just need to sit back and enjoy it."

She looked up with a hint of her sassy grin.

His princess was back. "Sit back and enjoy, huh? What are *you* planning to do while I'm just sitting back?"

He tipped her chin up with his fingers and kissed her gently, then with more intensity. They both knew what he was doing. He was keeping her from analyzing their great sex by initiating more great sex. And they were both good with that for tonight. She fell back against the pillows, her robe coming undone. Shane was coming undone, too. Mel was undoing him one kiss at a time.

They made slow, sweet love right there on the sofa. At this rate, they'd have every room in the small apartment covered by morning. She cried out his name when she came, then curled up against his chest and fell asleep. He lay there and held her, watching the sky through the gaps in the blinds go from black to orange to yellow to soft blue. They had to talk before reality came crashing through her door in the form of her family and her dog and all the people who cared about her.

He nuzzled her ear and whispered her name until her eyes swept open, nearly stopping his heart. This woman. He kissed her lips softly. This incredible woman. He brushed his lips across her temple as she stretched and sighed in his arms, coming awake. Would he ever be able to walk away from her?

"Good morning." Her voice was raw with emotion. Was it possible she was feeling it, too?

"Mornin' sunshine." He sat up and she followed, pulling her robe around herself.

She stared at him until he wanted to squirm. "We never did answer last night's question. What now?"

"Now? We make coffee and get dressed. And after that?" *Yeah, genius, what comes after that?* "After that, you and I are going to take this a day at a time, with no strings and no rules. How's that?"

One lovely eyebrow rose high. "No *rules*? Trust me, if we're doing this, there's going to be at least one rule—there's no one else as long as we're…"

As if he'd ever share this woman. As if he'd ever want anyone else after having her.

"That's a given. Okay, maybe not a given. Let's agree that it's a rule—no sharing. You said you didn't want a relationship, and I don't, either. But whatever this is stays monogamous." It felt wrong to say he didn't want a relationship, but he ignored the sensation. "My time in Gallant Lake is very limited, and who knows where you'll land. So we'll be friends with…aw, shit, I hate that phrase."

Mel smiled. "Benefits? I always thought that sounded like an insurance deal." She stood. "Look, we're both adults. Let's call it what it is. A temporary…relationship, for lack of a better word. We know each other pretty well now. We trust each other. We definitely have that chemistry thing going on. So let's enjoy it while it lasts. One day at a time. Kind of like that other relationship I have." She noticed his confusion. "One day at a time? Twelve steps?"

A troubling thought occurred to him. "Is this… relationship…going to stress you? Is it unhealthy? I don't want to do anything that will…"

Her hand squeezed his arm tightly. "What was it you said last month? You wanted to 'set expectations'? Well, we've set our expectations. And yes, you set the bar very, very high, Mr. Brannigan, and achieved it." His chest swelled accordingly. There was something primal in knowing he'd satisfied her. "Once Tori goes back on tour, you'll move on and I'll be here and we'll both have to deal with it. But we know it going in, so it's okay. Right?"

"You're really serious about staying in Gallant Lake?" Wouldn't it be great if he could convince her to come to Boston with him? "What are you going to do here?"

"I'm thinking of opening that little dress shop I said someone should open. Maybe buy a house.

This feels like a safe place for me right now." She looked down at his nakedness. "Although I never thought I'd have a naked man in my living room. Go get dressed before someone comes knocking."

"It would be a shame to waste all this nakedness, Mel. There's still one condom left."

Her eyes darkened.

"We don't have a lot of time."

He folded her into his arms.

"I can work with that."

"So, LET ME get this straight." Amanda was perched on the very same kitchen island where Shane had destroyed Mel two weeks earlier. It was very distracting. "You guys have been together all this time and you didn't tell any of us?"

Nora looked around the apartment. "Ew. You guys are having sex in my apartment?"

Mel wondered what Nora would say if she told her what had happened on the stairs to the loft last night? A smile tugged at her lips.

"Oh, boy. I know that smile." Amanda pointed at her and laughed. "That's an I'm-getting-great-sex smile, and it's *recent*. Was he here last night?"

She turned away to hide her wide grin. "We have good chemistry. It makes for some fun times."

Nora refilled their glasses with sparkling water. Mel and Shane hadn't been working all that hard to hide their relationship, but they hadn't advertised it, either. She didn't want people worrying about her, and he didn't think it was anyone's business.

He didn't understand that in a small town, *everything* is everyone else's business. When Asher had walked out his shop's back door two nights ago to toss some trash into the container in the parking lot, he'd caught Shane and Mel on the hood of Shane's Lincoln. They'd been fully clothed, of course, but their position had left little to the imagination.

Asher had just laughed and told them to "get a room." But, of course, he'd told Nora about it when he got home, and Nora told…everyone. So here she was, being grilled by her cousins. Shane had received a formal invitation to the town poker game—which Nora's fiancé and Amanda's husband were also attending—so she imagined he was being grilled, too.

Amanda squinted at her. "So how strong is this 'chemistry' you speak of?"

Nora was always the more practical one. "What is that 'chemistry' going to lead to? How serious are you guys?" she asked.

Mel stared into her glass for a minute.

"I don't know. I mean, we've become…friends, I guess. And the sex is…well, it's incredible. And constant." Her cheeks went warm. "And did I mention incredible?" She took a sip. "But as far as 'serious' goes, I'm not sure. Tori left for the tour a week ago, and he's still showing up. But he's been talking to some big talent agency in LA, so who knows?"

"Why is he talking to another agency? Aren't he and Tim doing well enough on their own?"

Mel frowned. That was the real question. Shane and Tim had been arguing about Shane's plans for days. He wanted some big agency to buy them out, but Tim wasn't interested. He liked their business just the way it was. Shane kept saying they'd always planned on doing this, but Tim said that was *Shane's* plan, not his. And Tim swore Shane had never mentioned it before his father's death. It hurt her heart to see the two friends at odds.

Luis, of course, was staunchly in Tim's corner. The men were dating and playing it casual, but Mel suspected there were deeper feelings growing there. Naturally, Luis didn't want Tim moving to LA any more than Mel wanted Shane to go.

"Shane has his goals all tangled up with his father's expectations, and it's really complicated."

Nora pushed a plate of ginger cookies her way. "Define complicated. Because, you know, I've *done* complicated in relationships. In fact, I've done complicated in this very apartment...and the one next door."

Amanda laughed. "Maybe it's the apartment! Maybe this place is really a little love shack, and people who live here find their true love."

"You and your romantic ghost stories." Nora waved her off. "But seriously, Mel, what's up with Shane and his dad?"

She told them about the man who had never once told Shane he'd done a good job at anything. Who'd told him he was a loser for representing athletes who didn't come from addresses like Beacon Hill. Shane resented his father, but Mel had come to realize he was still trying to live up to the man's idea of success. Shane kept talking about a corner office and less challenging clients, but he thrived on problem solving and he wasn't the kind of guy to like being chained to a desk. He and Tim had a flourishing business, and she didn't understand why he'd think about giving it up for corporate trappings that didn't fit him.

"Have you tried to talk him out of it?" Nora emptied a bottle of sparkling water into Mel's glass.

"We don't spend a lot of time talking business."

Amanda snorted. "I'll bet."

"No, I don't mean it like that. We just don't see eye to eye on each other's business plans. He thinks I'm crazy to consider opening a dress shop here. I think he's crazy to give up his life's work and sell out to some corporation." She shrugged.

"So we've agreed to stay out of each other's career decisions."

Nora frowned. "That sounds like a pretty heavy limitation to put on a relationship. If you don't talk about your careers and your life goals, what do you…?"

At Amanda's naughty giggle, Nora just rolled her eyes. "Oh, yeah, well, there is *that*."

Mel laughed along with them, but she agreed with Nora. She and Shane *said* they were keeping things light and fun and sizzling, but she knew they were dancing around the subjects that could impact their lives and their relationship.

She had a feeling that dance might trip them up eventually.

CHAPTER TWENTY

MEL ROLLED OVER and squinted at the bright sunshine flooding into the loft. Damn, she really should have closed those shades last night. But she'd been too busy trying to pull Shane's pants down around his ankles as he'd struggled to beat her in a race to the bed. Laughing and cursing at the same time, he'd stumbled to his knees and watched as she'd run past him to the loft. He could have snagged her leg, of course, but he'd told her later…much later…that he hadn't wanted her to scrape her knees on the metal steps.

Then he'd pointed to his knees, bloodied by the impact when she'd tripped him up. That had led to her kissing his wounded knees, then kissing her way up his thighs until she'd found a way to take his mind off his injuries. And it had worked very well. She smiled to herself. Yes, very well indeed.

"You look pleased with yourself this morning."

Shane walked out of the bathroom, wearing nothing but a towel wrapped low on his hips, his hair wet and tangled. He hadn't shaved, and the copper stubble just made him look sexier.

"Well, I think I have good reason. You don't have any complaints from last night, do you?"

He grabbed her arms and shook his head, spraying water all over her, laughing as she squealed and tried to get away from him. Finally, he pushed her back onto the bed and crawled over her with a wide smile. "Yes, princess, you definitely should be proud of yourself. That was quite a masterful achievement." He kissed her hard and hot. "But you know what they say— practice makes perfect."

Before he could continue with that thought, Nessie landed on the mattress beside them, clearly ready to go outside and get her day started.

"Damn that dog!" Shane dropped his forehead to Mel's shoulder. "Do you know she ate one of my Ferragamos yesterday? Actually ate it. She's like a goat that barks."

Nessie nuzzled her head against his, whining loudly. Mel laughed and reached up to push her away. The dog had reluctantly welcomed Shane into their lives over the past few weeks. Some days he was her favorite human, and some days she ate his shoes. Only his shoes. Never Mel's. And only one shoe from a pair. Never both.

"See? She's apologizing! And you know better than to leave your shoes where she can get at them."

"Yeah, I'll try to remember that the next time you start tearing my clothes off in the kitchen. From now on, I'll have sex with my shoes on."

Mel pushed on his shoulder. "That would be a sight to see. Let me up and I'll take her out."

"No, I'll take her." He sat up and grabbed his pants from the floor. "You can start the coffee." He looked at her sprawled across the mattress, naked. "Damn, woman, you are a sight for sore eyes. Forget the coffee. Just stay right there while I walk all the way down two flights of stairs to let your damn dog do her business and back up again, and if I still have the strength, we'll pick up where we were before she interrupted us." He whistled through his teeth at Nessie and pointed to the steps. She galloped down, clearly in a hurry to go.

Shane shook his head. "That is not an apartment dog. You know that, right?" He kissed her forehead.

"I've been thinking about getting a house." His eyes went wide.

"Here? Why?"

Nessie barked downstairs. Mel nodded toward the sound. "She's one reason. And if you don't get downstairs, you're going to be cleaning up after her, so *go*."

Mel went into the shower after she heard the door close. Shane had told her to stay in bed, but even after three weeks of spending nearly every night together, she wasn't much for following orders. Her elbow bumped against the back of the marble shower stall. Amanda had redecorated the loft for Nora last winter, and it was lovely. But Amanda and Nora were petite, and Mel wasn't. She needed more space, not just for her long limbs, but for her peace of mind. She'd walked around a house on the water yesterday that Asher had remodeled, and she couldn't stop thinking about it.

From the road, it was a charming bungalow with weathered cedar shingles and bright blue shutters. There were two big rocking chairs on the covered front porch. But the back of the house featured a contemporary wall of glass facing the lake. Two decks ran the length of the house, divided by a large screened porch. Looking through the windows, she could see the open floor plan with a modern kitchen and a fieldstone fireplace.

She'd turned away and walked to the water's edge. Off in the distance, she could see the resort and, beyond that, the round towers of Halcyon, Blake and Amanda's home. She could imagine herself sitting on the deck with Shane, watching the sun rise over Gallant Mountain. And if she started that dress shop…

The shower door swung open, startling her out of her daydreams. Shane stood there with no shirt and low-riding jeans, eyes hooded and full of desire. "I thought I told you to stay in bed."

She grinned. "And I thought I told you I don't work for you."

"Such a defiant woman. Are you done in there?"

"Yeah."

"Good." He tugged her out of the shower and up against him, kissing her senseless. "Mmm... you're all squeaky clean now. You wanna go back to bed or grab some breakfast? Or maybe we'll do both." He winked at her. "Maybe you'll be breakfast."

Mel snuggled against him, skin to skin, and it felt as natural as daylight. He hesitated, then pulled her close, wrapping his arms tight around her. He knew she just needed to be held sometimes, to feel safe. To feel wanted. To feel grounded. His voice gentled. "Hey, princess."

They stood there in the bathroom, her naked and wet, Shane nearly naked and now damp. She could feel his heart beating slow and sure. And she knew. She was falling in love with Shane Brannigan.

Someone knocked on the door downstairs, and Nessie started barking wildly.

Shane nuzzled her hair with his nose.

"Tim? Luis? Nora? Amanda?"

Before she could guess, they heard the door open. She looked at Shane in mock horror and hissed at him. "Oh, my God, I'm naked! Go see who it is!" He sneaked one more kiss before he grinned and turned away, snagging his T-shirt off the foot of the bed and pulling it over his head as he went down the stairs. Mel was tugging on a pair of jeans and hopping on one foot when she heard Shane's shocked voice.

"Mom?"

Mel almost hit the floor, jeans in a knot around her calves, but she was able to grab the corner of the dresser and save herself. *Whose* mom? *His* mom?

SHANE STOOD AT the bottom of the stairs, trying to understand what he was seeing. He blinked a few times, but she was still there. His mother, fending off Nessie's leaping greeting. In Mel's apartment. In Gallant Lake.

"I… What… Mom…what the hell are you doing here?"

"That's a fine way to greet your mother, Shane. Really nice." Eleanor Brannigan struggled to keep Nessie from jumping on her. Shane finally snapped out of his stupor and walked over to grab the dog's collar. Nessie immediately sat and lifted one paw. She'd cornered the market on being adorably sorry after she did something wrong.

"Mom, how did you…?"

"Find you?" She brushed yellow dog hair from her tailored trousers. "I'm more resourceful than you might think, darling. After waiting weeks for you to show up, I decided to come looking. Timothy was a hard nut to crack, but he finally caved and gave me the name of this town. I drove here last night and stayed at that lovely resort on the lake. The lady at the desk said you gave up your suite there after your client went back to golfing, but she thought I might find you in town." His mom walked to windows overlooking Main Street and the lake. "So I drove to town this morning and the nice man in front of the hardware store told me you lived here above the coffee shop. He even gave me his spare key."

Shane closed his eyes. Freakin' Nate, getting even with Shane for beating his ass at poker last night by sending his mom up here. And freakin' small towns, where everybody had spare keys to everyone else's place. Who *did* that?

"Oh! Hello! I didn't know you had company, dear."

Shane's eyes snapped open. Mel was halfway down the stairs. Her hair, still wet from the shower, fell in damp strands down the front of her pink knit top. Her eyes were fixed on his mother.

He was in a room with two proud, strong-willed women. This could take a bad turn at any moment.

"Actually, *I* have company, Mrs. Brannigan. This is my apartment, and Shane is my…guest." Mel walked down the stairs, sending him a wide-eyed "what the hell" look as she passed him. "I'm Melanie Lowery. It's wonderful to meet you." She was in warrior princess mode, shoulders back and head high. She wasn't going to be intimidated by his mom. *Go, Mel.* "Would you like some coffee?"

His mom seemed to be in a state of shock, watching Mel walk into the kitchen, talking away as if she'd been expecting her for tea.

"I'm sorry about the dog. She gets excited when we…" She glanced at Shane. "When *I* have company." She started the coffee maker and opened the fridge, pulling out a plate of her favorite ginger cookies. Nora had delivered them last night after the shop closed. Shane knew this was a major sacrifice on Mel's part—they were her favorites. He'd teased her about preferring ginger cookies and ginger men.

Mom sat at the kitchen island and sampled one, then smiled. "Delicious! You have a lovely place here, Melanie. I can see why Shane finds it hard to get away long enough to visit his mother." Both women turned to stare at him. Oh, shit.

He stepped away from the stairs and cleared his throat. "Mom, I've been calling every week like I promised. You know I've been busy…"

She looked at Melanie and arched her brow. "Oh, yes, very busy."

"Mom, I was in Dallas last week. I'm not…"

"Shane, don't argue with your mother." Mel flashed him a quick smile. "Why don't you set the table and I'll make us all some breakfast. Unless you had something else in mind?"

Yeah. He definitely had something else in mind, and she knew it. He had Mel naked in bed in mind. He had that amazing blow job she'd given him last night in mind. He'd been planning on returning the favor this morning, but that wasn't going to happen now.

Not with his mom sitting in the kitchen.

CHAPTER TWENTY-ONE

"So you were naked, and his *mom* walked in?"

Mel shushed Amanda, looking over her shoulder to make sure Shane hadn't heard. They were
at Nora and Asher's mountain house for a Saturday night cookout. Shane was on the patio with
Asher and Blake, watching the grill, as men do.
Nora opened the refrigerator to pull out the salad.

"His mom didn't walk in and *see* us naked.
We just happened to *be* naked upstairs when she
walked in. Well, I was naked. Shane had his pants
on."

Nora set the bowl on the counter. "What happened?"

"It was okay, actually. It took an hour or so
for the weirdness to wear off, but once she and
Shane got their apologies sorted out, we had a
nice time. We took her to Hunter Mountain and
rode the ski lift to the top to take in the views.
Shane said she'd never get on the lift, but she did.
She had fun, too! We took some pictures and had
lunch at a German place the next town over. It

wasn't Beacon Hill, but she wasn't at all snobbish about it."

Mel had finally gotten Shane to stop apologizing to his mom for the small towns and small res-
taurants and small whatevers. Once he'd gotten
over that, she was pretty sure he'd had fun, too.
He'd even agreed to walk the little nature trail behind the restaurant, and Mel had taken a picture
of him and his mom on the sleek new wooden
bridge that crossed the stream back there. In the
photos, Shane looked relaxed and happy, his arm
around his mother's shoulders and a big smile on
his face as he pointed out the deer coming down
to the water for a drink.

For all his complaining about the Catskills,
Shane was making friends here. He even said he
was looking forward to skiing at Hunter Mountain, and he'd never once compared it to Vail,
where she knew he'd skied last winter.

Amanda got up to refill their glasses. "How
long did his mom stay?"

"She headed home Monday. But I think she'll
be back. She loved the resort. And the town. And
I think she liked me, too. She pulled me aside
and said she thought Shane was happier than he'd
been in a long time." Mel winked at her cousins.
"I didn't tell her it was probably all the sex!"

Nora didn't laugh along. "It's more than that,

I think. You two are really good together. Have you talked anymore about the long term?"

Mel shrugged. "We're still taking it one day at a time, just like we promised each other."

"Are you sure that's what you want?" Nora picked up a stack of dishes to take to the table.

Of course not.

"I think it's good for both of us to keep it light. We're both being realistic, and that works for us."

Nora didn't look convinced, but Amanda, thankfully, redirected the conversation. "How's our girl Tori doing?"

Mel filled them in on Tori's strong showings at her first tournaments and how she texted Mel every day with some little tidbit of news or gossip or just a random thought she'd had. Her aunt was traveling with her as a chaperone these days. Shane had insisted her family had to find a female companion they could all trust, and the aunt was happy to take the job.

Hours later, after a dinner filled with laughter and stories, Shane and Mel headed down the dark mountain road to her apartment. He was grumbling to himself behind the wheel, and she finally asked him what his problem was.

"Are you kidding? Look at these roads! Actually, don't bother looking, because you won't see anything. Why don't they put some streetlights up out here?"

Mel started to laugh, then realized he was serious.

"Shane, it's a *mountain* road. Streetlights would make it look…"

"Civilized?"

She sighed loudly. "That's not the word I was thinking of. More like…commercial. Or suburban. People move out here to get away from all that."

"Away from what? Safety?" He slowed to go around a tight curve, with the side of the road dropping sharply toward rocks and the lake she knew was below, even if she couldn't see it in the dark. "Do you really want to live like this, Mel?"

"We're two hours from Manhattan, Shane, not in the outback. And no, I don't want to live up on the mountain." She looked out the window as the shadows of trees passed by. "This is a little too 'pioneer' for me."

Nora loved it, of course. Or at least, Nora loved Asher, and he loved it, and that was enough. Mel felt a tug on her heart. Nora had given up the comforts of suburban Atlanta to move to Gallant Lake, and she had given up her apartment in the village to move up on the mountain with the man she loved. That's what happened when people fell in love. What was she willing to give up for Shane? And him? What, if anything, would Mr. No Rules ever give up for her?

"But you're still talking about house hunting. I don't get it. How can you go from Miami to this?" He spat out a few curse words when a raccoon walked into the road in front of them, making him slam on the brakes to wait for it to cross. "You're bigger than this place, Mel."

"What?"

"Come on, you have to know it. Don't get me wrong—" he navigated around the slow-moving raccoon and continued down the mountain road "—this is a nice place, and the people are great. Really great. But the sidewalks roll up at six o'clock. There's nothing to do. Nowhere to go."

She reached over and tapped his thigh with her fingers. "We always find something to do." She could see his grin in the glow from the dashboard lights. "I like it here. I especially like it here with you." Maybe this was the wrong time to bring this up, but she had to try. "You told your mom you could run your business from anywhere. So why not from Gallant Lake?"

Shane laughed a little too loud and a little too long. As he turned onto the main road into town, he said, "Seriously? Come on, Mel, in a few months you'll be bored here. You and I are the same. We need the bright lights of the big city."

Mel shuddered. "The big city isn't my friend

anymore. Been there. Done that. Got the scars
to show for it."

His voice gentled. "I didn't mean it like that.
But we could find a house anywhere. You could
open a boutique anywhere." He pulled into the
parking lot behind the apartment, turning to her
after he killed the engine. "I want us to have a
future. I don't know what the future looks like
yet, but I want us to have it together, princess."

Her heart jumped. "A future?" Was it possible
he'd fallen in love the same way she had?

"Sure. The big house, the fancy cars, the corner office—the whole deal. Together."

Her heart fell with a thud. "Shane, those are
your dreams, not mine. In fact, they're not even
yours. They're your father's."

He stiffened. "Now you sound like Tim. It's
always been my goal to build the company and
sell it or merge it. And now we have a shot. This
could be everything we've been waiting for."

"We?"

Shane got out and came around to open her
door, ever the gentleman.

"Yes, *we*. This was the plan. This is my shot."

She grabbed his arm. "You see what you did
there? You just went from 'we' to 'my.'"

He drew her in for a kiss, scattering her
thoughts for a moment. "Semantics, baby. Don't
worry about that. Let's just chase that dream,

okay?" He kissed her again. They'd made a deal
not to interfere with each other's business decisions, so she melted in his arms and ignored the
warning bells ringing in the back of her mind.

SHANE LEANED BACK in his office chair and stared
at his best friend in disbelief. "Tim, do you really
want to split the business like this?"

"It sure as hell isn't what I want, but I also
don't want to work for some bureaucratic law
firm where we can't make our own decisions."

"Look around, man. We could have so much
more than a three-room office suite in a Boston
suburb. We don't have to keep babysitting our
misbehaving clients." He leaned forward, ignoring the stubborn set to Tim's chin. "We could be
respected."

"You don't think we have *respect*?" Tim waved
his hand in dismissal. "You've been blind to reality ever since you got this idea in your head.
If you want a fancy office, get one here. We can
afford it. We already have success, dude—more
than we ever dreamed of." Tim pushed away from
the small conference table and started pacing.
"You're starting to think of our clients the way
your dad used to. And you're just as wrong now
as he was then."

Shane bristled. "This has nothing to do with

my father." He'd had this same argument with Mel just a few days ago.

"Bullshit. This has *everything* to do with your dad. Ever since he died, you've been less and less satisfied here. You built this company from the ground up, and you never used to think our clients were a problem until your father died. Now it's like you're trying to become him, and I'm really ready for you to stop."

Shane jumped to his feet, directly into Tim's path. "Did you just say I'm becoming my father? Are you out of your mind? Damn it, Tim, I'm just trying to take us to the next level…"

"The next level of *what*? And once we get there, what comes after that?"

Tim didn't back down. Shane had a size advantage, but Tim could take him down without breaking a sweat, and they both knew it. Businesswise, Shane could force the closure of The Brannigan Agency, and they both knew that, too. They stood there glaring at each other.

Shane finally turned away, slapping his hand hard against the wall. He ran his fingers through his hair and spit out a string of curse words. He simply couldn't ignore the engine inside him that kept pushing for more. He turned to the friend he'd known since they were nine years old.

"Okay. If I can make this work with Bolton, I'll set up an agreement that allows *this* agency to stay in place. You can buy me out. We'll let our clients decide where they want to be." This felt so wrong, but what choice did Shane have?

"So you've taken care of me all nice and tidy. What about Melanie?"

His chest tightened. "She has nothing to do with this. You don't make your business decisions based on Luis, do you?"

"Actually, I'm thinking about it. It would be tough for Luis to leave the fashion district, but I can work from anywhere. So can you."

"Mel isn't as tied to a specific place as Luis is."

Tim shook his head sadly. "Are you sure about that? She seems pretty tied to Gallant Lake. Luis said she's been house hunting. Have you discussed this with her at all?"

"We've agreed to stay out of each other's business decisions."

"Even when they involve moving across the country? Do you think that's smart?"

"It's working for us." Shane knew he didn't sound very convincing. *Was* it working for them? He was falling for Melanie Lowery. He was falling fast and hard, and he had a feeling she felt the same way. If they really loved each other, they'd be able to sort things out.

That was how love worked, right?

CHAPTER TWENTY-TWO

SHANE SLID THE phone into his jacket pocket and got out of his car. After their recent meeting in New York, Calvin Bolton had just called with the offer he'd been working for his whole life. A surge of energy pulsed through his veins. This was it. He'd done it. He'd made it to the big leagues. He was moving to LA. He'd be representing the very best athletes in the world. Maybe even a movie star or two. He was going to have that corner office that was always so important to his father.

He stopped at the bottom of the stairs behind the coffee shop. That corner office was important to *him*. This wasn't about his father. This couldn't be about his father. This was *his* victory. This was everything he'd worked for.

Tim was still angry, but that really wasn't fair—this had always been the plan. Build a stable of athletes and go to a big-time agency. Except now, Tim wasn't interested. And neither were some of their clients. In fact, most of their clients were staying with Tim. But Calvin Bolton didn't care. He wanted Shane Brannigan at Bolton & Bolton. He'd finally made it.

The only missing piece right now was Mel. He jogged up the stairs with a smile. He hadn't seen his girl in a week, and he couldn't wait to hold her again. All he had to do was convince her to move to LA with him and things would be perfect. Her apartment door opened before he knocked. She rushed out and threw her arms around his neck while the yellow dog ran laps around the two of them, barking.

"I thought those were your footsteps I heard! I'm *so* glad you got back today—I have the *best* news!"

Shane swung her around in a circle before setting her down and kissing her.

"That's great, princess, because I have some awesome news of my own! I…"

"Me first! Come on, I can't wait to show you. Nessie, you go back inside, sweetie." Bemused, he let her lead him back down the stairs and past Carl's liquor store, then through the narrow alley that led to Main Street. His normally cool and composed lover was practically bouncing with excitement, and he couldn't imagine what her big news was. Had she bought a new car? Had she managed to get someone to paint that tired old gazebo by the water she kept fretting about? Maybe she'd done something for him? But what could she do for him in this little 'burb? Open a cigar bar?

She stopped in front of the empty old general store she was always saying "someone" should do something with. Maybe "someone" had finally bought the place, and she thought he'd care. He didn't, except for the fact that it made his girl this happy. Maybe the new owners would make it into a cigar bar. *Snap out of it, Brannigan.* His thoughts were all over the place after that call from Calvin, and he needed to focus on Mel's joy right now. She was unlocking the front door to the building.

Wait.

She was unlocking the front door to the building.

"Mel, what…"

She ran inside and spun around in the center of the store, sending dust bunnies scurrying across the floor. She stopped, facing him, her arms open wide.

"I bought the five-and-dime!"

He heard them, but the six simple words just echoed in his head and refused to compute.

"You *what*?"

"I bought the store!" Mel laughed, her violet eyes shining with joy and confidence. The beauty of her left him momentarily speechless. She, however, did not have a problem speaking.

In fact, the words poured out of her as she paced around the dirty old dump. "I'm going to open a boutique in Gallant Lake like nothing anyone's ever seen. I'll call it Five & Design. Get it? Like five-and-dime, but with *design* for the fashion part?"

Her hands moved all around, accenting the words and setting off alarms in Shane's head that he tried to ignore. "Asher said the building is structurally sound. He's going to do the renovations, and Amanda will help me decorate, and Luis is helping with merchandising. We'll rebuild that beautiful staircase and put a fancy design studio upstairs, then I'll put my office on the third floor, which has this amazing arched window overlooking the lake." She wrapped her arms around herself and squeezed tight. "Oh, Shane, isn't it amazing?"

Amazing wasn't exactly the word Shane had in mind. What the hell had she done? And why? Why *here*? Why *now*? Okay, he needed to focus. He also needed to close his mouth, which had dropped open at those first six words and hadn't closed since. He swallowed hard. Okay, every problem had a solution. This wasn't a deal-breaker, just a bump in the road. He forced a smile onto his face. Mel was happy, and he had to be happy for her. He *was* happy for her. And they could work with this. Of course they could.

"Wow, princess. You really did it." He pulled her into his arms and kissed her. She pressed tight against him and for a moment the only thing he could think about was how great they were together. How soft her lips were. How much he loved that little moan she did when they kissed long and wild like this. Sure, she'd done a crazy thing by buying this dilapidated place, but he loved this woman, and he was going to make this work. Somehow.

She rested her head on his shoulder and sighed happily. "It's amazing, right?"

There was that word again. "Um…yeah. Definitely amazing."

Her head popped up and her eyes narrowed. "What's with the tone?"

"What tone? It's…amazing. I'm agreeing with you."

Mel stepped back and pointed at him.

"You aren't agreeing with me. You're just parroting my words back at me, and I want to know why."

He blew out a long breath and scrambled for the right words. Now that her euphoria had worn off, she'd know if he was lying to her.

"Look…you know I've never seen what you see when you look at this place. You see white walls and pretty dresses. I see rat droppings and toxic dust. I don't get it." He raised his hand to stop her protest. "But I trust your vision." He glanced around warily. "I'm *trying* to trust your vision. That's about the best I can offer right now. I can still be happy for you even when I have no clue why you did this."

She tipped her head, her hands on her hips. A slow smile started to grow.

"Fair enough. But when it's all done and you can walk right into my vision in all its glory, I'm going to say 'I told you so.'"

He stepped up and pulled her in for another long, simmering kiss. "I don't doubt *that* for a minute. Who's going to run it for you?" She stiffened in his arms.

"What?"

"Do you have someone in mind to run the place? Is there someone local or are you recruiting to bring someone in?" He had no idea what her body language and miffed expression were about. "Sweetheart, I may not be able to envision the finished product yet. I may not be your best choice for swinging a hammer or holding a paintbrush. But I *can* offer business advice. It's kinda my thing." He made a funny face at her, but she didn't laugh.

"Shane, *I'm* running the shop."

"Well, yeah. I know you're the owner and manager and boss and all that. But who'll do the day-to-day grind? It's not like you're gonna live in Gallant Lake forever."

Now it was her turn to blow out a long low breath, clearly trying to remain calm. He knew he was in trouble when she gave him that talking-to-a-small-child tone of voice.

"I already live in Gallant Lake."

"For now, yeah. But I'm talking long term."

Because, sweetheart, you're about to move to LA.

"Short term. Long term. This town helped heal me, Shane. It feels like…home."

Shane looked through the filthy windows to see an older couple walking by, hand in hand and laughing. Across the street, Nate was helping Maggie move a table of children's clothes out to the sidewalk. A sheriff's car was parked nearby. Dan was leaning against it, sipping coffee and listening to Mrs. Sheffield prattle on about something. Two young boys were playing at the gazebo, jumping from the top of the steps to the ground and chasing each other as their mothers sat on a bench talking. It was almost like an afternoon on Beacon Hill, but without the sound of endless traffic and tour buses going by.

Yes, he'd made friends here. Yes, he'd come to enjoy poker nights and dinner at the Chalet and walking along the lakeshore at night with Mel. There was a sense of community here. A community that was starting to wake up and get more business-savvy and successful, and that was interesting to watch.

But even if Gallant Lake did feel *slightly* like home, it didn't matter. Because LA was going to *be* home. He'd find Mel a nice little neighborhood like this, maybe near Venice Beach. Quirky and friendly, close to the water, with older homes and shops. She could even open a shop out there. He started to smile. That was it. He'd find her a great little boutique in California, she'd love it, and everything would be fine.

"Shane?"

"Hmm? Oh, sorry, baby. Yeah, Gallant Lake's okay. I was just thinking about *my* news…"

"Oh, God! I'm so sorry—you told me you had big news, too, and I totally hijacked the conversation, didn't I?" She wrapped her arms around his waist and looked into his eyes, rubbing her hips against his like the temptress she was. "Tell me your news, and we'll celebrate together, all night long."

Celebration sex sounded awesome, so he did his best to ignore the sense of foreboding he felt.

"I took a job with Calvin Bolton at Bolton & Bolton. It's the biggest entertainment agency in the business, and he wants me to run their new sports division. It's everything I've been working for, Mel. Corner office. Vice President of Sports

Operations. And finally dealing with athletes who don't need the constant hand-holding."

"Wow. I knew you were trying to reach out to other firms, but…"

"I didn't have to do anything. *They* came looking for *me*. They threw everything on the table to make sure I took the deal, and then I asked for more. I made 'em work for it, babe. It'll be red carpet all the way." He knew he was puffing his chest, but damn it, this was his gold-medal moment.

He studied her face. She was hanging on to a smile, but it looked like a struggle. "Of course they wanted you—you're the best. So where is this big corner office of yours?"

"The job's in LA, Mel. I'm moving to the West Coast, and you're coming with me."

MEL KNEW THE floors were old in this shop, but Asher had assured her they were rock-solid. So how could they be falling away under her feet like this? She pushed back from Shane, trying to get a foothold. Trying to understand what he'd just said to her.

"You took a job in LA? I thought we were…"

She'd *thought* a lot of things, but apparently she'd been wrong. Shane held up his hands, trying to stop her retreat, but she shook her head and turned away. She tried to put this news together in a way that made sense, but she couldn't.

"Mel, it'll be great. You're a city girl, and LA is the city-est city in the world! And we'll be together. That's what we want, right? You can open a little dress shop anywhere..."

"I don't *want* to open a store anywhere!" She spun around and smacked her hand down on the counter, ignoring the cloud of dust that rose up. "I want *this* store. This is my dream, right here. I've got a business plan, I've got a scheduled opening date, I've got..." She echoed his words. "This shop? In this town? The sense of peace I feel here? It's everything *I've* been working for, Shane."

They stared at each other, letting the words hang there between them. She could see them, intermingling and trying to come to agreement until the letters just fell to the floor in defeat. They didn't stir an ounce of dust when they landed with a thud she felt deep in her chest.

"What about Tim? What about the business you two built? What about Tori?"

What about me?

"Mel, we can make this work. We have to." He ran his fingers through his hair until it practically stood on end. "Tim could have come with me, but he wants to stay with our agency. I'll have to divest myself from it. Tim will run everything.

Keep it small. He'll do okay." Shane hesitated. "A lot of our clients are staying with him. Including Tori, probably. Her parents want someone on the East Coast."

"Doesn't that tell you something? If this corner office is so great, why isn't anyone else coming with you?"

"You are. That's all that matters."

"No. I'm not."

He looked stunned. Then hurt. Then angry.

"You can't be serious. Why not?"

"Shane, I have a life here. I was going to wait and surprise you, but I found a house, right on the water. It's everything I want."

"And what about what I want, Mel?"

They'd agreed not to interfere with each other's career choices. But now those choices were interfering with them.

"Shane... I'm sorry, but I'm not leaving Gallant Lake. It's time for me to live the life I choose for myself." She was done letting other people make those decisions for her.

"I thought we wanted to be together, to take the next step?"

"I do, Shane. But that doesn't change my answer."

"That's the stupidest thing I've ever heard!"

"Really? You love your business. You love Tim. You love your clients. You love your mom.

You love…" She caught herself before she put words in his mouth. He'd never actually said he loved her. "You're walking away from *all* of us to chase some dream that isn't even yours."

He growled and stepped toward her, eyes like ice.

"What the hell does that mean?"

"Is the corner office your dream or your father's?"

"Mine." She saw the glimmer of doubt in his eyes before they hardened again. "This was always the plan—build the business until we could get in the door of a major agency. And I did it. This was always the plan."

"Are you trying to convince me or yourself?"

He turned away, walking to the front windows with long, angry strides.

"Don't play cute with me, Mel. I want to be at the top of my industry, and this job gives me that."

"Working for someone else puts you at the top? How does that work, exactly?"

"Stop twisting things around. Bolton & Bolton is the big dog in this business, and they want *me*."

"Look at me, Shane." He stared out the window, shoulders tight, neck muscles straining to contain his anger. He didn't budge. He refused to see what he was doing. Her voice softened. "Look at me."

He turned slowly, chin set stubbornly.

"*I* want you. You don't have to do this. You don't have to walk away."

"Actually, I do. And I'm not walking away—I *asked* Tim to come with me. I'm *asking* you to come with me. So don't put this on my back."

"You won't be happy in LA, even if I say yes. You won't find what you're looking for. You can't win approval from a ghost."

"What kind of psychobabble bullshit is that supposed to be?"

He was like a lost little boy, so hurt and angry and afraid. Lashing out to protect himself. He recoiled when she walked over and rested her hand on his arm. He stared at some spot over her shoulder, refusing to meet her gaze.

"Your father's gone. He was a fool not to recognize the amazing man you are. It was cruel, and I hate that he hurt you. But it's too late to change his mind, Shane. He's *gone*. The only reason you're taking this job is because you think this is something he'd approve of. Even though he probably wouldn't."

"This isn't about my father. This was my plan all along…" Moisture glistened in his eyes. "Come with me, Mel. We'll be happy there, I promise." He cupped her face in his hands. "I'll make you happy."

She let him kiss her, and she even returned it for a moment, knowing it might be their last.

"I'm already happy. Here. With a shop to open and a future to build. I finally know what I want to do, and it's something I'll be good at."

He looked around the store in confusion. "If you really love this old place that much, fine." Her quick burst of hope was quickly squashed. "Open it and let someone else run it. You can open another one in LA, where there are people with money. You've moved in circles with the rich and famous before, Mel. They know your name." He was warming to his solution to her problem. "Call it Mellie's! You could open a whole chain of them. Or we'll franchise it. Calvin Bolton could put it together for you with his legal team. Honey, we'll conquer the hell out of that city."

He moved in for another kiss, but she quickly stepped away, covering his lips with her fingers. Did he really think that was something she'd want? To go back into the jaws of the jet set?

To become Mellie Low again? To conquer a city? Her skin started to twitch and burn just at the thought of it. She slowly counted backward from one hundred, trying to slow her pulse and beat back the tension. She made it all the way to sixty before she could put her thoughts into words.

"You want me to be Mellie Low again?"

"What? No, not like that. You don't have to be-come that person. Just use the name for market-ing, you know? Or not. I don't care, baby. Call it whatever you want. Just come with me. We can do this."

"I can't believe you'd even suggest that. How desperate can you be?"

How could he? Hadn't he been listening to her?

"So you'd rather stay here in some converted haberdashery selling handbags than come with me?"

"LA is your dream, not mine. I loathe cities—don't you remember what happened in New York? Not only do I think I *can't* do it, I don't *want* to. Not just because it's a city. I won't go to LA and watch you be disappointed. Chasing your father's goal is never going to bring *you* satisfac-tion. You can't find peace chasing something that can never be caught."

He scoffed and turned for the door. "Peace. That's all you talk about—finding *peace*. As if you can find that in a place. You're not trapped here just because you found some peace here. Didn't my love give you any sense of peace?" They both froze. He'd said it. Mel's eyes burned with tears. He might love her, but he didn't un-derstand her at all.

He turned to face her. "Yes, I love you. That's why I'm so desperate to have you with me. Come on, Mel. I know you're afraid to go back out into your real world again, but I'll be right there for you."

"First, I'm not afraid of that." She was afraid of losing him. She was afraid of seeing him hurt. Of him hurting her. But she wasn't afraid of the world anymore. She just didn't need it. "Second, you'll be in your precious office all the time, not with me. And third…" She blinked at the tears that appeared out of nowhere, but she knew she was doing the right thing, even if it tore her heart out. "I'm opening a boutique in Gallant Lake with my family and my friends. It's not just peace I found here, Shane. It's happiness. It's a sense of belonging." She walked to the doorway where he stood, his hand on the heavy brass doorknob. "And you know what? I'd gladly walk away from all of that and follow you if I thought you'd find your happiness out there. But you won't."

"You could have everything, but you're staying in Gallant Lake." His voice was thick with a mix of anger and sorrow.

"Stay with me, Shane. LA isn't your dream."

His head shook slowly back and forth, in direct contradiction to his words. "This is what I've always wanted. This is what I've worked for all my life. I have to go."

"You know where to find me when you realize what you *really* need."

There were no goodbyes. They just stared at each other sadly for a long time, until Shane finally yanked open the door and walked away from her without another word.

CHAPTER TWENTY-THREE

"Mel, I think it's clean enough."

She flinched and blinked at Nora in confusion.

"The window? You've been rubbing that same spot for ten minutes now." Nora took the cloth from Mel's hand. "Come sit and have a cup of coffee. You look even more pathetic than I did when Asher left me back in March."

"No, she doesn't. You looked worse. *Much* worse." Amanda walked over and sat on one of the folding chairs by the windows of Five & Design. Nessie trotted over and plopped down on the floor at her feet. "Mel's a little spacey, but you were downright scary. Your hair…"

"Okay, okay, you've made your point." Nora cut Amanda off with a glare. "I was a wreck, but I had an injured, pregnant, hysterical daughter on my hands who'd just been dumped, too. Asher was only gone for a week, but it wasn't easy." She handed Mel a coffee. "Not that what you're going through is easy, honey, but…"

Mel really didn't want to talk about *anyone* being dumped, especially her.

"Speaking of pregnant, I haven't heard from Bree in a few days."

Nora waved her hand dismissively. "She texted me this morning, threatening for the hundredth time to kill me if Asher and I get married before the babies are born. As if I'd get married without her."

Mel didn't really want to talk about weddings, either, but anything was better than talking about Shane.

"Have you set a date yet?"

"We're in no hurry. We've been living in sin for months now, and it works for us."

Amanda snorted. "Now there's a sentence I never thought I'd hear my proper Southern cousin say."

Nora leaned back and propped her feet on a box. "No longer Southern. No longer proper."

Mel looked at her two cousins and couldn't help smiling. "Look at us, all grown up. Amanda's married and raising her family in an actual castle. Nora's a grandmother proudly living in sin. Bree's married to a farmer and about to pop with twins in North Carolina." She lifted her coffee in a toast. "And I've got a dog, and I'm opening a dress shop."

Amanda sat up straight. "Mel…"

"I didn't mean that as a pity thing. I'm *happy.*

All of us are happy, and we all got here in such different ways. It's great, right?"

Of course, the other three had gotten there by finding someone to love. And, in a way, so had Mel. She wouldn't have had the strength to do any of this without Shane. He'd helped her learn to trust herself. He'd helped her learn how to laugh again. How to love. He loved her enough to do all that. He just didn't love her enough to stay.

"It *is* great, *chica*." Luis stepped off the staircase and walked over to give Mel a much-appreciated shoulder rub. Those big hands worked magic, and Mel was briefly jealous of Tim. "In order to find happiness, you have to see where you were meant to be, and you were meant to be right here. This place is going to be a hit."

Luis had just arrived the day before, exhausted from Fashion Week, but thrilled with the reception his collection had received. He promised Mel he was all hers until he had to leave for Paris at the end of the month.

She looked around and nodded. In the past three weeks, they'd scrubbed and stripped every surface and removed any fixtures that were in the way. Asher had repaired the staircase. A coat of pale ivory paint on the walls and ceiling had done wonders for the place. The volunteer labor was helping her save precious dollars. Between buying the house and the shop, she was running her bank account down to the bone. But Luis assured her last night that he'd be returning her investment in his company with interest as orders came in. The timing was perfect.

She was hoping to be open while the leaves were turning and the tourists were coming to the Catskills in carloads.

"I'm excited about it." Three pairs of eyes studied her intently. "What? I am!" Whether she wanted to or not, she was going to have to talk about Shane. "Seriously, I know I'm doing the right thing. Gallant Lake is home. I'm closing on a house next week, for crying out loud. And this shop brings together all the things I do well, other than posing for pictures, and I'm done with that. I'm *glad* I'm done with that. I'm *happy*, okay? I'm not even at level two right now. I'm *good*."

They didn't look convinced. "I miss Shane. Of *course* I miss Shane." Just saying his name out loud caused a sharp, stabbing pain in her heart. "But going to LA with him was never an option. Even if I could survive that circus, he can't. And when it falls apart, he'll be off to chase the next big thing to try to please a dead man. I love him, but I can't watch him destroy himself." She stood and patted Luis's shoulder. "I made the right choice for my recovery, and for me. I'm… I'm happy. I'm also heartbroken. But let me do that part in private, okay? If things get bad and I need help, I promise I'll call one of you."

"Does that go both ways?"

Tim stood at the base of the stairs, cell phone in hand.

"What do you mean, both ways?"

"I'm assuming you were including me in that promise…"

"Of course."

Tim was missing Shane almost as much as she was, but he was determined to keep the business going, which meant a lot more traveling than he used to do. Luis was none too happy about it.

"So if I call you for help, you're there, right?"

"Absolutely. What's up, Tim?"

"I need to fly to Boise." Tim raised his hands when Luis muttered something under his breath. "I know you just got here, but it's Tori." He turned back to Mel. "I might need your help."

"What happened?"

"Someone's been whispering that she's using PEDs."

Nora frowned. "Peds?"

"Performance-enhancing drugs. It's not true, but it's gained enough momentum to reach the ruling association, and the press caught wind of it this week. Social media is blowing up. Tori's hysterical, and she and her parents are holed up in a hotel room like prisoners. They can't make a move without cameras in their faces. And sponsors are threatening to 'examine their current relationship' with her. This thing is snowballing fast, and we need to get a handle on it."

"Have you called Shane?" The girl had been one of his favorite clients. Surely he'd be able to get her out of this. He was The Dealmaker—he'd have a solution.

Tim's face sobered. "Yeah. He said his hands are tied because we're still in the process of severing his ties to the agency. He told me it would be a—" Tim held his fingers up in air quotes "—'conflict of interest' if he got involved. Can you believe that bullshit?"

Shane was completely blinded by that shiny new corner office of his. He'd lost himself already. She looked at Tim.

"When do we leave for Boise?"

He gave her a quick smile of relief. "Tonight."

THE MEDIA ROOM at the Emerald Valley Country Club was packed wall-to-wall with reporters. Everyone was talking at once, and the lights were blinding. It was pure chaos, and Mel had a flicker of doubt about how Tori would handle it. They'd been up all night deciding what she should say and what she should wear and how she should use her body-acting abilities. She was selling the true story of a teenage girl who was the victim of a horde of jealous "mean girls" spreading lies. She was a *victim*. Despite a handful of pictures still floating around the internet showing her last year with a beer in her hand and pills on the table next to her, Tori Sutter had her life together and was focusing on golf. She was a professional. Because of this upsetting situation, she was so concerned about online bullying that she was going to announce a foundation to address the issue for teens.

It was going to be fine. Tori was ready. Her hair, pink streak still in place, would be worn down and natural so she'd look her age. Her clothing was age-appropriate and conservative— a soft pink golf shirt with white bermuda shorts and sparkly sandals. She'd read through the statement a dozen times. She knew where to pause, when to look up into the cameras, when to smile and when not to. She was ready.

They'd be fine as long as there were no surprises. Tori didn't seem aware of the possibility, but the adults all knew there was a very real threat out there that could derail all their efforts. And they hadn't figured out how to control the Gary Jenkins factor. If her ex-coach was even involved.

Tim walked into the room and up to the microphones. Voices started to hush. He saw Mel in the back and winked. He looked tired but determined.

"Ladies and gentlemen, thank you for coming today. I have handouts for everyone with the text from the statement my client is about to give you. She will not be answering questions." There was a loud communal groan. Tim held up his hand. "She's a sixteen-year-old girl, folks. She's the victim of online bullying, and it's been a very emotional week for her. She's also a professional athlete who has a tournament to prepare for. But I will make myself available in the back of the room after Tori has spoken if you need anything clarified." He looked sternly into the cameras. "For the record, like other players, Tori has been drug-tested at multiple tournaments, and she has passed every single test without issue. The ruling body has determined that no fines or actions will be taken against Tori because there is not a shred of evidence that she has done anything wrong. This is a smear campaign against my client, and it won't be tolerated." He looked around the room, seeming to make eye contact with every person in there, and he clearly meant business. "We will be watching all social media mentions about our client, and we will take legal action whenever necessary. For now, we just want this circus behind us so Tori can focus on winning this weekend's tournament. And here she is."

Tori walked out with her parents, and, after blinking at all the lights, she stepped to the dais and performed exactly how they'd rehearsed. Tim joined Mel at the back of the room. She leaned close as Tori started to speak and whispered to him.

"She's doing great!"

"Yup. Now we just need to avoid a blindside."

Their eyes met. They knew there was a chance this was more than a "mean girls" episode. They'd talked about it on the flight here last night and had discussed it with Tori's parents. That's why they didn't want to allow any questions today. Tori was innocent, but there was at least one smoking gun out there that, if produced, could destroy her career.

CHAPTER TWENTY-FOUR

SHANE LEANED AGAINST the door frame, arms
folded across his chest. Outside the hotel windows, he could see mountains in the distance
beyond the Boise skyline. Inside the hotel room,
Gary Jenkins was sitting at a desk, reading the
document Shane had shoved in his face as soon
as the door had opened.

A woman sat on the sofa in the opposite corner
of the room, watching TV while she waited to no-
tarize everything. On the screen, Tim was talking
to the press mob. He was handling the situation
just right. Bring the rumors out into the open, address them and move on. Gossip only lived in the
dark, and a good PR plan would protect Tori, as
long as they didn't get caught off guard. Which
was why Shane was here in Idaho.

He'd been sitting in Calvin's office when Tim
had called about Tori. Calvin had stepped out,
but the door was open, his assistant was sitting
right there, and for all Shane knew, the room was
bugged. He'd had no choice but to toe the com-

pany line. He'd hated what was happening, and he'd *really* hated telling Tim to handle it himself.

Calvin Bolton was paranoid as hell, but maybe that just came with his level of success. People were always trying to poach clients and profits, so the guy had to be tough. Shane could respect that, but the atmosphere at Bolton & Bolton was light-years from he and Tim throwing Nerf balls at each other across The Brannigan Agency office while they discussed business decisions.

When he'd landed at LAX to start his new life ten days ago, a limo had been waiting to whisk him to the hotel suite where he'd be living—at the company's expense—while he looked for a place of his own. The limo would be at his disposal, as well as a rental car that drove like a polished rocket on wheels. His suite was all chrome and glass and marble and leather. It was ritzy but cold. And quiet. And lonely. Whenever the doubts crept in about his decision, he held on to the slim hope that Mel would change her mind and come join him.

His office was everything he'd expected it to be. It was huge. It was in the corner. And the views of LA and the mountains in the distance were breathtaking. He'd been meeting with HR on and off as he got settled in, working out tiny details in his final contract. The head of HR seemed to think they were *very* tiny details that could be clarified later and had quietly questioned whether Shane was intentionally stalling. But Shane had assured her he just wanted to be sure everything was as clear as possible before he signed. And they were almost there. But not quite.

"This is a load of nonsense." Gary sat back and glared at him. "I'm not admitting to any of this. I'd be unemployable!"

"Yeah, that would be a real shame." Shane walked over to the desk and pulled out a page from the bottom of the folder. "You sign *that*, and I'll sign *this*, agreeing that your statement stays locked away forever. Unless, of course, you decide to cause any more trouble for Tori Sutter. That happens, and I'll release your signed statement saying you illegally obtained prescription drugs in a minor's name, without her parents' consent, from a sleazy doctor who'd never met the girl. And you're going to put his name and address right there on that blank space, so I can pay him a visit. You're going to swear that Tori refused to take a single pill from you. And let's not forget that last paragraph, admitting you started this whole media shit-show in the first place, by saying something to one of Tori's competitors."

"But I didn't…"

"Don't lie to me, Gary. One of the first online mentions of Tori taking pills was from the sister of one of your clients. It's pretty easy to follow the trail back to you. Why else would you be in Boise this week, if not to cause a stir by producing a photo of some prescription with her name on it?" Shane leaned over Gary, smirking when he shrank back so far he almost fell off the chair. "Have you shared any pictures, Gary?"

"No. What? No! I haven't taken any pictures of anything. That would be career suicide for me." Beads of perspiration appeared on his balding forehead. "I let something slip in conversation by accident, and Suzannah and her sister ran with it, and then I didn't know to reel it back in. I had no idea it would get this big. If anyone puts Tori and Suzannah together as both being my clients, I could be finished. I just want this to go the hell away." The guy was turning green, and Shane started to believe him.

He glanced up when he heard Tori's voice on the television. The kid looked and sounded perfect. Tim was going to do fine with their clients. With *Tim's* clients. That thought felt sour, but he shrugged it off. Pretty soon he'd have his own stable of athletes to keep him busy, and hopefully at this level he wouldn't have to worry about putting out fires like this every other day. Although he was pretty damn good at it.

"Sign the papers, Gary, and it goes the hell away. The girl looks like a superstar right now, and we can all move on as long as you keep your mouth shut."

Gary's shoulders slumped in defeat. He picked up the pen and signed his name. Shane did the same. While the notary was stamping the documents, Shane watched Tori finish her statement. She looked tense but composed. Her commitment to fighting online bullying surprised him, and he nodded in approval. That was a nice touch. The camera swung around to show the crowded room, and he caught sight of a tall brunette in the back. It was enough to make his knees go weak.

Mel was here. In Boise. In this hotel.

She'd come to help her friend Tori. She'd come to help her friend Tim. She had a whole circle of people who cared about each other and took care of each other, and he was no longer a part of it. He'd walked away from them to follow his dreams. He frowned. There was nothing wrong with wanting to be the best. Even if it meant you weren't with the people who were the best *for* you. Right?

He finished up his business with Gary, reminding him to keep their agreement, and their meeting, quiet. He wanted to pound the guy into the wall for causing pain to people he cared about. But that wouldn't help anyone, so he had to satisfy himself with a very, *very* firm handshake. The color drained out of Gary's face when he squeezed, and Shane was pretty sure he wouldn't be able to grip a golf club with those fingers for a day or two.

Shane called the concierge on his way out of the room. He needed to get back to LA. As it was, Calvin had been very unhappy with his sudden departure for a "personal matter," and if he ever found out Shane had come to Boise to help a former client who chose *not* to join him at Bolton & Bolton, he'd be in a ton of trouble. Best to make a fast, clean getaway.

And he almost made it. The elevator doors swung open on the ground level, one level below the lobby packed with reporters. He could see his limo waiting for him.

"Shane?" Tim stood by the concierge desk. "Let me guess. It's a total coincidence that you're in this particular hotel in Boise today."

Shane tugged Tim to the side, around a corner and out of sight. "I was just leaving."

"Yeah. So I see." He hated to see that look of betrayal in his best friend's eyes. "Were you afraid I couldn't handle it? That I'd screw up? Why do you even care, Shane? It's not your company anymore, remember?"

He bristled. "I haven't signed anything yet, remember? So technically, it *is* still my company."

Tim brushed him off with a wave of his hand. "You have a non-compete clause *and* an addendum about our agency in your Bolton contract, so there is no way in hell you should be in this hotel. Why *are* you here?"

Shane didn't bother telling Tim he hadn't signed the Bolton contracts, either. He'd been busy, and cautious. It didn't mean he wouldn't sign them all eventually.

"Look, Bolton doesn't know I'm here. And you shouldn't have known, either. Why aren't you with Tori?"

Tim's eyes narrowed dangerously, and for the first time Shane wondered if he'd pushed their friendship too far. Would Tim ever forgive him for going to LA? Would Mel? But this was what he'd always wanted, damn it. It was what he deserved.

"Not that it's any of your business, but Tori's upstairs with her parents. I came down to get something from my rental car. Now, why don't you answer my question? What. The. Fuck. Are. You. Doing. In. Boise?"

Shane reached into his satchel, pulled out the folder full of papers and handed them to Tim. They belonged with Tori's agent, and that wasn't him any longer. Tim frowned as he scanned the documents, including the one that said Shane wouldn't release them without provocation. He looked at Shane in confusion.

"You promised not to expose this asshole? Who gave you the authority to do that?"

"I gave myself the authority. Look, if this goes public, Tori's name gets dragged through the tabloid mud for months. The best way to protect her is to keep it out of the news. Gary gave me his word he's done working with minors. If his adult clients are stupid enough to use PEDs, then that's on them. And I never said I wouldn't drop a few anonymous tips to the association on who might need a drug test. This deal keeps Tori's reputation clean. And if it doesn't, I'll bring that son of a bitch down so fast he won't know what hit him."

Tim stared at him for a minute, then a smile spread across his face.

"You came here to protect Tori."

"Yeah. Does that really surprise you that much?" It hurt a lot that it might.

Tim's hands lifted in an amused shrug. "I don't know, man. You've been a pretty big jackass lately. But now I'm wondering if you're not missing the thrill of troubleshooting. Is that corner office too dull for Shane Brannigan, The Dealmaker?"

"My corner office is just fine, pal. Everything I wanted." Those last words came out with less enthusiasm than he'd intended. "Life is good in LA. But Gary Jenkins was a loose end and I wanted to make sure he was contained. Now he is. So now I'm off to La La Land."

"Mel's here."

Shane's eyes closed as he absorbed the pain of those words. "I know."

"You're not even going to see her?"

"There's no point. We both made our choice." He couldn't help asking, "How is she? How's the dump—I mean, dress shop—coming?"

"She's good, man. Sad, but good. The shop is opening in a couple weeks, and everyone's working hard to help her make it a success." He didn't have to say it—everyone but Shane.

"Good." There was really nothing else to say. "Good. Um, I gotta go. My car's here and I have a flight to catch. I'm glad we saw each other, Tim. You handled this whole thing just the way you should have. Tori's statement was spot-on."

Tim looked at the papers in his hand. "But you're the one who handled the real problem. We knew that shithead was probably behind this, but we weren't sure how to handle him. You, of course, went straight for the jugular, and it worked." He extended his hand. "Thanks, Shane. I know you're not supposed to associate with me anymore business-wise, but…stay in touch as a friend, okay?"

Too overwhelmed with emotion to reply, Shane just shook Tim's hand. He'd only gotten a few steps away when Tim's final words hammered into his heart.

"When you finally get your head out of your ass and realize where you belong, give me a call. I'll help you get your girl back. Unless she's figured out what an idiot you are and it's too late. Then you'll be on your own. Literally."

CHAPTER TWENTY-FIVE

THE TEMPERATURE CLIMBED to over one hundred degrees for the third day in a row. From his hotel suite, Shane could see the heat shimmering as it rose above the LA traffic.

His phone chirped, letting him know his driver was waiting. And the car would be air-conditioned. Hot days in LA were no different from cold days in Boston—you spent as little time outdoors as possible. He straightened his tie in the mirror and ran a comb through his hair. If Mel were here, she would have immediately mussed it with her fingers. She didn't like him looking "all buttoned up" and had taken every opportunity to bring him down a notch or two whenever she'd noticed him getting too cocky.

After he'd made that comment one night about the mountain roads needing more streetlights, Mel had made it her personal mission to point out his snobbish attitude when it came to Gallant Lake. She'd told him the only reason he complained so much was because he didn't want to admit he was falling for the place.

He flinched when his phone chimed again. It was nothing new, losing himself like that in thoughts of Melanie Lowery. He'd tried to set them aside, but after seeing her on TV in Boise with Tori and Tim, he was having a hard time moving on. But he had to. This was his life now, and the fact that everyone he cared about had decided to stay on the East Coast didn't mean he'd been wrong.

People could say what they wanted about his father's aspirations for him, but the old man had been right to push. Shane grabbed his leather satchel and headed out the door. Who wouldn't want a job like this, with a luxury suite and limo at his disposal? There was no doubt about it— Shane Brannigan had officially *arrived*.

In the elevator on his way up to his thirtieth-floor office, he scrolled through his schedule for the day. One meeting after another.

Shane greeted his secretary, a quiet woman named Karen, and opened the door to his office. The view from his hotel suite had nothing on the panoramic view from his corner office. The heat and haze made the colors a little more muted today, but it was still breathtaking, with the San Gabriel Mountains in the distance. They were more rugged than the Catskills, but they still reminded him every single day of Gallant Lake. He pulled out his laptop. Who was he kidding? He didn't need to look at mountains for that town to cross his mind. Or the people in it.

Was Dan stopping by Nora's for a mid-shift cup of coffee right about now? Had Nate ever gotten Hank the parrot to stop using the word Shane had taught him as revenge for giving a key to Shane's mom? Had Asher finished building the fancy new poker table he'd been working on for their weekly game in the back of his shop? Blake and Amanda were talking about expanding the resort farther along the lake, but they were worried about pushback from the locals. Considering all the jobs the resort had brought to the town, and the support the Randalls were giving the improvement efforts along Main Street, Shane had a feeling the expansion would go just fine.

He walked to the windows, ignoring the work stacked on his desk. He knew his own contract was in the middle of that pile. The contract he hadn't signed yet. He'd come on board with a probationary agreement that gave him time to move to LA and sort out his departure from The Brannigan Agency. That probationary period ended this week.

Once he signed the final contract, he'd be permanently severing ties to the firm he and Tim built together. The non-compete clause would be firmly in place. The finality of it all weighed on him. His signature on those papers was the point of no return.

If only Tim had come to LA with him, instead of splitting the company. If only Melanie had come with him, he wouldn't be having these conversations with himself.

Damn it. He had to stop thinking about her. Somehow.

He turned to his solid mahogany desk with an exasperated sigh. This office was so over-the-top masculine that even Shane had cringed the first time he'd walked in. The first thing he was going to do once the contracts were finalized was hire a decorator. For now, dark paneling covered the walls, with framed impressionist paintings of British hunt scenes. The leather desk chair threatened to swallow him, and he was a pretty big guy. Bookcases lined one wall, and a thick oriental rug covered most of the hardwood floor. Shane looked around and the corner of his mouth tipped up. He could almost hear Mel if she ever came here.

Is it possible even the air in here is infused with testosterone?

He gave himself a sharp shake of his head. Shane had fought for this office alone, and he'd moved into it alone. Mel wasn't here. And he doubted she ever would be. This was *his*. He'd achieved his goal, and he was happy. *Happy*.

Even if he did crave the scent of lilac perfume to lighten this space.

The phone on his desk beeped, saving him from disappearing down another Melanie rabbit hole.

"Mr. Brannigan..." He'd told Karen almost daily that he preferred things on a first-name basis, but it hadn't sunk through to her yet that he wasn't joking. He wasn't used to having a staff ready to leap into action for him. He was more about teamwork, a hands-on kind of agent. "Mr. Bolton is on his way to your off—"

"Brannigan. I'm glad you're here." Calvin strode into his office and closed the door behind him. It had only been a few weeks, but Shane knew Calvin only did that if he was there on serious business. He walked around the desk to shake his boss's hand. Having a boss of any kind was a new experience.

"Hi, Mr. Bolton. Here to talk about the upcoming meeting with our future star quarterback?" Calvin liked his employees to boast of their accomplishments. He thought it created a more competitive atmosphere in the office. Shane thought it fed into insecurities and encouraged unethical behavior to become the one on top, but he knew it was too soon to buck the Bolton system. "I'm betting we'll have a signed contract within the week."

Calvin sat in one of the tufted leather chairs in front of Shane's desk and gestured for him to take the other. The older man was taller than Shane, but much leaner. His dark silver hair was as perfectly styled as the silk handkerchief in the breast pocket of his bespoke suit.

"I'm not here to talk about football."

Shane frowned. "Okay. What's up?"

Calvin didn't answer right away, brushing invisible lint from his pant leg, then looking around the office.

"Where did you go a couple weeks ago, when you said you needed personal time?"

"I'm sorry?" Shane hadn't told anyone with the agency that he was flying off to help a former client. He'd stayed behind the scenes in Boise not only to protect Tori, but also to protect his job. He didn't say anything further, hoping Calvin was just fishing.

He wasn't.

"Did you go to Idaho, Shane?"

"I did."

"Why?"

"Tori Sutter was my client. There was a problem that had to be dealt with."

Calvin nodded, still not making eye contact. "And Tim Monroe couldn't deal with it? Isn't she *his* client now?"

Shane frowned. "I had special knowledge of the situation and the ability to resolve it."

"And did you? Resolve it?"

"Yes."

"And you didn't think I should know?"

Shane didn't respond right away. It seemed Calvin knew all the answers anyway, so what was the point?

"I used the personal time you gave me for moving, so I wasn't on your time clock." Shane leaned forward, resting his arms on his knees. "Calvin, I'm sorry. I couldn't turn my back on a sixteen-year-old client in trouble. Even if, technically, she wasn't my client anymore. That kind of loyalty is what you want in an agent."

"I want my agents loyal to *me*, not our clients. And definitely not loyal to other people's clients." Calvin sat back and stared hard at Shane. "Are you going to be able to do that? Put me first?" He held up his hand to keep Shane quiet, and gave him a rueful grin. "I have to admit, Brannigan, I never expected you to take this job."

"What?"

"I never thought you'd walk away from the agency you built from the ground up." Calvin shook his head. "I built this agency the same way, you know. I signed an unknown actress who landed the role of a lifetime a month later." He laughed. "Getting the role had nothing to do with me. The director saw her in some stupid fruit juice commercial and thought she'd be perfect for his sitcom. I negotiated a good deal and boom. I'm a talent agent."

Shane frowned, still unsure where this was headed. "I didn't know that."

"Most people don't. They think I've been a rich asshole forever." They both chuckled. "You and I are a lot alike, Shane. And that worries me. I know I could never go to work for some other guy, and I'm wondering why you think you can."

"You're doubting my ability?"

"Your ability to be an agent? No. Your ability to do things *my* way and not *your* way? Yeah." Calvin stood and walked to the windows, Shane joined him. "Can you look me in the eye and tell me you've had zero contact with any of your former clients?"

"I... Not professional contact, no." He'd driven up to San Francisco to have dinner with Riley and Emma Sue two weeks ago. He'd texted with Alonzo about a recent vote in DC. And Marquis had called earlier this week to talk about a car he was thinking about buying. But those guys were friends. He was allowed to have friends, right?

Calvin gazed out the window, looking far more relaxed than Shane felt. "I know you went to San Fran. Riley Chapman was your client."

"That was a personal visit. Are you having me followed?"

"Let's just say I like to know what goes on around me. How do you think I got here?" Calvin gestured around the office. "I don't understand why you walked away from an agency you built with your own two hands. You and your partner had it going on, man. What the hell are you doing in LA? Because if you're here on some whim, or because you got butt-hurt in Boston over something, I don't need you on the team."

Shane started to object, but Calvin stopped him. "I called Marquis Jackson yesterday. You probably know his wife is an aspiring actress, and she's a client of ours." Shane groaned to himself. He knew the first, but not the second. "Marquis and I know each other well enough for him to take my call. I asked him why he wasn't following you here to Bolton & Bolton. He just laughed and said you'd never stick. Said he'd be waiting for you when you snapped out of it and came back to The Brannigan Agency."

Shane swallowed hard. "I'm not going back…" He looked out at the LA skyline and thought about a sleepy little town in the Catskills, and the woman who told him she'd be waiting.

Calvin pointed to Shane's desk. "Somewhere on that desk is a contract. It's ironclad. And it's due tomorrow." His eyes met Shane's. "I want you here. But I need you here for the long haul. Your time, your *life*, will belong to this agency. *My* agency. If you seriously think you can do that, then sign the papers and let's get going." Calvin put his hand on Shane's shoulder. "But here's the thing—I've had buyout offers of my own through the years, merger offers…whatever. A few were even tempting. But I could never give up being the boss. I could never walk away from *my* company. So take a day to think about what you really want. And if this isn't it, no harm, no foul. We'll part with a gentleman's handshake, and hopefully you'll leave me with some names of people who might be willing to take on this office and my ego."

Calvin walked to the door.

"The choice is yours."

CHAPTER TWENTY-SIX

FIVE & DESIGN WAS filled with flowers, customers and sunshine for the grand opening the second weekend of October. Mel was frantically busy, but she did her best to remember every little moment. This was her store. This was her future. She was planting her stake in the ground here in Gallant Lake and making a life for herself. This was a big deal.

Becky was helping customers with selections— Nora's daughter had a good eye for fashion. Amanda and Nora were at the cash registers, laughing as they competed to see who could ring up more purchases. Blake and Asher were awkward but charming greeters and hosts. They took turns manning the entrance and keeping the line of people entertained as they waited to come in. Mel couldn't believe it, but yes, there was a *line* at opening time and for a few hours after that, and they had to keep the fire code in mind. Especially since Sheriff Dan was there to offer his support with traffic and parking.

Luis, fresh from the Paris shows, was upstairs

in the bridal and evening wear salon, where his
new collection was on display. There was steady
traffic up and down the grand staircase to see the
fashions and place orders, and Tim was helping
him keep track of it all. Luis had worked mira-
cles creating buzz for the store opening, and Mel
knew he must have called in a lot of PR favors.
People had driven up from the city to little Gallant Lake just to check out Mellie Low's boutique. *She* never referred to it as that, of course,
but when people heard what the former famous
model was up to, they were curious. They were
also willing to spend their money, so she for-
gave them.

Blake told her the only thing the guests had
been talking about at last night's swanky wedding at the resort was her grand opening. The
bride's mother had finally given up and arranged
for a shuttle to bring them all to the shop after
today's brunch. That small busload alone had put
sales over Mel's goal for the day.

She smiled nonstop, helping customers, accept-
ing congratulations, posing for selfies as people
held up their bright blue bags. The day had been
more than a success. It had been triumphant.

This was her home run, her championship
event, her gold medal. And yet…something was
missing. Some*one* was missing. Shane wasn't
here to share it with her. He'd called and texted

a few times right after he went to LA, but it was too painful to pretend things were okay between them. It had been a few weeks now since she'd heard from him. Not since Boise.

Tim told her Shane had been there, and what he'd done. It stung that he hadn't tried to see her, but she understood. It would have been too hard to say goodbye all over again. They were truly over, and she was just going to have to accept it.

It was late afternoon before traffic slowed enough that she could sit and nibble on one of Nora's sandwiches. Amanda joined her on the settee in front of nearly empty racks.

"I hope you have more clothes in the back room."

"We've gone through nearly everything, but there's another delivery coming on Tuesday. Luis insisted I'd need to replenish quickly, and I'm glad I listened." She was taking a mental inventory. The cashmere sweaters had sold out already, so she should reorder a wider variety of colors. It may have been too early for the wool trousers, since there were still quite a few on the shelves. That teal dress she'd loved so much had sold out, but the brown one hadn't. Maybe if she displayed them with some colorful scarves…

An odd hush fell over the shop. Even the customers seemed to stop in their tracks. She looked up and cried out in surprise. Amanda's hand grasped hers, but Mel pulled away, standing up and fighting the urge to run. The question was, which way should she go? Out the back door? Or straight into the arms of the ginger-haired man standing in the doorway?

Shane stared at her, ignoring everyone and everything else. It was as if the shop had emptied, leaving just her and him. His mouth quirked up into that crooked grin she adored, and it caused a shot of pain to her heart. He wasn't hers anymore. She had to remember that. His life was in LA. He'd walked away from her. She straightened her shoulders, barely aware of Tim's voice coming from the stairs behind her. He sounded more amused than surprised.

"Well, look who finally decided to get his head out of his ass."

Shane gave Tim a barely perceptible chin lift and stepped inside. His voice boomed across the shop, making more than one person jump.

"I'm looking for the owner of this building." He pointed at Nora behind the counter. "Are you the landlady here?" Nora shook her head with a bemused smile. He looked at Becky, who was folding the boatneck tees at the front table. "Are you the owner? I heard the woman who bought this old place was beautiful. Where is she?"

Mel didn't know what game he was playing

at, but her emotions were too volatile to let it go any further. She was afraid it might break her.

"I own this building." She wasn't going to move toward him. She wasn't going to say another word. Let him do whatever he was going to do. She wasn't going to make it easier for him. But if he moved any closer, surely he'd hear her pounding heart and it would give her away. She wanted to be in his arms more than anything. But she stood firm, and there was a flicker of admiration in his eyes.

"Well, the rumors were right about you being beautiful, ma'am. And I'm not talking about pretty." He stepped closer, and she couldn't help her sharp intake of breath. He heard it, and his smile deepened right along with his eyes. "I'm talking about *beautiful*. The kind of beauty that comes from a person's heart. The beauty of a person's mind, like someone who could envision this—" he gestured around the shop, where they were very much the center of attention "—from looking through a dirty window into a decrepit old building and dreaming. That's a rare kind of beauty, and it can't be captured in any photograph."

She'd read once that a hummingbird's heart rate was over two hundred and fifty beats per minute. Her heart was fast approaching that, and it felt like she had an actual hummingbird flailing around in her chest. Shane's smile. His heated eyes. His smooth words. What was he doing here? What was he *after*? Was he here to ask her to go to LA? Forever the negotiator, going for the win?

"Why are you asking for the owner?" Not bad. Her voice only had the slightest tremor.

He shrugged with a little too much drama to be sincere. "Well, I heard you were only using two floors of this place. I thought you might want to lease the third floor for office use."

"You have an office. It's in LA."

He held her gaze as if he was daring her to look away. And damned if she couldn't.

"Not anymore."

She had no idea what that meant. He played the silent game on her, and she broke before he did.

"I don't understand..." This time the tremor couldn't be controlled, and Shane reached for her shaking hands, folding them into his strong, steady ones.

"Mel, I'm here to stay. I quit LA. The Brannigan Agency has a Brannigan in it again."

I'm here to stay. She was too afraid to believe what that might mean.

"What does that have to do with the third floor?"

"The Brannigan Agency needs a new office. One that's closer to the things—the people—who are important to me and Tim." She glanced toward the staircase. Luis was there, with his arm casually over Tim's shoulders. They were in on this. She narrowed her eyes on Luis before turning back to Shane.

"You're moving your corporate offices to a third floor walk-up in Gallant Lake?"

"This will be a *satellite* office. Desk. Phone. Computer. The main office is relocating to a converted Brooklyn warehouse." He nodded toward Tim and Luis. "It has a nice big loft above it, and I've been assured it would make a great apartment for some lucky couple."

Mel's hand rested on her chest, trying to get that hummingbird and all his friends to go perch somewhere so she could breathe. She offered the weakest of protests.

"I was going to put my own office up there."

He tugged on her hands, and she was finally, blissfully, in his arms again. He wrapped them around her and held on tight.

"Even better. We can work together." He grazed her ear with his lips. "And eat together." A soft kiss on her temple. "And ride together." Another kiss, on her forehead. "And live together." This kiss fell on the tip of her nose. "And sleep together." He rested his forehead on hers, staring straight into her eyes.

"I'm sorry, Mel, for being such an ass." A customer who, like all the others, had been listening intently, let out a snort. "You were right about everything. LA wasn't what I wanted, it was just what I thought I had to have. Christ, you were so right. I got all the way out there and realized I was missing something far more important than a job title and a corner office." He kissed her lips gently. "I was missing my heart. I left it here in Gallant Lake with you, and that little shit refused to come back. It *couldn't* come back, because you had it wrapped up in velvet chains." His hands cupped her face. "I need my heart, princess. Take me back. Tell me I didn't ruin everything. Tell me you love me. Because I will love you every day until there are no more days if you'll just tell me that."

Mel started to smile. The hummingbirds were gone, replaced by a slow, steady drumbeat of purest joy. She slid her arms around his waist and rested her head on his shoulder. *Now* she was home.

"I still love you, Shane. I tried not to, but it's as much a part of me as breathing."

"Thank Christ." His head rested on hers and they stood there for a moment, overwhelmed with emotion and unable to move. Someone started a slow hand clap, and others joined in. Mel raised her head and looked around, flushing red at the realization they'd just played out their most intimate moment in front of a shop full of people. Some of them were holding up their phones and recording it all. Shane noticed that, too.

"Do you want me to tell them to stop?"

"No. I've had plenty of viral moments I'm *not* proud of, but this is different. I don't care if the world knows how much I love you." She winked at him. "And you admitting in public that you were an ass is too good not to share."

He laughed and pulled her in for a kiss, deep and sweet and hot and tender. It earned them a second, and much more enthusiastic, round of applause.

SHANE DIDN'T WANT to let Mel go, but there was only so long they could stand there while friends and strangers applauded their kiss. Pretty soon they'd be holding up score cards. He took one more taste of her before stepping back.

She'd forgiven him. She loved him.

A huge weight lifted off his shoulders. It wasn't just the burden of his fear over whether she would reject him. It was the lifelong burden of never being *enough.* Never *having* enough. The constant, gnawing hunger of chasing some invisible, impossible achievement was just…gone. He felt lighter than air, and the sensation left him feeling unsteady.

"Shane?" The scent of lilacs swirled around

his head again. He'd never tire of that. He'd never tire of her. She was his forever.

And now he was getting so sappy he wanted to roll his own eyes. *Snap out of it, Brannigan!*

He took her hand and smiled. "Can I get a tour of the place?"

Happiness radiated from her as she tugged him toward the front of the store. She'd built her own dream right here in Gallant Lake, and from the look of things, she had a success on her hands. He was so damn proud of her.

She was talking enthusiastically about silks and wools and colors and accessories and he had no clue what it all meant. He just knew some of the racks were empty already, so she'd clearly selected the right merchandise for her market. Luis had told him once that this was her strength—putting a "look" together. Shane disagreed. Sure, she could do that. But it wasn't her greatest strength. Not by a long shot.

"Are you even listening to me?" She was showing him how she'd converted the old five-and-dime cubbyholes into purse displays behind the counter. They were behind the counter because some of those leather bags cost a few *thousand* dollars. Just because he loved a woman didn't mean he'd ever understand them.

"I'm listening, princess. It's amazing. Really."

Blake walked over to shake Shane's hand and

give him a man-hug in welcome. Asher did the same, and Shane talked to them briefly before he realized he'd turned his back on Mel in the middle of her tour. He looked at her and she arched a brow as if to say *finally*.

"What? You wanted me to make friends here, right?" That brow didn't budge. "Sorry, baby. I really am impressed with everything. Are there more clothes on the second floor?"

"That's the more upscale salon."

"More upscale than a three-thousand-dollar pocketbook? Is there a gold mine in Gallant Lake I don't know about?"

Mel laughed. "No one calls them pocketbooks anymore. And I have fifty-dollar handbags, too. There's something for everyone. Luis will even come here to do custom design work for the right clientele." They headed up the wide stairs, nodding at a woman headed down with a big smile and a bright blue garment bag over her arm. "Don't forget Gallant Lake is becoming a tourist town again. An *upscale* tourist town."

They turned the corner at the top of the stairs and came to an abrupt halt. The studio was all white and pink, with lace curtains on the windows and one of the biggest oriental rugs Shane had ever seen. Luis and Tim were standing in the middle of that rug, locked in an intense kiss and oblivious to their audience. When Tim's hand slid down toward Luis's butt cheek, Shane cleared his throat loudly, causing both men to jump back.

"Do you boys want me to get you a room somewhere?"

Tim scrubbed his face with both hands, then shook his head. "No thanks, smart-ass." He glanced at Mel. "Sorry."

She did her best not to laugh at two grown men acting like schoolboys caught under the bleachers, but it was a losing battle. Before she could speak, Luis did.

"Don't apologize to them. They're the ones who put us in this romantic mood to begin with." He walked over and shook Shane's hand, holding it longer than necessary. "That was quite a speech downstairs. You meant it, right?"

Shane started to bristle, but he knew he deserved that question. And he didn't ever want Luis to stop protecting Mel.

"I meant every word."

Luis nodded and released his hand.

Mel showed him around. More dresses and frilly things. All he truly cared about was her pride in it all. There was a fancy round table in the center of the room, topped with a huge floral display. Mel tugged the card out and handed it to him to read.

Congratulations, Mel! Since you agreed to learn golf, maybe I'll have to learn how to de-

sign clothes? I can't wait to come shopping in Gallant Lake this fall. Love you! Tori.

He didn't hear much of what she was saying, because he couldn't stop thinking about Tori's note. Not about Mel golfing, although that would be fun for them to do together. But Tori and design and Mel and clothing and a popular sports star and marketing and…well, no one said he was going to stop being The Dealmaker. And he smelled a deal in the works. It was time Tori moved on from Winthrop Athletic, and went with a company who'd give her a line with her name on it.

Mel showed him the three fancy dressing rooms with their pink upholstered chaises, and that was finally enough to chase deals out of his head. He pulled Mel close and kissed her, making her eyes go wide in surprise, but her mouth was enthusiastic. When he finally raised his head, she grinned.

"What was that for?"

"First, get used to me kissing you for no reason at all, because I'll be doing that a lot. And second, I can picture you stretched out on that velvet chaise right there, naked and waiting for me. And that makes me want to kiss you. You and I are going to have some fun in this room after closing time."

"In that case, I can't wait to close up shop."

CHAPTER TWENTY-SEVEN

"DAMN IT, DOG! Those are three-hundred-dollar shoes! Give 'em back!"

Nessie galloped down the hall and into the great room, skidding across the hardwood floors with a loafer in her mouth. Shane was hot on her heels. As soon as Nessie saw Mel by the windows, she dashed over to her. Her wide eyes made it clear she wasn't sure if she'd won or lost by stealing the shoe.

Shane grabbed for it, but Mel stopped his hand.

"If you tug on that, she's going to clamp down and your shoe is toast. Use your words." She ignored his skeptical expression. "Get her attention and give her the command."

Shane glowered at Nessie, who was unimpressed. She wanted to play, and she was ready to bolt if he took another step. Because playing tag was fun.

"Eyes." Shane pointed to his face, and Nessie automatically looked up at him. He lifted his forefinger and calmly commanded her. "Sit." Her fanny hit the floor so fast that Mel had to look away to keep from laughing. She didn't want to interrupt this training moment. For man or dog. He reached out and tapped under Nessie's chin. "Drop it."

She looked crushed that he didn't want to play anymore, but she obediently opened her mouth and released the shoe. Shane straightened and turned to say something to Mel, but she held up *her* finger. At him.

"You're not done with her. What's her motivation to obey?"

"Obey? She's the one who stole my shoe!"

Mel lifted a brow and waited until Shane let out a sigh of defeat. He looked at Nessie and scratched her ears, which brought her immediately to her feet.

"Good girl, Nessie! You're a good girl for giving me back *my* shoe that you stole from me." He grabbed Mel's hand and tugged her against his chest. "So is this how I get good behavior out of you, too? What will you do for me if I promise to tell you you're a good girl?"

"I think I was already a good girl for you this morning." Mel kissed him lightly. "Remember when I joined you in the shower? And you 'dropped' the soap? And as long as I was down there on my knees, I…"

Shane's kiss was anything but light. He folded his arms around her and pressed her back to the picture window overlooking the lake, taking her mouth like a conquering hero and leaving her breathless. What were they talking about again?

"I remember." He traced kisses over to her ear. "You're right. You *were* a very good girl this morning. And I should probably reward you with a treat to encourage more good behavior in the future, right?" He was working his way down her neck now. Her head thunked against the glass. Damn, he was good at this.

"Shane, we can't. Not now. Later maybe. Definitely later. Oh, God…" His hand slid beneath the hem of her shirt. She reluctantly extracted it and pushed back against his chest. "We're meeting everyone at the office in fifteen minutes." He nodded, obviously just as disappointed as she was.

But they'd been waiting over a month for this—the unveiling of their new shared office space on the third floor of Five & Design. Asher had drawn up the plans and done the work, while Amanda had selected the paints, fabrics and furnishings. Mel and Shane had approved the plans and the general design direction, but Amanda had wanted some of it to be a surprise, so they hadn't been upstairs in two weeks.

The shop didn't open until noon on Mondays, so Mel locked the front door behind them. She and Shane headed up the staircase hand in hand. They could hear voices up above. The stairway to the third floor was no longer walled in and dark. Asher had designed floor-to-ceiling panels of wood with cutouts and carvings of flowers— lilacs, to be exact. That had been Shane's idea. Stained in shades of ivory and violet, it was more like a wooden screen than a solid wall. An antique door at the base of the stairs with stained glass panels kept the offices private from shoppers. The door was standing open this morning, and Mel squeezed Shane's hand. He was looking at the very feminine floral screen and frowning.

"I hope the whole third floor isn't completely girlie. This is a man's office, too, you know."

"*Upstairs* is a man's—and a woman's—office. This staircase is in my salon, which is intentionally 'girlie.' Relax. I'm sure Asher gave you an adequate testosterone comfort level up there."

He didn't seem convinced, but he followed her up the stairs. Asher, Nora, Blake and Amanda were all waiting by the huge arched window overlooking Main Street and the lake and mountains beyond it.

Shane had once told Blake he was envious of Blake's massive home office, and Amanda had clearly paid attention. The wall on the right was all built-ins, just like Blake's. Bookshelves, credenzas, cupboards and even a copper wet bar sink with a small fridge below. On the exposed brick wall on the left were two large flat screens and a drafting/design table with an antique wire and muslin mannequin dress form. Two solid cherry writing desks were in front of the windows, facing opposite walls. One had a chandelier above it, while the other had a dark green glass shade.

Amanda had saved the room from feeling like a gentlemen's club by staining the built-ins the color of heavy cream. The curtains framing the window were a blue-and-ivory-striped damask, with a delicate floral design woven among the stripes. The wide plank floors had been sanded down and left their natural light oak color. A round conference table sat toward the back of the office, with dark blue leather chairs. Several colorful oriental rugs were scattered around the floor, and a tufted leather sofa sat facing the windows. Two modern recliners in bright coral faced the TV screens, with a small glass table between them to create a seating area.

Shane seemed as overwhelmed by it all as Mel was. Neither of them had spoken, and her effervescent cousin couldn't take it anymore.

"*Say* something, damn it! Are you in shock? Like what-the-hell-have-they-done shock? Or are you speechless with delight? I can't tell, and it's killing me!" Amanda's hands gestured dramatically. Nora was more composed, leaning against one of the desks and smiling proudly.

Mel gave Amanda a quick hug, then turned to

do the same to Asher. "It's beautiful! And practical. And...beautiful. Don't you think, Shane?"

"Yeah. Uh...wow." He was standing by the recliners, turning slowly in a circle to take it all in. "I figured this would feel like a funky little converted attic, but this is crazy. I could be standing in the coolest loft space in Soho right now."

Asher nodded. "That's pretty much the look Amanda had in mind. She had me design the built-in wall similar to Blake's, but we added some glass and rounded edges to keep it from being too much like a man cave."

"Hey! I like my man cave!" Blake dropped his arm around Amanda's shoulders with a grin. She looked up at him, smacking him lightly on the chest.

"The only reason you have a man cave office is because you don't have to share it with anyone else. I have my own office. This was different."

"This is perfect for us." Shane pulled Mel into a quick hug. Nora nodded toward the wall. "Did you see the pictures?"

Mel looked above the desk that sat below the charming crystal chandelier—there was no doubt this was her space. There was a large framed photo on the wall of Luis and her. It had been taken in Switzerland the day he'd picked her up from the rehab center. They were sitting on a low stone wall, with the snow-frosted Alps behind them. It wasn't a professional photo—Luis had just handed his phone to a staffer. She wasn't even wearing any makeup. But she was laughing into the camera. It hadn't been an easy four months, but on that day she knew she'd beaten the demons. She'd won, and there was a sparkle in her eyes and a freedom in her smile that said she knew it. Shane's fingers intertwined with hers and held tight.

"I loved that picture the minute Luis showed it to me. You look like my warrior princess there, laughing at the rest of the world because they have no clue how freaking powerful you are."

It made sense that Shane had selected the picture, since Amanda had asked *her* to find a fun, meaningful photo for Shane's desk. At the time, Mel thought her cousin was talking about something to sit in a small desktop frame, not a huge picture like this. But it was perfect. She and Shane turned to his desk.

Shane's mother had sent her the picture of Shane and Tim, telling her it had been taken shortly after Tim's release from the VA hospital. They were on the rocky beach at Chatham, and Shane's arm was wrapped around Tim's shoulders. Tim had been a little thinner then, but he was smiling and at peace with the titanium leg clearly visible beneath his shorts. Shane was smiling, too, but it was a fierce smile. It was a smile that said "if you mess with this friend of mine, I will hurt you." That smile was everything Shane was—loyal, strong, protective, happy. She looked up through her lashes for his reaction.

He was somber at first, but then a smile slowly spread across his face. "That was Tim's first trip to the Cape after his injury. He'd just received the fancy new leg. We walked down to the beach with Nana, and Tim admitted he'd never thought he'd see Cape Cod again. Never thought he'd see me or Nana. Never thought he'd survive. But he did, and he said he was damned well going to enjoy his life."

"I love that we both picked photos with our best friends in them."

Shane huffed out a short laugh. "It'll be awkward as hell if they break up."

"Don't be silly. I think they're just as deep in love with each other as we are." In fact, the two were grabbing a quick vacation together in the Caribbean now that all the fashion shows had wrapped up.

Mel turned to Amanda. "Thank you, honey. It's all perfect. Every detail."

Shane's arms wrapped around Mel's waist from behind, and his lips brushed that special spot right below her ear. The one he knew made her melt.

"You're right, princess. It really is perfect.

And it's going to stay that way, because we're together."

She turned in his arms and smiled into his sparkling blue eyes.

"Yes, we are. Forever."

* * * * *

Get 4 FREE REWARDS!

We'll send you 2 FREE Books plus 2 FREE Mystery Gifts.

Harlequin® Romance Larger-Print books feature uplifting escapes that will warm your heart with the ultimate feel-good tales.

FREE
Value Over
$20